Creatures in a dream

'I wasn't sure what wakened me as I heard the first faint noise . . . It was not the step of a man. That is, if it were a step at all . . . The soft scurry of light feet came to mind . . . the pitter-pat of shoes, dancing shoes . . . the sort worn by a young girl. I could almost see the white dress flutter through the hall towards my door.'

Nick Morell is camping at Longwood, the empty Georgian house he is renovating before his marriage to Sarah, and he's not at all disturbed by the noises that so unnerved his decorators. The sounds, which somehow conjure up the people who make them – a brisk military man, an eager girl – seem to welcome him, draw him in, reassure him that he, Longwood's latest owner, is wanted there.

And so, he finds, he is – his dream-like companions have work for him. His efforts on their behalf, tentative at first, then strenuous, are rewarded with enchanting glimpses of them as they urge him on. Enveloped in their loving approval, Nick hardly notices as everything outside Longwood recedes into insignificance: his friends, his job, even Sarah . . .

How powerful is illusion? Can the past intrude into the present? Ian Stuart Black's subtle and absorbing novel explores these questions as Nick's struggle between fantasy and reality builds to a violent and terrifying climax.

Also by Ian Stuart Black

In the wake of a stranger (Dakers, 1953)
The passionate city (Heinemann, 1958)
The yellow flag (Hutchinson, 1959)
Love in four countries (Hutchinson, 1961)
The high bright sun (Hutchinson, 1962)
The man on the bridge (Constable, 1975)
Caribbean strip (Constable, 1978)
Journey to a safe place (Constable, 1979)

We must kill Toni: a comedy in three acts
  (Evans Plays, 1953)

Ian Stuart Black

Creatures in a dream

Constable London

First published in Great Britain 1985
by Constable and Company Limited
10 Orange Street, London WC2H 7EG
Copyright © 1985 by Ian Stuart Black
Set in Linotron Plantin 11pt by
Rowland Phototypesetting Limited
Bury St Edmunds, Suffolk
Printed in Great Britain by
St Edmundsbury Press
Bury St Edmunds, Suffolk

British Library Cataloguing in publication data

Black, Ian Stuart
Creatures in a dream
I. Title
823'.914[F]   PR6052.L3

ISBN 0 09 466200 2

For Anne

I

'Strictly speaking,' said Mr Bennett, 'these belong to you.'

He had a cardboard box full of papers. 'They were behind a wall mirror in the stables. According to our contract we are required to dispose of all rubbish before handing over the house to you.'

'It's in splendid condition,' I said.

He was a punctilious old gentleman. 'The mirror was badly cracked and we decided to remove it. It came to pieces as they took it down. A pity. A good country piece. Late Georgian, but badly wormed. It went on the bonfire. Behind the mirror was a recess, not exactly a secret cupboard, but it served a similar purpose. A bundle of papers were stacked there. I'm afraid the men began burning them before I realized they might be of some interest to you.' There was no hurrying him, though we were standing in a sharp wind outside the stables.

'A few were destroyed,' he added. 'As you can see, we rescued this one from the flames.'

A collection of papers lay on the top of the box, some pages charred almost black.

'I'm sure it doesn't matter,' I said. He and his wife were leaving the house for the last time in an hour. At the rate Bennett did the rounds we would never complete the 'handing over tour', as he called it.

'There are quite a few more,' he added. 'Not in very good condition. In the stables . . . in the tack room.'

I was about to move on when I saw the sheet under the charred pages. It was a drawing of the house. I picked it up.

'We take that to be an artist's impression of Longwood as it was originally built, probably between 1830 and 1840, but in a slightly older style. That was only to be expected in the country. They lagged behind the fashion, you know. Good solid people with no desire to move with the times.'

The drawing differed in several respects from the house as it was now. I looked at Longwood fifty yards away along the drive, slightly elevated, a dell to one side of me and the walled gardens to the other.

'As you can see,' said Bennett, 'there have been considerable improvements over the years. We have ourselves extended and modernized the kitchen. The people before built the conservatory. The portico is a Victorian addition.'

'There is a portico, here,' I pointed out.

He peered short-sightedly at the paper. 'Ah yes. But very much smaller.'

'More in keeping with the proportions as a whole,' I said.

He looked at me sharply. 'We prefer it as it is. My wife and I have had very few complaints. And we have lived here fifteen years.'

I nodded. There was no point offending the old man. He was upset enough at having sold his house, which he was about to leave in the possession of a much younger man who probably didn't appreciate it. I didn't dare tell him that all his improvements were about to be demolished – that the following day contractors would arrive to start pulling down those extensions. What so delighted me as I examined the drawing was the accuracy with which my architect had sketched what he assumed to be the house as it was first built in this sunny, peaceful weald of East Sussex. His picture and this old drawing in Bennett's box looked near enough the same to me.

We moved on, but I was no longer listening. First the builders, I thought to myself – and then the painters . . .

'I'm not staying in this bloody house again,' said the painter. 'Not on my bloody own I'm not. Not another bloody night.' He was up a ladder in the hall.

'Why not?' I asked. I saw he'd done a remarkable amount of work.

'I'll tell you why not,' he said.

Sarah came in from the car, carrying things. 'Hello,' she said, peering over her bundle. 'You *are* getting on well.'

The painter waited for her to disappear down the corridor. 'You know about this place?' he asked me.

'Like what?'

'You know *anything* about it?'

'Of course.'

'You know its history? People what lived here before? What's happened here?'

'What's happened?' I asked.

'I'm asking you,' said the painter. 'What do you know about it?'

'It's been surveyed.'

'Not like that,' he scoffed. He was still up the ladder holding his brush, the paint tin resting on a rung beside him. He hadn't moved off the step since we arrived. 'No,' I said, 'I don't know anything special about it. It was built at the beginning of the last century, but I think it must have been on the site of an earlier house.'

'A bloody long time ago,' said the painter. He had come down the day before with us, and we'd left him to get on with his work.

'What's the problem?' I asked.

The sitting-room was one of three rooms leading from the spacious hall. 'I had a kip down in there,' he said.

I nodded. On an earlier trip to the house Sarah and I had slept on the floor in the same room. It was large, warm, and welcoming. As the centre of the house it had seemed the right place to sleep before furniture, carpets, curtains, or anything else arrived.

'We slept there, too,' I told him.

The painter gave me a steady look.

'Then you heard what goes on,' he said.

I frowned. The man was being silly. The builders had finished work some weeks ago, and he had agreed to stay on by himself until he completed painting the rooms – all nine of them, and all large. And this hall, with its arches, three doors

9

and a corridor. If he was now going to be difficult, the schedule was going to go by the board.

But he wasn't joking.

'Come on, Mac,' I said, 'what are you talking about?' I hated the drive I'd just done across London. It gave me a headache. I had a flask in my pocket, and had been looking forward to a whisky.

'You didn't hear nothing when you were here?' He looked at me sharply.

'I heard a lot of things,' I said. 'If you're in a big empty house . . .'

'Look, mate,' said the painter, 'big and empty's got nothing to do with it! It's not things at a distance I'm talking about. Course you hear things at a distance. That's not it. It's things quite close to you, things near at hand!'

Sarah went past again, heading for the car outside and another bundle of the essentials we had brought down.

'You're doing that beautifully,' she told him, indicating the walls.

'Thanks, lady,' he said.

We heard her rummaging in the car. I knew the painter was a London man, an East-Ender, at that. He had been recommended to us by friends and was striking out on his own. This job for us was the first he'd undertaken on his own behalf. We'd left him alone for a night in the country, where the silence at night was balm to the soul. But perhaps the loneliness and quiet had shaken him. I didn't relish the idea of trying to make arrangements for another painter at this stage of the proceedings.

I took the flask from my pocket. 'Let's find a couple of glasses,' I said.

He had in fact done an enormous amount in less than a day. Later I realized he had thrown all his alarm and energy into the familiar action of painting.

'I'll show you where I was,' he said. He came down the ladder. 'In here,' he said. He headed into the sitting-room, a beautiful room, high ceilings, nicely proportioned, with windows overlooking the main lawns. Banks of rhododendron bushes ran for a hundred yards along the far side of the garden, cutting it off from the country road beyond. Another window on the other side overlooked two dells that had been hollowed out from the slope around the house. They were planted with trees, a beech, an oak; the copper of a Japanese maple shone on the edge of a rockery. All magnificent, but the painter had no eyes for them.

'I just had blankets; these here rugs and cushions underneath. I stuck them under the window. I've slept on worse.' I could see I was going to get the whole story.

'Well, what happened?'

He gave me a quick look. 'I won't say I wasn't – well . . . After you left yesterday, I didn't fancy it here. Not used to being on my own.' The painter was about five foot ten, wiry in build, quick and spare like a boxer. His hands were rough and his appearance that of a man who could look after himself. 'Anyhow,' he said, 'when you and your fiancée went, I noticed it was bloody quiet. I'd only been here once before,' he went on, 'that time I did the estimate. You know, when you walk through a place with someone, it's different.' He took a mouthful of his whisky.

I knew he had to get it off his chest before he'd go on working, and I had a removal van coming down in three weeks.

'Anyhow, yesterday I got started. The hall first. Sun doesn't go down till late still. So I kept at it. I wanted to do a good job.'

'Oh, I know,' I said.

'Then you've got that kitchen all the way down that corridor. When you're married your missus is going to get tired going back and forward in this house . . . That is, if you stay,' he added.

'Why not?' I was irritated by his implication.

'Right,' said the painter. 'You stay or go. That's your business. But I know what I'd do; I'd get rid of it fast. Sell it again. I reckon this fellow that sold it to you knew what he was doing.'

'He lived here fifteen years,' I told him.

'Did he?' He sobered down a little after that. He went on, 'I'm not used to the country. So I was out of my element, as you might say. I was thinking of going to the pub in the village. Save cooking a meal.'

'*Did* you make a meal?' I asked.

He shook his head. 'That's it, you see. Just didn't feel like it. Didn't feel like walking through the house. Didn't want to stop working. Then when I came in here, I didn't want to go out there again.'

'Why?'

'Can't rightly say. Least, I didn't know at the time. But I'm glad I didn't go out, bloody glad.' He went on. 'Well, as I had this feeling, I just lay down on that rug. Wasn't cold. But I had a bit of a shake. You know – like I *was* cold. Then I told myself not to be a bloody fool. Anyone who came creeping round this place, I could settle him! Been in a few rough spots in my time. Well, anyway . . . I must have gone to sleep. It was dark outside when I woke, but I could see all right. What with there being no curtain.' He glanced at the windows.

'Was there someone outside?' I asked.

'In the house,' said the painter.

'Someone in the house?' I looked at him sharply.

'Blimey, I'm not making this up!' he said.

'Who was it?' I asked.

'I don't know.'

'Then how . . .'

He interrupted. 'He was out there, whoever he was. But I didn't feel like going to look.' The painter nodded towards the hall. It was hard to know what to say. Automatically I poured him another whisky.

'There was someone in the hall?' I asked.

'That's right,' said the painter.

'But you didn't see him?'

'No.'

'Just heard him, I suppose?'

'That's right,' said the painter.

'But how would anyone get in?'

'I don't know,' said the painter.

I had an idea. 'Did you go round the house this morning?'

'Very carefully,' said the painter.

'And which doors or windows were unlocked?'

'None,' said the painter.

'How could anyone get out and leave a locked door behind them?' I asked. Surely he'd seen the logic of that? Then I added drily, 'That is, I presume he's not still in the house?'

He looked at me sideways. 'I don't know about that.'

Sarah looked into the room. 'I'm making tea. Have you eaten, Mr Mac, or would you like a couple of eggs?'

'That's all right, lady,' said the painter. 'Tea will do nicely.'

Then she went out, and I was prepared to make clear the flaw in the painter's story. 'Look,' I said, 'if there was anyone else in here last night . . .'

The painter was thinking on quite another plane. 'I'll tell you what it was like,' he said. 'I heard this noise. In fact, I think I heard it first in my sleep. Probably thought it was a dream, so I didn't wake at once. Not till it got quite loud. Quite near.' He stood by the window, indicating the place where he'd lain. 'When you're on the ground you hear things in a different way. You get the vibrations, so to speak. I suppose I had my head on the floor, that's why I heard this getting nearer.'

'What was it?'

'Like someone walking,' he said simply. 'You know, someone who wasn't bothering to keep quiet. Someone just walking through the house. Like he had a right to be here.' He made it sound very real.

'Where was this?'

'Must have been down the corridor. Quite a smart step. Very loud in the night. God! I sat up all right!'

I had to clarify everything; it was the only way to make him see that it must have been a dream.

'You heard this loud step in the hall?'

'I was going to shout,' he said. 'Just to give him the tip to clear off. Couldn't get a croak out of my mouth.' That seemed to impress him.

'Go on.'

'It came right up to the door. Quick steps. Right to that bloody door! One more step and it would have been in the room.'

'It?' Now he said 'it'! Previously he had spoken of the noise in the house as 'he'.

'It! He! What does it matter, mate?' said the painter. 'The bloody thing was out there. One hand on the handle . . .'

'How do you know that?' It was impossible for him to know what had happened outside the room, out of his sight. He was fantasizing, deliberately inventing this nightmare!

'No, I didn't know that,' he admitted. 'It's what I felt was happening. You know, when the steps stopped just there . . . at the door . . .' Course I thought it was going to open.'

'Did it?'

'No.'

'What happened?'

'I was screwing my eyes up trying to watch the handle in the dark. Watching to see it turn.'

'Well, did it?' I asked.

He shook his head. I found this an unsatisfactory end. 'So what happened?'

'I don't know,' he said. 'I suppose it just went away.'

I was going to say something to him, but I realized it was useless.

Sarah came in with a tray of tea, bread and butter, eggs. The very ordinariness of the meal was a relief. She asked, 'Sugar? Milk?' She was so happy, smiling, eyes bright, amused, her fair hair shining as the sun streamed through the curtainless windows, full of life, full of the promise she was bringing to me and to this house.

We sat on boxes. 'It's like a picnic,' said Sarah. 'What do you think, Mr Mac?'

He allowed himself a faint smile. 'Thanks, lady. That was very nice.' He went back into the hall, and we heard him go up the ladder and the sound of him painting.

'Anything wrong?' Sarah whispered. She pointed to the hall.

I didn't want to disturb her. 'A bit jumpy,' I told her. 'Never been on his own before. Needs mothering.'

She leaned across and kissed me. 'Hold it,' I said, 'we haven't got the curtains up.' She grinned. The nearest neighbours were two fields away.

It was later in the afternoon that I solved the painter's mystery.

'Just a minute,' I stopped him as he shifted his ladder round the hall. 'What time did this manifestation walk?'

He frowned, suspecting mockery. 'Like I said,' he said, 'after dark . . . close on midnight.'

I went down to the cellar and had a look at the central heating. When I came up again he was at the top of the ladder. 'The boiler is on a clock,' I told him. 'It cuts out at night, just after eleven o'clock.'

He stopped painting and frowned at me. I think my lines of thought were as mysterious to him as his were to me.

I went on, 'If the heating cuts out at night then all the pipes will cool down, the wood throughout the house will contract – and there's a huge run of pipes in this place.'

He was still looking down at me, puzzled.

'My suggestion is that all this contraction must have made the wood shrink. And when it does that there's bound to be a noise. It might go crack! crack! crack! along in a line . . . Down the corridor, for instance, one contraction leading to another. It would sound like someone walking. And as the place is empty, it would echo. It must have sounded frightening. I tell you what I'll do: when we come down next week, I'll carry out an experiment. I'll turn off the heating – let it cool down – then I'll promise you, the floorboards will shrink as the pipes cool, and we'll get that noise. We'll hear the man – or whatever it was – walking to the door. All these things have got explanations. Don't worry, Mac, there's no one else here. You'll be all right.'

He didn't contradict me. But he just said flatly, 'I'll be going back home with you this evening. You can drop me off in Islington.'

I protested. 'You said you'd stay down here till the job was done.'

'I'm not staying here another bloody night,' said the painter. 'I told you. Not on my own. I'll come back again Monday. I said I'd do this job, and I'll do it.'

'Then you'll have to stay here to do it in time.'

'That's all right,' said the painter. 'When I come back

Monday I'll bring a couple of lads. We can all stay here. It'll be different then. It'll be all right with a couple of the lads.'

So we ran him back to London when we went that evening, and brought him down again on Monday morning. This time he had a couple of assistants with him, an older man, Joe, and Alfred, little more than a boy. 'Don't worry,' said the painter. 'We'll get it done faster this way. And it won't cost you any more.'

We left them working very hard on Monday evening. The painter didn't intend to stay there any longer than necessary, even with the company of his mates.

We had agreed to collect them that Friday and run them back to London, so we drove down to Longwood that afternoon. They had done a remarkable amount of work. The painter had got in an extra hand from the local labour exchange, but he had lasted only a few days as he wasn't up to their standard.

'These windows need fixing,' said the painter.

'What's wrong with them?'

'Wouldn't keep a kid out,' said the painter.

'Any signs of a break-in?'

'Nothing like that,' said the painter. 'It's just for your own good. You want proper locks put on.'

Alfred was already on the job of repairing locks. Joe, the assistant painter, was silently dedicated to his task.

I joined him.

'What's it like down here?' I asked.

'All right,' said Joe.

'Any problems?'

'Nothing much,' said Joe. He didn't stop work.

I found Alfred. 'Find it lonely here?' I asked.

He shrugged.

There was a subdued atmosphere amongst the three of them. I guessed the cause of it.

'Still sleeping in the sitting-room?' I asked the painter.

He nodded. 'Convenient,' he said.

'Any more footsteps?'

'Of course,' he said.

'Oh, come on. We've been into that.'

'Well, you asked.' He looked at me drily.

'You're all so tight-lipped about something,' I said. 'What have you got to be brave about?'

'Look, Mr Morell,' he said, 'you know this is the first job I'm doing under my own steam. I can't let you down . . . Doesn't matter how I feel.'

'That's what annoys me,' I told him. 'I don't want you making sacrifices, especially as you don't have anything to make sacrifices about.'

'That's what you think,' he said.

'Well, have you?'

'It's all right with Joe and Alf down here.'

'Good God, man, it's all right without them.'

'I don't fancy it,' said the painter. 'Not with someone having topped himself.'

'Someone topped himself? You mean, committed suicide?'

'That's right.'

'In this house?'

'That's right,' said the painter. 'Longwood.' He looked at me coolly and defiantly, as much as to say, 'You asked for that. Now disprove it!' Then he went on with his work.

I was sure – absolutely sure – this wasn't true, but at the same time I guessed he believed it. I certainly didn't want him passing on such a story to Sarah. Not that she would pay it any attention, she was far too level-headed for that; but it would leave a bad taste. I had to find out where he'd got the idea from.

He was mixing paints in the kitchen. 'Who told you that tale?' I asked him.

'The local chap.'

'The painter you got from the labour exchange? The one you sacked?'

'That's right.'

'What did he say?'

'He said I could stuff the job. He didn't want it anyway. Said he wasn't that keen to work in a place where a bloke had topped himself.'

17

'Look, he didn't say that till you fired him. It's his way of paying you out.'

'He'd been a bit jumpy all the time he was here.'

'That could be for a million other reasons.'

'He knew the story.'

'What was it?'

'A fellow did for himself. Blew his brains out some time during the war. Lost his son or something in the fighting.'

'What name?'

'Now he did say . . .' The painter thought. 'Harding, he said, I think. Yes. That's it. Old man Harding.'

I had seen the deeds of the house; I had a box of documents with my solicitors in London. The names of past owners in ornate handwriting went back over a hundred years.

'I can't remember a name like that,' I told the painter.

He shrugged, still stirring the paint. 'That's what he said. Harding. Topped himself. Fits, doesn't it?'

I felt certain he had got the story wrong, but I had no facts. It wasn't the sort of detail one checks when buying a house. I supposed I could check it now. I could phone the county council, or the police. Some department would have a record. But I was unwilling to do anything as formal as that. It was treating the idea with too much respect. It couldn't have happened. Not here, not in this sunlit corner of England.

I saw someone go past the window. It was the gardener we had inherited with the house, who came three days a week, worked in the walled garden, cut the wood, kept the hedges trim, and did everything except use machinery. He was a slight little man called Bridges, who spoke with a Sussex accent that I was learning to understand. I guessed he didn't know what to make of me yet, viewing me as a foreigner, a Londoner – remaining suspicious and taking his time making up his mind if he was going to accept us or not. I went out after him.

He didn't stop till I called. 'Didn't know you were here, sir. Thought you was one of those painters.'

'Can you tell me something, Bridges. Ever heard of a man called Harding?' He nodded immediately. My heart dropped. 'There was someone of that name?'

'Yes, sir. Not here very long, he wasn't, sir. Had an accident.'

'An accident?'

'That's what they said, sir. Accidental killed himself.'

'Lost his son in the war?' I wanted to be sure of the facts.

Bridges nodded. 'Nice young feller. Got some medal. Mr Harding had this accident soon after. Caused a bit of talk.'

'I didn't see his name in the deeds of the house.'

'You wouldn't, sir. Not this house. Longwood Farm.' He pointed across the two fields to the wealden timber-framed house on the crest of the ridge.

'*Not* this house?' I was irrationally delighted.

'No sir. Turnball was here at that time. The big shipping man. Harding was a timber merchant. Cut down most of these trees you see missing.'

I knew what he meant. 'Thanks,' I said.

I went back into the house.

'Harding lived at Longwood Farm,' I said, 'not at Longwood. He killed himself, as you say. But it was an accident. Anyhow, I don't see that what happens a couple of fields away is anything to scare you.'

The painter was with Joe and Alf. They looked at me impassively.

'Next door?' said the painter thoughtfully.

'Ask the gardener,' I said.

They all looked thoughtful. 'Then who's here?' said Alf. 'Walking about, and all that?'

I looked at the painter sharply. 'I don't see any point in filling his head with that talk.'

'He didn't need me to tell him.' The painter was equally sharp. 'Heard it for himself.'

'Heard what?'

'Footsteps,' said Alf.

'Oh, for God's sake!'

'It doesn't bother us much,' said Alf.

'You want to hear your footsteps now?' I asked.

'Not particular,' said the painter.

'Well, you're going to,' I said, and hurried down to the cellars. They ran the length of the house, a wide corridor through the centre with big cellars on either side, furnished with stone benches, wall cupboards, and meat-hooks hanging from the ceiling. The oil-fired boiler throbbed quietly in the second cellar. There were two other cellars at the end of the corridor; both with old fireplaces indicating the rooms the servants had used as living-rooms. I went into the boiler-room and turned off the switch that controlled it. The boiler cut out. I waited a few moments before I went upstairs.

The three had started work again and paid me little attention.

'In a few minutes,' I told them, 'you'll hear someone walking through the house.'

'Don't get that till dark,' said Alf.

'You listen.' I went off and left them.

I was in the kitchen when I heard the first contraction as the heating pipes began to cool down. Not long after, the floor-boards cracked. A noise in the woodwork seemed to cross one of the rooms above. When I went back, the painters were listening intently.

'Well?' I was pleased with the experiment.

They were quiet for a bit, still listening. I got the feeling they were being as impartial about this as they could.

'Did you hear that?' I asked them. There was a contraction almost below us.

'That's not it, guv,' said Joe. He was usually very silent.

'Not what?'

'Not them footsteps. That's noises, all right, I'll admit that. But different.'

They were being stubborn. Perhaps they wanted to believe this fiction they had created. Perhaps it added a little spice to the boredom of their work.

'I turned off the heating,' I explained. 'The noise is caused by the shrinking wood and metal. Of course it won't be identical each time, but the principle doesn't change. That's all there is. The rest you imagine.'

They looked at each other. 'All right,' said the painter, 'you have it your own way.'

We didn't say any more on the subject. They worked silently. Sarah made us a meal. I handed out cans of beer.

'Very nice,' said the painter. He would have liked to have been friendly, but something prevented him. The fact that he and his friends shared an experience, and I denied their mystery? They saw magic; they saw shadows; they heard footsteps – while I insisted there was nothing?

Alf helped wash up after the meal. The painter and Joe finished off the room they were working in, then they prepared to return to London for the weekend.

I carried in my suitcase from the car.

'Miss Foster's driving you back tonight, lads,' I said. 'But don't worry, she's steady as a rock.'

They looked at me blankly, unwilling to accept the implication.

'What about you, guv?' asked Joe.

'I've got one or two things to do here over the weekend.'

'You staying the night?' interrupted the painter.

'Three nights,' I told him. 'I'll be here Monday morning when you get back.'

They looked at me. The painter was uneasy. He wanted to say something, but he couldn't bring himself to speak in front of Sarah.

'You don't want to stay here on your own,' he said finally.

'Why not?' Sarah laughed.

The painter flushed, but he was determined. 'Gets a bit solitary,' he said. He was trying to signal to me. I followed him out of the room a moment later. 'Don't you do it, guv,' he said. 'Even if it is just noises, it gets on your nerves at night. I tell you I wouldn't spend another night like that one by myself. The lads' first night was jumpy.' I was touched that he should be concerned, but I couldn't help grinning. There was something old-womanish about our painters.

'What you *think* makes a difference,' I suggested. 'I think I'm quite safe, so I'll sleep like a log.' The painter shook his head. 'Thanks all the same,' I said.

Alf was admiring. 'More'n I'd do,' he said. Joe said nothing. He stood outside the house in the dusk, slowly glancing round at the darkening garden. The banks of shrubs fascinated him. He scrutinized them, a man peering into a jungle, apprehensive of what they might shelter.

Sarah kissed me lovingly. 'I wish I could stay,' she whispered. 'I love it here.'

We were in the hall. I indicated the three men outside in the dark.

'Someone has to take them back to their wives and sweethearts,' I said. 'We aren't the only people who are in love.'

I watched them disappear down the drive towards the road. As they turned off along the country road Sarah played a tattoo on the horn. Then the car engine accelerated and faded into the distance.

The first thing I noticed was how quiet it was. The painter was right about that. In busy, crowded England, with humanity packed into every square mile, here was silence, and peace, and seclusion. It occurred to me that those were soon going to become some of the most precious commodities on this overcrowded globe.

I walked through the empty rooms, conscious of my pleasure, enjoying the fact I was alone. A special aura came off the place at night. It had a fragrance, as if offering a gift. Different places had different flavours. A house was like a person, perhaps having acquired its character from the people who had lived in it. It had its own spirit.

There were three sharp reports on the stairs, and another series of cracks, like the brisk tread of a military man somewhere in the house. It reminded me exactly of the painter's description; like someone walking through the place, someone with every right to be here. The *crack! crack! crack!* of a soldier, heading towards me. I stopped shock-still in the centre of the room. No wonder the men had been alarmed. Anyone who was prepared to be frightened would have found cause for fear. That was undoubtedly someone on the move, if you were to conjure up that vision. No wonder the painter had expected the handle to turn. Instinctively I glanced at it myself. The room was gloomy. There was no electric bulb in this socket yet. I was quite taken aback. Was the handle turning? Did it move? I crossed and opened the door. The empty landing beyond breathed gently and reassuringly in the dark. But what if I had been the painter? Or Joe? Or Alf? What might one not have managed to imagine?

I went slowly along the corridor. Until we had fitted lights through the house it was foolish to walk in the dark. We had left boxes all over the place and a dinner service on the floor of one of the rooms. I would stay downstairs where a few lights functioned, I decided. But I moved slowly in the dark. Cautiously, yes. But also a little languorously, for I realized how pleasant it was to be absorbed in the great well of the house; it cradled me, as if with protective arms.

I made a bed for myself in the sitting-room, sleeping under the great windows, black with night, where the painter had slept. Shadows pressed close outside. Stars winked over the tall pines on the far sides of the lawn. This had been an elegant estate in years gone by. Even thirty years ago it must have been a rich way of life that could afford to keep up such a place as this. The cellars below indicated that a troop of servants had once run it. Now we had taken it over, Sarah and myself, part of a rootless generation, passing through, borrowing this elegance as it fell to our good fortune. Vagabonds and rogues found themselves in palaces from time to time.

I remembered I had turned off the central heating. I thought that I ought to switch it back on or the house would be cold by the morning. The noises had ceased, for the most part. Every now and again something would move in the dark, upstairs, downstairs, outside, not only the noises I had explained to the painters but also birds roosting on the roof, a night bird just outside the house. An owl. There were moles on the lawn; I'd seen the earth they threw up. The owls would be after them. There were all the night sounds of the country. No wonder my painters had had their fears.

I went down to the cellar to switch on the boiler. The lights weren't working down there either. I didn't know my way and groped along with a hand against the wall.

Someone had left something on the stair – a brush, as I saw later. But in the dark I didn't see it. My foot twisted as the brush rolled over under my foot. I threw out my hands to stop myself, but I didn't have a chance. I pitched forward into the dark. I wasn't sure what held me. But I was checked – caught – given a chance to steady myself, getting hold of something on the wall. It felt like a man's jacket, perhaps an old coat hanging on a nail . . . I found one there in the morning. It was a lucky chance. The odd thing was that I took it all in my stride. I had no feeling of surprise, I expected to be protected. *Nothing* could happen to me here, even if I walked blindfolded, and I was little better than blindfold now. I had slightly twisted my ankle, but I limped to the boiler and switched it on.

I went back to the sitting-room, and lay on the camp bed I'd brought, nursing my ankle. The sounds of the house were a lullaby. It was as if I and someone else, I couldn't think who, were sharing a joke. I had ample proof that the painter was wrong. There was nothing to be afraid of there; nothing to alarm one in the dark. The very opposite! The boy Alf had asked something like, 'Who is it in the house then?' I fell asleep without knowing the answer . . . but the strange awareness was, I realized, that there was an answer to be given.

2

I knew I was dreaming, and that a bell was ringing. It seemed to take a long time and a great effort to drag myself into consciousness. The phone was still sounding somewhere in the house.

It took me a moment to remember where it was. The room designated as a study was the next one off the hall. I climbed out of my camp bed and hurried to answer it. I felt a twinge of pain in my ankle, and remembered the accident of the evening before.

'Where were you?' It was Sarah's voice. 'I was beginning to get anxious.'

'Why?'

'You took long enough to answer.'

'I was asleep.'

'Do you know what time it is? Nearly nine! Not like you to sleep so long!'

'Must be the fresh air,' I said. 'How are you, love?'

'Missing you,' she said. 'And a little worried.'

'What is it?'

'Oh, Mac and friends.'

I was annoyed. 'Idiots! What have they been saying?'

'Don't blame them. I made them tell me. They sat in the car all the way back to town, hardly saying a word. Just mumbled about you staying. I made them come out with it. I said I'd turn around and come back if they didn't say what the matter was. I began to imagine all sorts of things.'

'There is absolutely nothing wrong,' I told her.

'I know,' she said. 'They've talked themselves into a three-man mass hysteria. They were almost making *me* hear things. What sort of a night did you really have?'

'Slept like the dead,' I said. And that made us both laugh.

'Anything else?'

'I fell down the cellar steps. And a good fairy swooped in and caught me before I hit the cold stone floor.'

'Did you really?'

'I just tripped over something. We'll have to put lights in all these sockets. I twisted my ankle. Next time I could break my neck.'

'Darling, you need me to look after you.'

'I know.'

'Shall I come down?'

'What's that?'

'I could be there in a couple of hours.'

'Good Lord, no. You've got things to do. You've got to see Freddie – and the solicitors. And look in at the office. Mac and his mates are out of their minds!'

'I meant because of your ankle.'

'It's nothing. I shouldn't have mentioned it.'

'Maybe I'll get things done quicker than we expected. I'll call you to see how you're getting on.'

'Sarah, everything is splendid!'

'Well, anyhow, if there's nothing to keep me tomorrow, I could come for Sunday.'

'Someone has to bring Mac and the others down on Monday,' I reminded her.

There was a slight pause. 'Don't you want me to come?' She sounded a little subdued.

'What a question! It's boring without you, you know that. Everything is. Life's boring without you! If you think you can do all you have to do today, you drive down *tonight*!'

'Darling.' That seemed to be what she wanted to hear. 'I'll call you later. I'll let you know.'

I went back to the sitting-room and folded the blankets on the camp bed. Then I stacked it against the wall. I did this slowly and thoughtfully, for I was a little puzzled by what I had said. I had been disturbed by the thought of Sarah coming back to Longwood. Why? Several reasons sprang to mind, but none of them seemed entirely true. It wasn't just concern about her driving backwards and forwards, it was something else, and I could not quite put my finger on it. Then I began to realize that I wanted to be there by myself. It was almost as though I had a secret assignation. I hadn't had an assignation for years! Not for three years; not since Sarah and I began living together. We were very happy with each other. As happy as a man and woman were ever likely, or entitled, to be. But I had never before rejected a moment of her company, and I had just said enough on the phone to dampen her thought of racing back to be with me.

It preyed on my mind as I went to the kitchen to make tea. Sitting alone having breakfast wasn't going to be much fun. I was used to seeing her at all times, especially breakfast. She was at her best then, it made the day start with pleasure. I knew there was a very easy way of solving the problem: I had only to call my apartment in London, and she'd still be there. She'd be down like a shot. She'd realize I was sorry to have hurt her feelings; I would tell her my ankle was painful – well, it was slightly. I needed her.

I went back to the study. There was nothing in it except the phone on a box lying on its side. Inside the box were a few papers. I could see some of them were the old plans the house agent had given me on my first visit. We had used very similar plans when we brought the builders in some weeks ago to remove the additions to the house made by later generations. An extension from the 'thirties had gone, a modern conservatory been pulled down, the portico rebuilt to match the original. Before the painters had set to work, Longwood was as its first owners had so confidently designed it. That gave me great pleasure. And it occurred to me that none of the builders had complained of anything strange. That must prove something.

I sat on the box by the phone and went through the documents. I spent a fair time putting them into order, to see how the place had grown and changed. It was like reading a dead person's letters . . . except that this house was certainly not dead. Then I remembered why I had come into the study. I glanced at my watch. It was just possible that Sarah had not yet left the apartment.

I dialled and heard the phone ring at the other end. I held on, listening, for a long time, feeling guilty about something. At any moment she would answer. But I knew she had gone.

The episode puzzled me. I walked through the house from room to room, not exactly admiring it but just being there; moving about in the big rooms, noting changes that had been made, checking with the earlier drawings and photographs.

There was one sepia photograph that I found very attractive, of faint figures on the lawn before the house. It seemed to tap some memory – some dream memory. It looked like a Victorian gardening party. Did they have such things? Faded shapes merged with the façade of the house – some clearer than others, none distinctly discernible. But there appeared to be a man with a well-kept short beard. A large and imposing woman stood near him with a garden rake. Three other figures posed on the steps to the front door, with a dog. It was all very formal, self-conscious. But so much in period that I felt a sense of

27

appreciation – almost identification. They had been previous owners of Longwood. I had inherited their home. They looked sure of themselves, self-possessed in a way I knew I could never be – sure of everything, by the look of that central couple. From what I could make out of the three other figures merging with the stone walls, one was in a uniform, one was plump and bald, one was a girl.

I think at that moment I became conscious of a sense of continuity. They had passed. I should pass. The house itself would ultimately pass, becoming rubble one day, but it did have a more enduring being than either I did, or these sepia-tinted owners of a hundred years ago. It would act as a shell for Sarah too, I reminded myself, and for others yet to come, as yet unborn, other people who would share these walls. I felt very close to someone – or something. I looked round the room. It was a very odd moment. I was especially aware of the seclusion, the silence. In a way it was magical! I glanced at the photo again. *They* had been here. *They* had lived in this room. They had spent days, nights, years, here probably; their essence, spirits, minds (whatever one liked to call the flow of life) *that* had been spun out in this place. Perhaps it never passed away. Time never really passes away, does it? They were still here. I was still here. I supposed in a sense the unborn inhabitants were still here, or were already here, however one liked to put it.

It gave me a reassuring feeling of the timelessness of life, something of my own restlessness, my need to be doing, achieving, drained away. Effort didn't seem to matter very much. It was enough just to *be*. To be here. To walk, rather like a spirit myself, from room to room, with the bundle of documents in my hand, lazily noting what time had done.

What I *did* note was the way Mac and his team had rejuvenated the place. The white paint, sparkling and glossy in the morning sun, mirrored the light. I would phone Sarah later. She might go back to the apartment for lunch.

It was Saturday. Even the spry old gardener wouldn't put in an appearance today. I would have the place to myself. Well, almost to myself.

The estate agent's brochure had described Longwood as a miniature country estate which was an exaggeration, though once upon a time it may have been. Now it had nine acres, and that was more than enough in my opinion. The grounds were mostly lawn round the house, and there were also a large walled garden and two big old-fashioned greenhouses. The drive came from the road about fifty or sixty yards away, swept past the front door, went on round the house to what were once stables and was now a garage with the groom's quarters as a flat above it. Some day I would put it in order. Ideal for friends and visitors. The drive finished there, but a path continued into the woods that gave Longwood its name. When the place had really been an estate it had included more of this wood than it did now. But I was still the owner of a long strip of trees on two sides of a stream which marked the border of the property. The path wound between rhododendrons and azaleas, high trees, pines, yews, the occasional beech. A magnificent oak stood in a field, which also went with Longwood. There were two other fields, but these were on lease to a neighbouring farmer. He had cattle in one, and some elderly horses in the other. It made for space and solitude round the house. Neighbours couldn't be seen. We were pleasantly isolated.

I walked past the stables; looked in at the walled garden; tasted the grapes in the greenhouse. It was September and summer was slow in leaving. The morning was warm. Bees invaded a vegetable patch that had gone to seed. Footsteps, my footsteps crunching on the gravel path, were the only sounds.

On the edge of the wood I stopped to look back. The house stood on the top of a slight rise, painted a pale rosy-white, with large sash windows, big eyes watching over its precincts, watching the stranger moving through its grounds.

The path led under the trees by the stream. Sun filtered through. Leaves and flowers were still nearly as thick, full, heavy as midsummer. The stream itself had dried to a trickle in rainless days, a mere whisper as it went over old ground. The banks were two or three feet apart, two feet deep; the water would be fast-moving when the weather broke. The area was peppered with springs.

Of course I had been down this rhododendron walk before, several times; but always with someone else – with the agent, with Freddie Dempster, my partner, several times with Sarah. This time the walk was different, I was very far away from the rest of the world. Strange, in a crowded country, with London fifty miles off and roads to the coast a mile from my door. Yet it was isolated; and more than isolated, it was timeless. Maybe the sound of bees is timeless, and the trickle of water. And I caught glimpses of the field through the bushes; horses are timeless, ambling about, necks stretched, champing the grass, throwing their heads up, shaking their manes, staring at me, on the edge of their territory.

The end of the path curved round a pond. It had been called 'the flight pond' in the agent's brochure, but now it was overgrown, motionless, muddy and dark. Little sunlight got under the high branches. It was four or five hundred yards from the house as seen across the fields, but it seemed a long way away. Another world.

There were signs of bygone days, overgrown, tangled with weeds and brambles. By a yew hedge I found a wooden bench rotting under the trees. It collapsed as I touched it. The path led further, but the mass of undergrowth was formidable. That was one part of the garden we were going to have to forget about.

As I walked back I enjoyed the same content I had experienced in the house. I didn't feel I had to go anywhere or do anything. To stroll back up the path was all one could ask for. This was unlike me. As long as I could remember I had been pushing on; hoping to achieve some position, looking for something. The feeling of the place – the atmosphere – made me relax. I didn't have to go on looking for anything. Had I found it?

The sun was warm, and it shone in my face as I came out of the trees. I was surprised to see anyone in the grounds on Saturday. Perhaps it was a neighbour, or a tradesman? Someone crossed the lawn at the front of the house; I saw him indistinctly against the light. A tall man by the look of him.

I called, 'Hello, there. Won't be a moment.'

I thought he had heard me, as he seemed to turn in my

direction. But he was some distance off and I had the big dell to cross – going down into it, then up again. I wasn't sure if he was still there as I climbed out, but I caught a brief glimpse of something. A shadow? He must have gone round to the front door. But when I got there, there was no sign of him. That puzzled me. Unless he had headed straight down the drive towards the road? There was no sound of a car, so he must have walked. Then I wondered why he had been wandering about on the lawn. What was he looking for there? I should have thought a visitor would have kept to the paths. I wasn't much concerned. What I had seen of him – or rather the impression I had formed – was of a solid gentleman, dark-suited, taking his time, walking about the premises as I had been doing myself. Perhaps the locals didn't know that Longwood now had an owner. He might be a neighbour who was in the habit of strolling round my lawns, and was embarrassed to be seen. I was sorry he had disappeared. I would have enjoyed a little company. He obviously appreciated the place.

I walked round the house again, just to be sure he had gone, and as I got back to the front door I heard the phone ring. It echoed through the empty rooms, but I wondered if I would have heard it had I been down in the wood. I'd have to have an outside bell installed. I guessed it would be Sarah.

'Mr Morell?' It was a man's voice, unfamiliar.

'Speaking.'

'Sorry to bother you. The name is Hedges. You don't know me, but we are fairly close neighbours.'

It was a 'solid' sounding voice; respectable, sedate.

'Nice of you to call.'

'Not at all. We weren't sure if there was anyone staying in Longwood yet . . .'

The penny dropped. 'Ah, so that was you I saw in the garden just now?'

There was a pause. 'I beg your pardon?'

'Sorry. I thought you might have been here a short time ago.'

'No, Mr Morell. Neither my wife nor I . . .'

'Sorry, I thought there was someone . . . Please go on.'

'It's just that my wife was driving past your place this

morning from the village and thought there was someone in the grounds. We knew there had been workmen there through the week, but understood they had gone. We get our information from The George, you know.'

I knew the pub in the village. Sarah and I had had drinks there a couple of times.

Mr Hedges was still speaking. 'She thought I had better check to see if there was anyone in the house. One can't be too careful nowadays, you know.'

'That's very kind of you,' I said. 'She would have seen me. I've been taking a look at things.'

'I hope you enjoy it there,' said Hedges. The voice was undoubtedly solid, almost pompous. 'It is, if I may say so, a splendid house . . . We knew it when the Bennetts lived there.'

'You must see it again when we have it in order,' I said.

I hadn't put the phone down more than a moment when it rang again. This time it was Sarah.

'Hello, darling. I am stupid. I didn't think about it until you rang off; then I wondered why you were falling over things in the dark when we brought down some light bulbs in that box.'

'Which box?'

'The one in the kitchen. You won't have nearly enough to go round, but if you spread them about you'll have sufficient light not to break your neck. And as well as that, there's a torch.'

'Don't worry about me. I can see in the dark.'

'Darling, you don't see very well even by day.'

That was true. I sometimes had difficulty seeing things not directly in front of me. She didn't sound concerned, but I knew what she was like.

'You're not still thinking about what the mad painters said?'

'Good Lord, no! What have you been doing?'

'Chatting with our neighbours.'

'Really?'

'A chap checking my credentials . . . How's work?'

'I saw Freddie. He says there are one or two decisions he doesn't want to take on his own. I told him you'll be back on Monday. There's nothing that can't wait till then.'

'Good.'

Sarah and Freddie could have run my business without me, but neither of them believed that. I was now delegating more to the rest of the management. I knew I had been working very hard for a long stretch. This was the first time I had backed off for five years, ever since the company had been set up. It was, fortunately, very successful. I knew now I could ease up, take a rest. And to be honest, I had begun to feel I needed to.

'But I don't think I'll get everything done in time to get down this week-end,' Sarah added.

'I'm sorry.'

'I'll go into the office first on Monday. So Mac and the lads will also be a little late.'

'Never mind,' I told her, 'I'm getting on with things.'

'Don't forget to put the light bulbs in.'

I spent a little time finding the right box in the kitchen. Sarah had stacked tins of food, soap, washing-powder, brushes and clothes on top. There were six bulbs and I took her advice and put them in the hall and corridors so I could see where I was going. I put one above the cellar steps in case I had to go down to the boiler again. And I kept one for the sitting-room where I slept. I put the torch beside my camp bed.

It was a pleasure taking my time, finding out how things worked, where we would keep things, discovering cupboards I hadn't seen before, or had forgotten. There was a scullery beyond the kitchen, with a butler's pantry boasting its own set of bells, shelves, and sinks and the old kitchen quarters with their splendid, scrubbed and polished surfaces, their array of brass and woodwork. I couldn't help feeling what a pity it was that such workmanship, such a solid way of life, such an era of richness, was passing away.

I was hungry by the time it started to get dark, and the village pub was a mile away. I knew I could get a meal there, and set off at a fair pace. The moon rose early, giving a white light. I kept looking back towards Longwood, but it was well back from the road and hidden by trees. They chose their building-sites well in the old days; sheltered, facing the sun, looking out over the property.

The George was one of several pubs in the village; the one

patronized by the 'in-comers', or 'them commuters' as we were called by the locals. There were a fair proportion of commuters in and around Longwood – mostly well-to-do people, who could afford to be in their offices as late as ten.

The landlord greeted me as a friend. 'Evening, Mr Morell. On your own?' There weren't many people in the bar.

'Your lads come down here some nights,' he told me. 'Quiet lot. Not too happy about the country.'

I realized he was talking about the painters. I nodded. 'Understandable. Dangerous after the safety of London.'

He grinned. He was a Londoner himself. He and his wife had taken the pub a year back, and it was turning out well. He chatted on. I went to an alcove where they served meals. They made a pretence of old English food, but you could get the same meal anywhere in London.

He had a brief chat as he brought the coffee. 'How's it going? Think you're going to like it here?'

'Very much.'

'Nice house, Longwood.' He nodded. 'Old, I heard. Get an old bloke in here knew it as a boy. Worked there when they had their own butcher. Makes you think, doesn't it? These big houses had a mass of servants. Their own butcher!' I was paying him. 'Well, anyway, that's all over.' He hesitated. 'Got a reputation, you know.' He looked at me as though he were asking a question.

'Oh?'

'Well, yes. All these old houses do.'

'What sort?'

'The usual. What those painters were saying in the bar one night. Can't quite explain some things going on . . . noises and the like.'

'I explained them,' I told him.

'Right.' The landlord grinned. 'If you want to frighten yourself, you can do.'

I walked the mile home. There, now, that shows how I felt about it! It was already 'home' in my mind. When I saw it in the moonlight – big black windows, dark pupils, watchers from within – it was with a glow of satisfaction to be back.

I had brought a bottle of Scotch with me from the pub. All I could find in the kitchen was a cup. But I sat in one of the few chairs by the window in the sitting-room, in the dark, without turning on my newly installed light, and the peace of the night was almost tangible. Birds fluttered on the roof. Something disturbed them, an owl? I stooped to pour a second drink . . . I was spending a long time over this nightcap . . . getting a lot of pleasure out of it. I froze! On the lawn, in the bright patch that lay beyond the shadows of the trees, something was moving slowly, low on the ground . . . On *his* ground, his patch, proud possessor . . . a fox! Just to see a wild creature! Then he turned, vanishing under the trees. So I wasn't on my own! I was not the only owner of Longwood. It was possessed at many levels. It belonged to a fox.

I went back and made sure all my lights were out, as there were no curtains on the windows. Then I made up the camp bed, unaccustomed to all this exercise, this walking, and suddenly tired. I had slept very deeply the night before. I remembered Sarah's call had wakened me. I had a feeling sleep would be as deep again.

The sound of the boiler cutting out for the night made me smile in the dark. It reminded me of the painters, watchful, wary at this time each night, no doubt. And I was ready for the cracking of the floorboards as the warmth of the house subsided. But the sound was a long time coming, and I fell asleep waiting for it.

I wasn't sure what wakened me. Nor did I know how much later it was. I reached for my watch on the floor beside me as I heard the first faint noise. I had been ready for the smart stride of what I thought of as my military man – the *crack, crack, crack*, the painter had heard, the crisp step I had demonstrated. But this sound was not that. This was not the step of a soldier. Indeed, it was not even the step of a man. That is, if it were a step at all.

It was, I reminded myself, the wooden floor contracting: there was no doubt about that. And yet, at the same time I had a vision of the hall outside my door, as if I could see what was happening there. In the dark I could hardly see across the room I was in, yet the hall suggested itself vividly.

It was the soft scurry of light feet that came to mind. The pitter-pat of shoes, like soft dancing-shoes . . . the sort worn by a young girl. The sound, of course, created the vision, I was aware of that. But it was effective. I could almost see the light dress flutter through the hall towards my door.

I sat up sharply. It was very real. The soft steps almost running . . . the hand reaching for the handle. Not that I had any apprehension. No alarm . . . no fear at all . . . only the sudden need to make my presence known. Illogically, as there was no one there, I had to give a warning of my presence.

'Who's there?'

But I was too late . . . the fraction of a second too late. Time for the handle to turn. I couldn't see it. But I guessed. And as I called, the whole house caught its breath. It was not just a silence that followed. Not a *silence*. It was an intake of breath! Of shock, startled alarm . . . of someone, something, else. Not me – I was totally at ease.

I had the light switch by my bed and pressed it. A blaze filled the room, artificial, abrupt, all-pervasive whiteness. For a second I could see everything. Then the bulb gave a 'ping'! The voltage, the power, something, was too much for it. The room was blacker, far blacker than before.

But I had seen enough. Quite what I had seen, I didn't know; but something. Someone was certainly outside that door, for there was no more movement. No light dance-slippers had scrambled away. The intruder was still there.

I crossed the room, snatched up the torch and threw open the door. I snapped on the torch and shone it into the hall. It was dark, silent, unruffled. And no one was there.

I stood, knowing this was true. In a sense understanding it, and in another sense unable to accept it; yet I had to. There *was* no one there. No one wearing slippers. No one dancing through the house. No party-dress swirling.

It was almost with disappointment that I went back to the room. What should have disturbed me, didn't. And, if I were honest, what should *not* have disturbed me, did very much. The strange thing was that I realized that in one way I – in someone's

36

eyes, or perhaps in respect of the house, the creatures in the house, the fox, the night birds, and whatever else – not they, but *I* was the intruder.

Silence, real unshocked silence, oozed back. The house breathed again. A deep, rhythmic, slow, pulse-beat; soothing, hypnotic, as in sleep.

3

Sunday morning, and the sound of drumming on the window woke me. I had seen Longwood in the sun of a dying summer; now it was being washed by rain blown in gusts against the glass. The trees across the lawn bent and swayed. The tops of the Wellingtonias – two giants guarding the drive – danced a swirling jig. Shallow water lay on the grass, wealden clay making it slow to percolate. Clouds, big heavy grey clouds, blew across the sky. I stood at the windows, delighted that all should be as attractive as in the warmth of the previous day. This excited, waving agitation! Blasts of air shook the bushes, the impact as they hit the house buffeting the front door, rattling windows.

I found one window not properly shut and a damp patch on the floor, and went round the house to see all was watertight. Longwood was a liner in a storm. On the top of a ridge, its curtain of trees battered by the wind, the house arrogantly faced anything the elements could fling at it. Wind howled down the chimneys. It made me feel well protected, warm, behind these thick walls.

Sarah phoned. 'What's it like?'

'Blowing a gale.'

'It's bad enough here,' she said. 'Any slates off?'

'Solid as a rock,' I said.

'Any more problems?'

'None at all.'

'Kept on your feet, have you?'

'I can see where I'm going now,' I said. 'I put the lights in as you suggested. Works a treat. Nothing like modern inventions to take the hassle out of life.'

I don't know why I didn't tell her about the footsteps in the night, but I didn't. Perhaps because it would be so hard to explain. Or perhaps . . . perhaps there was something about those footsteps – the dancing footsteps – so provocative, so special, that I did not wish to share it. I started to tell her, then I changed the subject. It would only alarm her. Besides the whole thing was fantasy, wasn't it?

'Have you had a look at the stables?' she asked.

That was one of the things I had stayed down to do. I wanted to find out how much neglect there had been in the building.

'I haven't got round to that,' I admitted.

'What *have* you been doing?'

'One thing and another. It all takes time, you know. You can't drive things along in the country.'

That must have reminded her of something, for she went on, 'Freddie has arranged for those Germans to be in the office on Tuesday. He needs you to discuss terms.'

'I'll be back,' I told her.

She was a splendid person to have as a partner. She made sure no aspect of my business was overlooked, and all my interests were her interests. It had always been like that, ever since we met, long before we realized we were in love, years before we began living together.

'You know what he's like. He needs support.'

'He'll have mine,' I assured her.

'Don't forget, I'll be late tomorrow.'

'I remember.'

She was ticking things off a mental list. She often did that. It left me smiling as I put the phone down.

When the rain eased off I went down to the stables about fifty yards away. The upper floor, the rooms the groom had lived in, were musty and cold. The rain had got under the eaves, and a wall was wet. Downstairs an area had been turned into the garage which had once housed a carriage. The manger was next door, with stalls for two horses. Further along was a comfortable little room. A label tied to the key read '*Tack Room*'. It was panelled in red wood, with some fine shelves; the fireplace contained old ashes, and a bundle of newspapers mouldered in a cupboard. The room was nicely proportioned, built for a servant but one of importance. I lit one of the papers and put it in the grate. It smoked a bit, then began to draw. An old Victorian chair, the worse for wear, stood by the fire. I tried it out, sitting there looking through yellowing newspapers. They were from the years before the war, so the rooms hadn't been lived in for a long time. It seemed a pity. I felt an obligation to do what I could to restore them. The structure was too good to leave to decay. I saw the mark on the wall showing where the mirror Mr Bennett had spoken of had been an ancient fixture. In the centre of it was the recess, in which were still a number of papers; farm records, notices of cattle sales, estimates for extending the drive, accounts from local salesmen. There was also a copy of *The Sphere* with a page turned down: a report about a hunt, with photos of the huntsmen marked. In the margin someone had written 'Bess of Longwood'. A splendid black mare was taking a gate.

The rain tailed off, drips falling from the broken gutters. I thought about going back to the house; or for lunch in The George before it was too late. Pushing the papers back into the recess I saw an ornate drawing of the gardens, clearly the layout of the whole estate as it had once been . . . The house, out-buildings, walled garden, flight pond, the folly. I had to turn back to look at that. The folly? What folly? I had never heard of a folly.

It appeared to be behind the flight pond, close to where I had been yesterday. I examined the plans. Yes, it looked as if it was just beyond the yew hedge, where I'd been stopped by the dense brambles. Perhaps there was another way through.

I hurried down the rhododendron walk.

I had the same trouble as the day before: the brambles were too thick to get through without hacking out a path. I went back to the stables to look for tools. Anything would do . . . a spade; a scythe. A rusty hand-cutter, like a sickle, the edge crumbled with rust, was all I could find. I went back down the path, beginning to appreciate just how much walking one had to do in nine acres. Everything was sparkling with the rain. The first few strokes at the long weeds soaked me. The blade was blunt and tore rather than cut, but I made a little progress; enough to encourage me. Somewhere just out of sight, round the other side of the pond, probably on the other side of the high thick hedge, was this secret place, this folly.

I had to stop after about ten minutes, unused to the effort, leaning on the tree beside me. It was a matter of getting my breath back. It didn't occur to me to give up the task; not even to delay it until I had the right tools. This inadequate little blade would do.

I went back on the attack with a little more skill, trying to conserve strength, taking it slowly, deliberately; but the going was back-breaking. After half an hour I had gone only a step or two into the undergrowth. I stuck the sickle in the ground, and stood, heart hammering, under the trees. I wasn't going to manage this, at least not in one day. It would take a long time to cut back the growth of years. I looked around. What a jungle it was! Weeds on weeds, trees seeded under trees, dark, all round the pool. Perhaps a hopeless task, not worth the undertaking. A lost corner in a huge garden. Searching for a building that might be long gone. That was the real folly!

As I was getting my breath back I had the feeling I was being watched.

I don't quite know what made me think that. I didn't hear anything. I didn't see anyone. But I had the sense that I was a centre of interest. There was an observer somewhere, motion-less, secretive, watching me. I looked round, slowly, cautious-ly, but saw no one. Two of the horses lifted their heads and viewed me from across the field . . . No, the feeling had come from somewhere nearer, quite close at hand.

I picked up the sickle again. Not as a weapon, I didn't need that; but the sickle showed I was working in this place, that I had a right to be here. Anyhow, the feeling I sensed was one of interest, not aggression, as though I had intrigued the genie of the place.

The wind blew the branches above, and I was showered with

raindrops. I would come back and finish this job. Having made my silent watcher that promise, I went back to the house.

The rain hung around for part of the afternoon, but by the time I set off for The George in the evening there were mostly clear skies, with a moon that came and went behind high clouds. The landlord greeted me with the news that there was something special on the evening menu. Local pheasant. He recommended it. And as I had a drink before the meal, he asked how things had gone.

'Anything to support your lads' alarm? Any strange happenings?'

I laughed. 'They must be out of their minds,' I said. 'Or I wouldn't be there alone, would I?'

He thought that proof enough, and it wasn't until I was by myself later in the dining alcove that I thought about my answer. I had certainly believed it, as I said it. There was nothing unusual about Longwood, either the house or the grounds. I had taken it all in my stride. Never for a moment had I been alarmed. Intrigued, yes. The feet dancing to my door had startled me; but it was a pleasurable excitement. And the second moment of unreality – the feeling of being watched – well, that wasn't anything very definite: lots of people have feelings that don't match reality. I didn't think of them as strange happenings. I didn't believe they were strange. They were very ordinary to me, normal . . . And yet it puzzled me that I had so accepted the two incidents, had played them down to such an extent, that they didn't occur to me when he asked the question.

I stayed later than I intended; and the landlord came over to make an introduction. 'Thought you might like to know there's a Mr Hedges here. And his wife. Said they'd had a word with you on the phone. I wondered if you'd like to meet?'

Mr Hedges was not as I expected. Fifty or sixty, he and his spare, spry wife were jolly and amusing. We had drinks together, then they ran me back to Longwood, as they had to pass it on their way home. I was glad to be spared the walk.

They dropped me off at the end of the drive. I went into the house, ready to check the landlord's question. It was as normal,

41

as ordinary, as I had said. No creaking boards, no whispered sounds. No shadows. Nothing. I went to sleep in my camp bed as soon as I got into it.

The painters and their alarms were ludicrous.

I half expected another call from Sarah next morning, but it didn't come.

I spent the time making notes for my meeting next day in London with the directors of the Munich company who were visiting us. I like to prepare myself fully before any important meeting. In the past I had been considered some sort of a whizz-kid (the term was of its time). Partners and competitors thought I acted spontaneously in business, with an instinct for success. The truth of the matter was that I spent time going over the eventualities, the permutations of a deal. It wasn't so much instinct as scheduling that assisted me. And that was what absorbed me on Monday morning as I sat in the hall and waited for Sarah to arrive with our little team of workers.

When they did arrive, the team was even smaller than I expected.

'Where's Alf?'

Mac shrugged. 'His mum wouldn't let him come.'

'His mother!' Alf was a grown man. I would have said, about twenty.

'She don't want him sleeping on the floor.'

I couldn't believe he was serious.

Sarah took me aside. 'Leave it. There was a hell of a row outside the house. Just inside, actually. But we could hear it in the car.'

'What about?'

'Oh, you know. God knows what he told that mother of his. But she wasn't going to have her lad exposed to the unknown.'

'Bloody hell,' I said. I had no idea they had taken things so badly.

'These two can manage,' she said. 'They're going to work night and day to make sure this contract is finished on time.'

'I admire that,' I said.

She shook her head. 'Not exactly what you think,' she said. 'They don't want to be a day longer than they have to.' I was very annoyed by this stupidity. 'Just leave it,' she repeated.

The two men were already at work, up ladders, and later on a plank slung between two ladders, silently covering vast areas of wall space with dedication. They moved from downstairs to the well of the stairs, hardly stopping at midday; and when they did, they soon got back to the job.

I told Sarah about my evening with the Hedges. 'Very old,' I said. 'Over fifty.' I was just thirty myself. Sarah was twenty-four.

We knew we were going to have to get back to London before the end of the day. The Germans were due in the office next morning first thing; first thing, when dealing with Germans, meant eight o'clock, well before managerial England was stirring.

I took Sarah round the gardens, anxious to show her everything, including the stables.

'Later on we'll make a flat out of that.' I pointed to the floor above.

'We don't want things too grand,' she smiled.

'Your brother can come and stay when he's in England.'

'I'm quite happy with you,' she said.

I was overcome with a desire for her. 'Nicky!' She pretended to be shocked. 'Not on this dirty, damp floor.'

'You wouldn't have said that two years ago.'

'I was young and hot-blooded then. We'll be back in our comfortable warm apartment tonight.'

'We're going to live here, you know,' I reminded her.

'When it's all nicely carpeted and furnished.' She went out of the tack room. I was inclined to agree with her as I followed.

The two painters had moved up to the landing on the stairs by the time we got back to the house. 'They're going at a lick,' I said. 'I should think – even just the two of them – they'll be done in time.'

'It doesn't really matter,' she said.

'It does. We planned it this way.'

'You planned it.'

'You didn't disagree.'

'No.' She sounded hesitant.

'Did you . . . I mean, are you going off the idea? Don't you want to get married?'

'Don't be silly. It's just that it doesn't have to be bound up with buying the house, settling down, everything ready.'

'In a way, it does. It's a new chapter.'

'I've been very happy,' she said.

'So have I. But this is a sign of the times. Passing time.'

'You're not *that* old.'

'Getting on.'

'Does it have to be bound up in this house?' she repeated. 'What if we'd never found Longwood?'

'We'd have found some other place.'

'You know I don't need gestures.' She took my arm.

'Gestures! This isn't a gesture. We've been together a long time. That's marriage, isn't it? I thought we decided to fix it the old-fashioned way.'

'Of course. So long as that's what we want.'

'Don't you?'

'Yes.' She kissed me almost protectively.

It puzzled me sometimes to find her so tender, as though she had to look after me.

Sarah was already thinking of leaving. 'We don't want to get mixed up in rush-hour traffic. I'll make tea for those two; I've got cakes. They deserve something.' She went into the kitchen.

On the spur of the moment I phoned the office.

'Give me Mr Dempster.'

Freddie was pleased to hear me. 'Everything ticking along fine,' he said.

'This meeting,' I asked, 'you know the score?'

'Yes. Why? Anything wrong?'

'Not really. The organization is a little out of joint. I made some notes. Could you jot a few of them down. Or put me on to tape.'

'You're on,' said Freddie. 'Why? Aren't you going to make it?'

44

'This is just in case,' I said. 'Best be prepared. I'll probably be home this evening . . . tomorrow morning at the latest.'

'God, you know these Germans. They're on a flight back to Frankfurt tomorrow evening.'

'I'll be there. This is just in case.' Over the phone I read out the details I had prepared that morning. 'Got that?'

'Loud and clear,' said Freddie.

'Think you can manage it? If I don't make it?'

'Of course. God, Nick, you aren't indispensable!'

'Don't frighten me,' I said. 'Good luck.' I'd already known I wouldn't be there as I put the phone down.

I had to tell Sarah as she was taking things from the car and stacking them in the hall. 'Just some more essentials,' she said. That was our joke.

'I don't think I'm coming,' I told her.

'What!'

'Not this evening anyhow.'

'But whyever not?'

I indicated the painters on the stairs.

'What's the matter? They're all right.'

'I don't think so. They are under some strain.'

'What difference will you make?'

I felt it would make a difference but I couldn't explain why. 'It will be one more person in the house,' I said lamely.

'That's ridiculous. And what about the meeting?'

'I've had a word with Fred.'

'When?'

'When you were making the tea.'

'Why didn't you tell me?'

'I was still making up my mind.'

She looked at me sharply. 'This is silly, Nicky. *They* don't need you. You have this business to attend to. The Germans will be offended.'

'I don't think so. Besides . . . I may be back before they go.'

'How will you get there?'

'I can hire a car in the village.'

She was unconvinced, even a little angry.

'You're being . . .' She shrugged and walked away.

45

'Don't go like that. I tell you I've given the details to Freddie.'

'You're the boss,' she said. She hadn't said that for a long time. She only said it when she was hurt. '*I* have to be there, anyhow.'

I gave her a kiss, but she didn't respond. For a moment I felt she didn't trust me.

'I love you, Sarah.'

She gave a smile as she drove away. I let the sound of the car die in the distance before I went into the house.

'You didn't have to do that, guv,' said Mac.

'I'd like to keep things moving,' I said cheerfully. 'We've got a schedule on this. You know – so many days to get it in order, so many days painting. There's a date fixed for the furniture to come down. We were supposed to be going off for a month after that.'

'Honeymoon?' said Joe.

I nodded. 'So I'd like to make it work.'

They didn't say anything else, but their backs expressed a lack of approval as they applied themselves to the job.

One of the rooms upstairs had been used as a billiard-room by the previous owner. The green-clothed table filled a large part of it. Cues and a scoring board had been left in a corner; coloured snooker balls were scattered round the table. It seemed to indicate how recently Longwood had been filled with life and activity; our own occupation of it was only a short time away.

Amongst the things Sarah had brought down on this visit was a briefcase of papers. On top was a scribbled note: '*Beautiful chimney in the stables. Have you seen it? Out of place. Idiotic. The best thing in Longwood.*'

I didn't know what she was talking about. I hadn't paid much attention to the flat in the stables . . . except to see that a lot of work was needed. '*Best thing in Longwood*'? Those musty little rooms? I put the briefcase in the sitting-room beside the picnic table. This would be my office for the time being. I had started business in sparser conditions nine years ago. Then I went off to the stables to look for Sarah's 'chimney'.

It was, in fact, a chimneypiece in the end room which had a good deal of plaster off the wall and two cracked and dirty windows shadowed by trees. No wonder I hadn't seen it. I wondered when Sarah had.

It was certainly out of period. The flat was modest, small; the chimneypiece dwarfed the room. It had been a labour of love and artistry, the art being of the twenties, the style that built Broadcasting House. A mantelpiece was held aloft by four naked figures, two men, two women, with a good deal to indicate the difference. Flat faces turned sideways, and heavy breasts helped to give the structure strength. Above the mantelpiece four more figures held up the lintel, framing three panels. These were painted with sunflowers and exotica. It was extraordinary to see this here, and, although it was not my favourite type of art, I realized it was exquisitely done. No wonder Sarah had picked it out.

I saw the gardener in the walled garden and joined him.

'Stayed down, sir?'

'For a bit.'

'Missus?'

'Not yet. Look Bridges, you know the flat in the stables?'

He looked up at it. 'Poor state,' he said. 'No one's been there since the war.'

'What about before the war?'

'Oh yes, chauffeur used to live there. And his wife.'

He nodded over that.

'What about that fireplace?' I asked.

'Fireplace?' That puzzled him. 'Oh, *that* fireplace.' He nodded again, a little grim, a little amused. 'That was the war,' he said. 'The soldiers. They were billeted here then. Didn't you know that? Yes, they were here then. They had the house. Ground gunners, they were. Trained in the field, and had the ack-ack where them horses are.'

'Soldiers made that fireplace?'

'One soldier. Mason or something. Made heads with clay. I wasn't here then; across the road, I was. But I seen him do the heads.'

'What was his name?'

47

'Can't say I ever knew it. But he was famous. Sold his pictures, and that, before the war.'

'What else did he do?'

'Didn't do a lot more after that fireplace. Got killed on the aerodrome. Knockholt, in Kent. Got killed there.'

'What did the owners do about it?'

'Nothing. Didn't need the place, did they? Didn't care for it. And Mr Bennett, chap before you, he hated it. He *hated* it.' Bridges went off chuckling.

The painters kept going until the light went. After that Mac called a halt. 'Don't get a true coat in the electric,' he explained. Joe would have gone on, but Mac firmly cleaned brushes and put everything away. He was so conscientious that I wished him well in my heart. I was just sorry he was still unhappy here.

They had brought tins of beer and stewed steak with them this time, having the cockney capacity to learn quickly how to make life tolerable, even in the country. I left them starting their meal. They were uncertain whether or not to invite me, but I told them I had arranged to eat at the pub. 'We're going to bunk down in the room beside the kitchen, guv. If it's all right with you? Smaller and don't get so cold at night.'

'Okay with me. I'll be in the sitting-room.'

The domestic details settled, they relaxed a little. As I left they were opening beer.

I got back late, and found the lights out in the kitchen and in the room beside it. I turned out the light they had left for me in the hall; and was soon in bed. I was getting used to this unencumbered life. I thought about what the gardener had told me, visualizing soldiers billeted in these rooms, living and sleeping like this.

I was at that moment when one is not certain if one is still awake, when I heard one of the painters come out of their room. I wondered if they had expected me to leave the hall light on. Whoever it was, he came tiptoeing into the hall, then went very softly up the stairs; occasionally a step creaked. What the devil, I thought, would either of them want on the floor above? There were lavatories and washbasins downstairs.

I waited for whoever it was to come back again. But there was no further sound. Then I remembered he could go through to the back, and come down a second lot of stairs by the butler's pantry.

I fell asleep waiting.

The painters were up before me in the morning. They had made tea and left the pot for me.

'Some there if you want it, guv.'

They both gave me a queer side-long look, a bit restrained. But Mac said, 'Hear that noise in the night then, guv? Hear that going up the stairs? What was that then? Sound of stairs cracking, was it? Woodwork cooling off again?' He looked at me drily. Joe had stopped at the kitchen door and was listening.

I got the message from nowhere. I grinned. 'Sorry about that,' I said. 'I didn't mean to wake you.'

'That was you then, guv?' Mac looked at me without batting an eyelid. 'That you up there?'

'Don't take it to heart,' I said. 'Just wanted to see how far you'd got.'

Neither of them said a word. Neither said I was a liar.

They were in full swing when I saw them later, and both looked at me as much to say they knew what I was up to. I was going to stand between them and anything that they didn't understand, anything that might threaten them. I don't know why they took comfort from that thought, but they did. The atmosphere lifted. Joe started playing his radio. The two of them chatted, chuckling over 'young Alf'. They stopped at eleven for a coffee, which I'd never seen them do before. They seemed to have unburdened something on to me; they felt I could cope with it. In an odd way, I felt the same myself. At last we had worked out a *modus operandi*. They could get on with the task; I was a shield against uneasy spirits. It went well. They loosened up, working just as fast, just as efficiently. They even began to enjoy themselves. I had no idea who or what – or if anything – had gone up the stairs in the dark, but I was grateful that the ice had broken and a sort of spring-time lit the house.

Mac allowed himself a joke. 'Nothing funny about this house, guv. Nothing that a few nails won't put right. Get them floorboards fixed down, and we'll all sleep safe.'

We got back the odd-job man whom Mac had fired, and he tidied up as they went along. Through the landlord at The George I got in touch with two women from the village, who came out to prepare the rooms for the arrival of furniture, the husband of one dropping them at the door from his car. They made a point of sticking together, moving from room to room in unison. They were both in their thirties, but giggled like young girls and jumped if anyone came into the room behind them.

'Cor! It's only you, Mr Morell!'

'What did you expect?'

'You never know, do you?' Peals of laughter.

The outcome was that the work went along faster than I had hoped for. Sarah was going to have to admit that it was a wise plan for me to have stayed behind. There wasn't much I could do personally in the house, but I had bought some garden tools. Bridges was critical. 'Don't need all those,' he said.

'I'm going to clear up the rhododendron walk,' I told him.

'Not been done for a long time,' he said. 'I reckon there's enough to do as it is.'

'I'll do this,' I said. 'Just the path round the flight pond.'

He wasn't impressed, and I noticed he left the walk to me. But as he came only on three days, he was right – he had enough to do. And I preferred things this way; I wanted to work on my own.

I had a mechanical cutter, but found it clumsy, noisy, and, besides, it seemed out of place; so I ran it back to the stables, and set to work with a hand-cutter, as lethal as a machete. It was a splendid tool, but the tangle of bracken, brambles, and weeds was formidable, and the sweat came running off me. I felt like a peasant – a farm-worker in an earlier century. We must have lost a lot of muscle in this labour-saving age.

The satisfaction I got was enormous as I saw some progress. Each small area cleared revealed more of the old path. There had once been an ornamental line of stones on either side. Most were missing or broken. I would reset them, I decided. The prettiness of the design, the pattern of the place, delighted me.

I would straighten up from time to time, not just to rest new-found muscles but to look with pride at my progress. I hadn't relaxed like this for a long time; I couldn't remember being so caught up in a game – for it was a game – since I was a child. I had thrown all my energy into work these last few years. I felt as though I had been swimming under water, and now was bursting to the surface with a shout of pleasure, playing, enjoying, doing something just for fun! What's more, the path made progress.

I was smiling at that thought, standing up to ease my back. Once or twice I had again had that feeling of being watched, which I ignored, putting it down to the fact I wasn't used to working like this. Besides, the horses cropped grass close by and a robin hopped about as I scraped at decades of fallen leaves. They had accepted me. I wasn't alone.

But now, viewing this first patch of path with pleasure, I did think I saw someone. I had heard nothing; I had no premonition, nothing like that, and there was no reason to expect that anyone was near me. It was just as I stood up, leaning back, I saw . . . I thought I saw . . . a man? Silent, watching, looking at what I was doing? I can't truthfully say I 'saw' him. It was too brief a moment for that. But I must have seen something, for I had the impression he was surprised. Now if I were to be able to get that impression, or any impression at all, I must have 'seen' him.

Of course it was an illusion. There was no one there. I had overdone the morning's work, that was all.

I went across to where he had seemed to stand. I couldn't quite get there as the bracken was thick, the brambles sharp. Anyhow, there was no sign of broken twigs, nor of leaves disturbed.

I got back to work, puzzled by the experience. Not that it disturbed me, but I wondered what would cause such a vision. Shadows under the trees? Sunshine? Branches? A trick of light? Reflections from the water in the pond?

I experimented. I looked up as before. Could I make him reappear? Was it I who created the onlooker?

51

But he didn't come back, and I wasn't surprised. It must be dead boring watching someone hacking at an old path.

I went back to the house to eat. The two women had gone; the painters had finished their cans of beer and sandwiches.

'Beer for you, guv, if you want it,' called Mac.

'Thanks.'

I was grateful for the way he always included me in his calculations.

I had my beer, bread, and cheese in the kitchen, my arms sore with the constant effort. I decided I'd done enough for the day, but I kept on thinking about the path in the wood. With a bit of determination I guessed I could clear another foot or two before dark. So I went back again, wondering at my own persistence. I wanted to get this area tidied up and back to what it must once have been. In a way I was hooked on it, but it was a harmless obsession.

I had a strange sensation as I walked down the path, as though I was on my way to see friends. As though I *expected* to see friends. My heavy cutter lay where I had put it; I picked it up and started where I had left off. In the wood round me was an air of excitement, pleasure – more, of amazement, jubilation! I was careful not to look up; not to try to see what caused this feeling. To do that might destroy it . . . and I found it exciting. Someone was watching again; someone was delighted by what I was doing. There was no sense of danger, nor harm. I was truly amongst friends.

I took my time during the afternoon. It was cool, the grass damp from the rain; and I wanted to stay as long as I could, to do as much as I could, to experience this sense of approval which wafted round me, which elated me. It was heady, intoxicating.

I cut old roots from my path, slashing back bushes. Working faster and more adeptly, I had another couple of yards cleared before the sun dipped. This job would be limited by light; evening came a little quicker at the flight pool under the trees.

I scraped the rubbish aside and wiped my machete, knowing what I was going to see before I looked up. He would be standing in the same place. He would be in shadow, then he would vanish.

I looked towards the spot, and saw a woman.

A woman this time! And previously a man! Surely that proved *something*. I wasn't imagining them. *Something* existed, something that on different occasions was different. Surely that was proof?

She vanished immediately, too quickly to be sure what she was like. Vague, vanishing pictures in an album flickered past. Middle-aged, dark, hair black on top of her head – powerful, imperious . . . Did I see all that? Did I guess it, or imagine it? My mind had taken a magical snapshot, and the inner image seemed to be all these things . . . to be looking on proudly, possessively, smiling.

Leaves rustled with a chilling breeze. The wood was empty, apart from myself. I put the machete back in the stables, and sat there as it darkened, not so much trying to make sense of those images . . . they already made sense . . . but wondering who the people were, a little surprised that I had accepted this experience so casually, without alarm. I had already decided not to speak of it to anyone.

4

And the next day was just as busy and effective, with Mac and Joe making progress in the rooms upstairs; the odd-job man oiling locks, washing windows, polishing metals; the two women from the village back for the morning. It was half-day at the nursery school and they both left at twelve to collect children. Before they went, a car stopped at the door. It was Sarah. She had a passenger, young Alf, shamefaced, muttering about his 'mum', carrying a sleeping-bag, anxious to get back to work before the other painters, straight-faced, could ask him mocking questions.

I was in the wood at the time, making progress, cutting a yard of pathway out of the Sussex jungle.

They sent Alf down to tell me Sarah had arrived and was at

the house, and I sent him back with the message that I would be there immediately. There had been no manifestations that morning, no visions, no appearances, but I had the idea that I was still the centre of an approving audience. However, they had kept out of sight, out of my senses.

It was only as Alf hurried back to the house that I was aware of anything unusual, any sort of presence. It was more than one. Several. All round me, as if I were boxed in, making it difficult to leave. It was a strange sensation; taking a step left me a little breathless. I stood getting my breath back, sticking the machete into a tree-stump, looking round to locate what was impeding me. It was like a web, but invisible. I found I was waving my arms – brushing something aside. It held me for a moment only – and then I was on my way back up the path.

But even then there was another despairing attempt to delay me . . . a sudden puff of air, a frail, ill-defined image, half-hearted in its presence, or lack of presence; a different image. But one that momentarily stopped me in my tracks. It was the dancing-shoes! I knew! (Though how I knew, I didn't know.) The wearer of the dancing-shoes! But oh! how vaguely; there, and then gone! Too faint to be effective. And yet . . . it was the way I had 'seen' her in the dark outside my door – in the hall – youthful, lovely, buoyant with life . . . Strange that that phrase should occur to me, but it was how I saw her, 'buoyant with life'. And then gone!

They were right to try. The charm was powerful, and she nearly took the resolution out of me. In any other circumstance I would have stayed, but not this time. Not with Sarah back at Longwood, waiting to see me.

I left the walk . . . and suddenly it was silent.

Sarah threw her arms round me. 'It's a transformation,' she said. 'How did you get all this done?' She was amazed to see the way the work had gone. 'What a crowd you've got. Who are they all? Those two women? And that other man?'

'They're from the village.'

'It's wonderful!'

'I'm going to get this finished, as planned, my love,' I said. 'I promised you. This place is my priority just now. No more fantasy about the young genius building a business empire.'

'*That* fantasy worked very well,' she said firmly. 'I must tell you about the German meeting. They loved your ideas; it all went through. I was wrong, you didn't need to be there. Freddie could do it.'

I was very pleased. 'Glad about that. But it was my second priority. I want this house to be right, I want this to work. I want you to be happy.'

'I've been happy for three years,' she scoffed. 'I don't need a house. I don't need to be married. I don't need anything except us. If you go on like this, I'll back out.'

'Come on, let's take a look round.'

'It's only a couple of days since I was here,' she protested.

'I've seen your chimneypiece,' I told her.

We went up to the flat in the stables and looked at the artistry of that unknown soldier, billeted here forty years ago.

'It's wonderful. Absolutely wrong. But I love it.' She was smiling as she stood looking at it. I knew how she felt, for there were things at Longwood which filled me with exaggerated delight. I nearly told her. I nearly said, 'Come and look at the flight pond,' but something stopped me, and we went back to the house.

'What fun finding that fireplace,' she said. 'It's my favourite thing.'

'Okay,' I said, 'I'll remember that.'

We went into every room in the house, Sarah marvelling. The painters were flattered. 'Had a bit of help, lady,' said Mac. 'Guv'ner helped, one way and another,' as though we were in cahoots about something.

'They're all together again.' Sarah indicated the three painters. 'You can safely leave them.'

'You're going back?' I asked.

'I have to. So do you. Really.' She looked at me, the smile going. A little serious. For the first time, a flicker of anxiety.

'What's keeping you here, Nicky?'

'Good Lord, nothing's keeping me.'

She watched me doubtfully.

55

'Don't worry,' I said, 'the business won't disintegrate if I'm not there for a few days.'

'Of course not,' she smiled. But she was uneasy.

She had made arrangements to drive back to London that afternoon. I was unwilling to let her go; one part of me longed for her to stay. But another voice, secretive, whispering, told me to let her go. I would be distracted by her. She was too much part of life; of the busy coming and going that had obsessed me for the last nine or ten years. Now I needed to be alone.

But I had a sharp stab of unhappiness as she left. We had been very happy these last three years. It had been my initiative to marry, not hers; it was a statement that I wanted to make. She was six years younger, six years less concerned with social gestures. I was the one who felt happier about – what? Settling down? God forbid! Making a statement about the permanence of our love? Perhaps. Perhaps at thirty, I felt I had played out one role and ought to be ready for the next. To be thirty before one was sure of one's emotions, of how real they were – surely that was late in life? Anyhow, I had made the running and Sarah had been happy to come along.

'Humouring his deeply conventional attitudes,' she informed our friends.

'About time,' they told her.

And now I felt that I was going a little shaky on the deal. Not exactly 'jobbing back', but losing my single-mindedness. Something else had crept in, as if I were infatuated by someone else, which I wasn't; there was no one else. I loved Sarah. No woman had affected me as deeply as she had done. No one else felt right to me.

I couldn't make out why I was summing up the past like this. With Sarah nothing was superficial; our happiness was never without arguments, without differences, some angrily, passionately felt. But even the troubles as they arose seemed an essential part of our lives. I never wanted to change any of it. I didn't want to change anything now . . . but I had never before been aware of this voice whispering at the back of my brain, advocating deception, betraying us. It was as if I were two people; each accepting the other, passing no judgements.

Once Sarah had gone, I felt relief and uneasiness. Perhaps I had caught the unease from her. But relief was the stronger emotion, and I went back to my task in the woods, quickly, immediately, eagerly. But the woods were empty. The walk was just part of an old garden, and a little dull. My task lacked interest or excitement. The urgency had gone. But I kept at it, cutting my way through bracken and briars, hands scratched, bleeding from thorns. I didn't let anything hold me up. This was a watershed. I realized that I had challenged my secret friends, had dismayed them when I brushed them aside. Now I had to win them back. This effort was a form of paying my way, buying myself into their good graces. If I kept on, if I showed them I was truly their ally, then I was sure I would be accepted again, I would regain their confidence . . . perhaps their love.

I had to stop at that thought. That was the real betrayal! That was the crux! For although I was faithful absolutely to Sarah, with no thought for any other woman, yet there was this excitement, not about someone, but about an idea, a mirage that had swum out of this dark wood. I had to be honest: I was in love with this mirage. I kept at the work until my hands were raw, and the scratched knuckles trickled blood. Surely they would see what I was doing? My bruises ought to be credentials enough?

I knew when they were there, easing back from shadows, tentatively, like candles spluttering; not all together but one at a time, growing in strength. Realizing themselves, becoming . . . being . . . I was careful not to acknowledge them, not to look up. If they were there, it was an act of their faith. I had to coax that along, give them time, allow them to become used to me again, to appreciate what I was doing. And this was what they did, with a growing enthusiasm. Theirs, or mine? Both, I decided. And with this enthusiasm they would perhaps drop their guard, become a little less nervous, not so ready to vanish like startled birds – and then the moment would come to admit to each other our mutual presence.

I had cut a path to the yew hedge, a long and back-breaking stint, and I had a twinge of pain by the time I finished. That was the warning: I had done enough. Slowly – very slowly – to give warning of my intentions, I stuck the machete in the ground, marked the limit of my progress, and straightened my back. As I did so I looked up. There was a flicker of uncertainty, like a gust of wind; shadows were blown, startled, surprised, doubtful. I caught all those feelings in one brief second, in a vision of flight . . . But uncertain flight. To vanish or not? And I helped to make the decision by holding my excitement in check – doing nothing, nothing to startle, nothing to alarm.

With what a reward! Out of the corner of my eye I saw a man. The same man I had seen that first time in the wood. And on the fringe of my vision I glimpsed the woman, dark, imperious, possessive. I looked at no one directly, but they were there. Only the two of them? There had been a third presence, the one that most intrigued me. She must be there as well. They were all as one, coming or going as one. If two of them were here then . . . I had to look round searchingly, I couldn't stop myself. With that one movement they were gone. Not vanishing in alarm or anger as they had done earlier in the day, but merely not there. I had moved out of focus. Yes, that was it. The secret was focus. Probably they *were* still there, but I couldn't see them.

I sat on a tree stump, marvelling. It was too consistent to be doubted; it was no trick of light; no illusion. No one, certainly not me, would believe that they were real in the way I was real. Nevertheless we were in communication. Tentative as yet; primitive – a morse signal that came and went in an uncertain atmosphere, sweeping towards the stars and back. It was certainly nothing to chat about over the bar or in my club. I didn't doubt the reaction I'd get! I grinned; even Freddie would vote to get me off the board! Who wouldn't?

Back at the house the painters were pleased with themselves.

'How about that then, guv?' Mac wanted to know. He displayed the walls above the staircase, the wide sweep of rooms at the top, the corridor to the back of the house. The conjurer had performed a major trick!

'Must be a record,' said Alf. 'Should be in the Guinness.'

I admired it, genuinely.

'Finished before D-Day,' Joe forecast.

Mac shook his head, calculating. 'No, be dead on time.' He was the professional. Then he looked at me. 'How you getting on then, guv? All them garden paths in order?'

'Bit by bit,' I smiled. He allowed a hint of mockery when he spoke to me like that. Was it just because the white-collar man was working? Or had I not fooled him? Did Mac, in the wisdom of his night alone in Longwood, know what I was really concerning myself with?

We had a small celebration at The George that evening. I phoned for a taxi which took us there, the three painters and myself; the odd-job man went home. I bought them all drinks and offered them a meal.

'Thanks, guv. We'll just have something at the bar.' Mac spoke for the three. They realized it was my way of showing approval, and they in turn approved of that. I had a few drinks myself, knowing things were going to change in the next few days. Mac and company would be finished; the house would be furnished. Sarah and I had arranged to take time off, a belated honeymoon. She had said we should leave things to the spur of the moment. We'd take a car to Europe, and drive where the spirit moved.

But the spirits had already moved! Spirits no one had anticipated. I wondered where and how far we would go? How far *could* I go? How far would they let me?

The painters were finished on time, but it was a close-run thing. A Harrods furniture van was due in a couple of days with things Sarah and I had collected for the house, and that left us with little over thirty-six hours for the place to dry out.

'More'n enough,' said Mac. 'What with this quick-drying, and the order we done things.'

I was grateful for the way he'd stuck to his job, remembering the look on his face the day we had driven down. At that moment another man would have walked out. I added a bit to his cheque.

'Thanks, guv. Didn't have to do that.'

'For over and above the call of duty,' I said. 'I thought you'd pack it in after that night.'

'Shows what a bloody fool I was,' said Mac drily. 'Lot of bloody nonsense, isn't it? 'Course stairs creak. 'Course in an old house you start thinking things. All them horror films. Shouldn't show them, should they?'

I wondered if he was still mocking me.

I'd been in touch with Sarah every day; she phoned me, or I her. She called now to see if I was coming back with the others.

'Not much point,' I said. 'I'll have to be here when the stuff arrives.'

'Are you all right?'

'What do you mean?'

'Alone?'

'Good God, of course! It's my home. It's *our* home.'

'I'll see you with the luggage,' she said, reminding me of our planned holiday together.

This departure hung over me like a cloud. I tried to ignore it but as the time drew closer I knew I didn't want to leave. Not that anything special had happened, there was no further development with my audience in the wood. I hadn't seen them, not actually *seen* them, though I knew they were there. I sensed the two of them, the tall, serious man and the imperious woman, always in attendance for some part of the day. I would be exhausted by my efforts, and at that moment I'd sense them, approving, affectionate, full of gratitude . . . As though what I was doing was throwing them a lifeline. A lifeline to the already dead.

The thought of leaving them concerned me. I had a strange feeling that if I weren't there they would starve. Only my presence, my efforts, were keeping those visions from vanishing totally and permanently. And if *they* vanished, the third vision would go also. Not that she had reappeared. But she would, I knew that. They were just waiting for something. I didn't know what that 'something' was, but I was certain it would happen. The accolade of approval, confidence, love, would be bestowed. One had to win the race to be given the prize. The gold medal went to the man as he stood on the winner's platform, not while he was still running.

And I was still running.

Now there lay ahead of me thirty-six hours of solitude. Not even Bridges, the gardener, would be there to share the grounds at Longwood. From the time that Mac and his team departed, a handshake all round and a promise to come back and work on the stables at a later date, from that moment I had the house and garden to myself. I strolled round the empty rooms, through to the kitchen quarters, the back of the house, the billiard-room, the cellars; all sparkling, transformed, as Sarah had said; no nook nor cranny that had not been swept clean, fresh painted. Nothing of the past resided there; nothing dark, nothing disturbing; it was high-ceilinged and elegant, with an air of timelessness. Other owners and their families had peopled these rooms before we established our moment of tenancy, brushing out cobwebs, renovating, laying claim, though perhaps a little tentatively. A more assured generation had built these rooms. Had I been challenged, how would I have defended myself? By what right was I there? It wasn't yet really home ground. Ours was a fluent and impermanent generation, not truly wedded to any one place.

My steps took me to the long wood, to the walk and the flight pond, even more secluded now that everyone else had gone. And as I strolled down the path, I realized I'd done a lot of work without effort and with energy generated by excitement and delight. These last few days had given me power; I could cut, swing the sickle, throw rubble aside. So it wasn't surprising to be back at work again – delay was frustrating.

When I'd started that first day in the wood I hadn't had any clear idea of what I hoped to accomplish. It had been a vague thought of clearing the overgrowth. I had just found the plans of the old estate, I remembered, and had been intrigued by the thought of that lost folly. Now I was within a few feet of rounding the yew hedge. If it still stood, I was within a few scythe-strokes of reaching my goal. A small reward for so much time, I asked myself? But such a question was preparation against disappointment, for I could hardly expect a garden ornament to have stood up to decades of weathering and neglect. After all, it *was* just an ornament. I remembered that there had been a time when people decorated their estates with bridges and artificial ponds, built fountains or put up buildings which looked like Greek or Roman ruins. This folly might be just as ludicrous, as ephemeral as the hundreds that had vanished from other English gardens.

But at the same time, I guessed this wasn't so. The watchers were there because of what I was doing. As my work pushed ahead, so their interest grew, their presence strengthened. If there was nothing at the end of this rainbow, there would have been no watchers. There must be something left of this folly, or why were they here?

But I wasn't ready for what I saw.

I don't think I had visualized what a folly would look like. Anything in this Sussex jungle would surely be out of place, anyhow.

But this . . . a Chinese pagoda!

It was about ten feet high, with three levels of roof. Perhaps four . . . it was difficult to see with creepers tangling over it. Each roof curved to uprising points at four corners. Coloured wood showed through the ivy and columbine. Fretted metal-work laced its delicate balustrades. A pastoral toy, lost and forgotten . . . a charming incongruity, a work of art. It was so unexpected, such a shock, a pleasure, that I laughed! I had even forgotten my unseen companions, and my plan not to startle them. It was too late to snatch back my amusement, which echoed through the trees. I guessed it would have my associates vanishing in a puff of dust, but I was wrong. It wasn't just *my* laugh that was sounding round the pond, bouncing from tree to tree, bush to bush, shadow to shadow. Another world was also laughing.

Two removal vans with a team of men exploded into Long-wood. They had been preceded by a smaller unit the day before, laying carpets, hanging curtains, deadening the now familiar sounds, and dressing, somehow softening, the rooms and corridors. Sarah arrived ten minutes after they had started unloading.

'Hold it! Nothing moves until the starting pistol.'

She had the operation mapped out on several sheets of paper, an officer with her troops. Before nightfall the house was draped in new clothes. Each room had changed character. I went through the house before the vans left, and my heart sank. It had become domesticated, habitable, comfortable, indeed just as we had planned it. But it had shrunk. No tall empty rooms. Something had gone. Spirit had gone.

'What do you think, Nick?'

'Bloody wonderful,' I said.

'As you expected?'

'Better.' How could I tell her about this missing quality?

'It's bigger than I thought,' she said. 'Our things look tiny!'

'They look absolutely right.'

'You think so? Good.'

We hadn't furnished some of the upstairs rooms, as we didn't need them. But they were all carpeted, all had been given a face-lift. They had Sarah's colour on them. My pictures. Our mark. You could no longer say the rooms belonged to the people of Longwood. They belonged to us.

5

This should have been a time for celebration: we had looked forward to this day from the moment we had seen Longwood. But now there was an uneasiness between us. We were playing parts; we spoke with the same apparent love and ease, but the rhythm had changed. There were false notes which we pretended not to hear.

The vans drove off leaving us with the lights full on, in the unreality of a stage set. Bedclothes heaped on beds; books piled on tables, chairs on chairs. We went into the kitchen. There was food in the deep-freeze. 'I think we should put this in order later,' she said.

I jumped at the opportunity. 'Right, let's go out for a meal.'

Were we anxious not to be alone together?

We went to The George, and the landlord was delighted to see us.

'So he's going to get proper meals, is he?' he asked Sarah. 'He's been eating this rubbish while he's been by himself.'

The 'rubbish' appeared on our table alongside some fairly strong drinks. The food was even better that evening, but what I needed was whisky. Sarah ordered brandy; she hadn't done that for some time.

'You down to stay permanent, then?' The landlord seemed pleased.

'It isn't quite settled.' She didn't seem to notice what she'd said, but it stuck in my mind. So it wasn't quite settled? Did that mean she wasn't staying? Or what? What wasn't quite settled? Guilty about my sudden sense of hope, I didn't ask her what she meant. It might have been a slip of the tongue.

We didn't talk much, and that wasn't like Sarah.

'You all right?'

'I'm a bit tired,' she admitted.

'God, yes. It has been a day!'

We got to the coffee. It was all so guarded; so disguised.

'Did you bring the luggage?' I asked.

'I brought your things. They're in the room.'

'What about yours?'

'They're still in town.' She didn't look up, staring at her coffee, slowly stirring.

I could have pretended to be surprised, but it didn't seem worth it; at least we remained *that* honest with each other.

No one had said anything about staying or going, about our plans, about the holiday we had long promised ourselves. It was a penance that stretched ahead of us now, which neither of us could face. But we hadn't even said why. Nor could we have given a reason – at least, I couldn't have given a reason, not a proper one. Not one that would have made sense to anyone, even to me. What *could* I say? That it was impossible for me to leave Longwood for even a few days, let alone three or four weeks, because I had to get back as soon as possible, as soon I was decently able, to the walk by the flight pond, to tidy up an old garden path? To take a look at the ruin of an old garden folly, a Chinese pagoda, the image of which was hardly ever out of my mind? The whole thing was too childish; yet the recollection delighted me.

'You're smiling,' she said.

'It's being with you.'

She gave me a sad look, a tiny shrug. 'I don't know what it is,' she said, 'or who. Or what's happened. And I'm not asking. But whatever it is, darling, it's not us, is it? It's not you and me.'

I could hardly drink my coffee; I was in a sweat. I wanted to shout out that everything about Longwood was nonsense, only Sarah meant a damn to me! But I felt my resolution drain away as if I were not master of my thoughts anymore, as if illusion were more valuable than reality. But it wasn't. I knew it wasn't. A voice in my brain was shouting, 'You're suffering from something! It's an illness, it will pass. Tell her. Tell her what's been happening.'

But I didn't. If I told her, or anyone, the world I had discovered would crumble . . . evaporate. And it was too precious to allow that to happen.

She was waiting for me to say something.

'What about tomorrow? What do you want to do?' I asked.

Again, a tiny shrug, another gesture of defeat. 'I'm going back tonight,' she said.

'Good Lord! So late?'

She got up. 'Goodnight, Nicky. I'll call from the office.'

'I'll call you,' I said. 'Another drink?'

'I have to go.'

I drove her back to the house. She didn't come in. 'There's nothing of mine there,' she said.

'It's all yours,' I said.

'There's nothing I want,' she said. I gave her a kiss, but there was no warmth between us.

She drove off, tail-lights disappearing at the end of the drive. I stood in the dark, absorbing the cool, comforting night air, wondering what was happening, what had vanished, what had taken over? I had to admit it was a deep pleasure to unlock the door and to be alone in the house again. The very atmosphere embraced me.

I had to resist the impulse to walk through the garden in the dark. The pagoda would be exquisite in this moonlight, but I had noticed that after nightfall the walk lost much of its charm. It always felt empty after dark. I would get up early in the morning and start work then. But I was restless, full of energy. I knew I wouldn't sleep; my brain was working at top speed, excited about a confusion of many things.

I went into the study. A bank of files was ranged along one wall, with duplicates of my work at the office. A partner's desk faced the door. Heavy curtains hung by the windows and I pulled them, shutting out the moonlight. Directly above the study was our bedroom. Now I could work and sleep; I felt very self-contained.

I began by going through things, checking to see what was there, but I was soon caught up with the problems of the company's affairs, of accounts, of campaigns which had not lived up to their promise. I sat at my desk and analysed those I considered failures. Then I took the ones that I felt could be salvaged, and spent the rest of the night working on them. It was nearly four in the morning before I finished. I had been invaded by a rush of ideas; everything seemed easy, full of possibilities, of promise. I had written out pages of instructions, for putting together another brochure, another schedule, a much more attractive proposition. I had hardly noticed the time, aware of a sense of being taken over. It amazed me. When I read through the work I had done, I didn't need to be told it was good.

I still wasn't tired. I had a fresh lease of energy but forced myself to stop. I put the stack of notes in an envelope and addressed it to the office. Though I didn't think I would sleep at this hour, I did – immediately.

I woke about four hours later to see Bridges working in the

garden. He had a bicycle in the stables, so I sent him off to post my letter.

'Moved in, then?' he asked.

'Mostly.'

He nodded and cycled away. I realized I would have to get Freddie to send me down my car – I couldn't stay out on a limb like this – but for the moment I liked the isolation. I was down in the wood before Bridges came back. He saw me across the field, but he never showed any inclination to find out what I was working at.

There was an air of expectation as I walked through the wood, carrying my machete and the small sickle I had bought in the village. I felt as though a burden had been lifted, and walked with a light step, surprised to see how eager I was to get to work, and flattered by the sense of wonder around me, as though I were a distributor of happiness. I felt like a conjurer about to perform a fantastic piece of magic before an audience, that was just out of sight, peeping through branches, edging closer in concentration, in their absorption, and forgetting the dreadful facts of their unreality, of the void between us, of universal laws that cannot be broken; forgetting everything in a shared obsession. All this raced through my head as I cleared the way to this hidden pavilion, trying not to show my awareness of them, trying not to compound the irregularity they were committing, that I felt might be explosive.

But I knew they were there, and I sweated to carry out the job I now knew was the reason for their shadowy existence. I was the hands, the living muscle, that could touch, lift, and hack, and drag aside. I could uproot bramble and burn rubbish. That was my function. I was their agent, bridging a gap in time.

A mass of ivy, creepers, columbine, honeysuckle, moss, nettles, docks, smothered the pagoda. Some roots were as thick as my arm. I attacked the lot! I wanted to make clear my intention: I understood this partnership, and would do what I could to carry out their thoughts, with dedication, so that the delicate and unstable relationship might be fostered. I didn't know if it would work.

It was noon before I risked the experiment. I'd been warning myself that if it didn't work the whole magical adventure might be over; but I couldn't put things off any longer.

The sun was almost above me, hitting the high trees, breaking into rays of light. But light didn't seem to bother these beings, they were not creatures of night. I had done a lot of work on the path, and could walk along it in comfort. I had even replaced the edging stones. I'd cut the yew hedge back, trimming it flush with the path. I had started on the pagoda. Now it was time to ask *them* for something. The good faith had to be on both sides.

I think they knew what was coming. Birds stopped singing; the breeze dropped. Shadows were black and still. I put the sickle down, leant it against a tree, added the big knife; there was no doubt what I was doing. I was stopping work, stopping this busy activity, taking my time about it, moving slowly, doing nothing to create alarm; and I turned to look impassively at the circle of trees around me.

But this time I looked in a different way; only a slight difference, but I guessed this difference was going to be significant. I was almost sure of it. I had noticed that previously I had seemed to catch sight of something out of the corner of my eye. I would become aware of a figure standing watching me, always in a moment of relaxation, when I was least expecting it. It was out of the corner of my eye, on the margin of my vision, that I had made contact. As soon as I had tried to concentrate, to see clearly, to look straight at the vision as I might look at something real, the image had faded, had ceased to be there. So now I would make use of what I had learned. The way to keep the onlookers in any vision at all was not to look at them too closely, not to look full at them. The way was to fix my eyes on a distant object, to look at something just ahead of them, or behind them, to keep them on this indistinct margin . . . to try and hold them there.

I looked round the circle of the pond. It lay, a black pool down the slope below me, the far end coated with dead leaves, sunshine on green slime on one side, shadows blurring the bank on the other. I focused on the pond, keeping my eyes on the part that glittered green, glittered then reflected a blinding patch of sun. And while I watched the water with this fixed stare, I let the side of my vision grow accustomed to the shadows round the pond banks.

Someone was there. I guessed the pattern in which they would manifest themselves.

First, I saw him, unmoving, watchful, looking across the water, uncertain, for all his power, for all his assurance and air of ownership. It was almost as if I held him there; prevented his image from vanishing. And it seemed to be working. I had not triggered the mechanism that had caused earlier alarm and evaporation, whatever the process was; for in this limbo the figure seemed to hesitate, dimmed, faded, returned. I still didn't look full at it, watching the sunlight on the water, but I saw enough to register this coming and going, these moments of insecurity. Then the vision took on more substance, a more determinate shape, as if it had settled to some wavelength. The picture steadied as if I had tuned in to a station on a television set. The man was standing under the trees on the opposite side of the flight pond, and he was watching me.

This was the first time I had been able to observe him in any detail, and I had to force myself to look away from him as I checked over his dress and appearance. He would be about sixty, perhaps just over, with fair hair receding to give him a broad, wide forehead and a rather formidable look. He had heavy eyebrows, a strong jaw, a small, short beard, and a broad face. He stood very straight, like a military man, his jacket buttoned up high to his neck and it looked like a good tweed cloth. It was long, and his trousers were narrow and smart. He seemed to have a starched collar. It was the dress of the last century. I would have said such a man lived and possibly died more than a hundred years before I was born.

The woman was a yard or so further away, slightly behind him, and to one side. It was difficult to see if she was firmly standing on the ground. She was as I had seen her twice before, darker than the man, with a rich mop of black hair firmly plaited on top of her head, with a dark lace cap. She was a few years younger than he, in her fifties, dressed in a wide skirt and a bodice with full sleeves. She would be about five foot six

69

inches while the man was six feet, but she exuded a sense of power every bit as potent as his. She was broad, strong, with a self-confidence, a determination, a charm, that I could sense from across the pond – which I could, indeed, sense across more than a century.

So that was the order they appeared in, first the man, and then the woman. Or was that merely the order in which I experienced them? The husband first, to face whatever dangers this strange experience might present, and then after him, very soon after, his equally purposeful wife? For that was what they were, there was no doubt in my mind: man and wife . . . past owners of Longwood, the property on which I had not made my mark, the territory in which I was as yet a stranger. Perhaps the original owners of Longwood, responsible for the building as it now stood; as they had built, I had restored. Was that the bond between us?

I was delighted by the way the experiment worked. All I had to do to keep the images steady was to observe without being seen to observe; to move my head slowly, make no sudden gesture, turn as I turned my body, stay as a piece, so that from across the sheltered wood I could be seen to be no threat; indeed, could be seen to be a friend.

But I was disappointed too. The man and wife were also father and mother; at least, so I thought. I wanted to see the daughter. I wanted that with as much determination and resolution as I could muster, still keeping motionless, still head averted, yet *willing* the third person to appear. Demanding it. The girl . . . *where was she?* I formed the memory of her in my mind. I *would* bring back, create, recreate that brief, fantastic image flickering with a sharp loveliness outside my door, and again here in this wood. I had worked like a serf to turn this forest back into a neat Victorian garden. I deserved my reward; I would not be obstructed by these two static figures. It was not exactly a struggle of wills . . . it was a moment of explanation, of silent explanation, in which they gradually came to understand. I would not go on, I would do no more work, I would not touch the decayed pagoda (something I knew they desperately wanted me to do), unless . . . And when it happened it didn't even seem to be part of a bargain, but a sudden welcoming into the hearts and arms of the family, overwhelming me with joy, not just because the girl had appeared, and even closer to me than the others, but because I was made part of them, absorbed into this splendid, special, longed-for world. A world given, though never promised, a dream world. It was a triumph. The bargain was clearly understood, and fairly struck. If I was to be their human hands – their *living* human hands – then I was to be given their confidence, or as much as was possible across a span of time.

She was as fair as her father, with long hair tied at her neck and falling loosely down her back to her waist; a white dress, long-skirted, long sleeved, reminding me of Alice in Wonderland; white soft shoes. Yes, now I saw them – the dancing-shoes! She had thin, darker eyebrows, high cheekbones, pale green eyes, fair skin, one or two freckles . . . she would grow out of them, for how old was she? My guess was eighteen, plus a hundred and fifteen years. But it was the look of the girl that riveted me: a smiling archness; to be honest, a little sly. She at least turned her eyes towards me, not quite a full look, but sideways, secretively, a little seductively. Perhaps it was merely the innocence of an innocent age. The message in the sidelong glance may have been unconscious; the lowered eyes and the half-smile might mean one thing in my century, and quite another in hers. Besides, what did it matter? One inadvertent gesture, one approach too close and the mirage would show itself to be a mirage. The girl was safe to play any part, make any promise, presage any seduction; we had only sight as a shared sense, no sound, no taste, no smell, and saddest of all, no touch.

But as long as I looked into the pond, or into the bushes beyond her, into the shadows round us, I could keep her in vision, on the perimeter of my sight; and I could also see the other figures, now more at ease, closer, larger, accepting, understanding. Best of all . . . welcoming. Perhaps the pleasure grew too acute, too unbearable to sustain. The need to look at her overcame me, and as I did she vanished. And with her, the wood went dark. I was suddenly very tired. I could hardly drag my feet up the path, across the garden, to the front door.

'You all right, sir?' Bridges called.

I waved. 'Okay, just overdone it.'

I managed to get into the house. I almost collapsed in the hall, on the stairs, at my door.

I fell on the bed. I thought my heart had stopped. I passed out.

6

Two days later the phone rang loudly throughout the house. I hadn't spoken to anyone during that time; I'd been cut off from the rest of the world, absorbed in my work. I hadn't even tried my experiment again: I didn't need to. I knew *they* were there; close to me, approving, equally absorbed as I continued clearing the pagoda. Besides, they were not a sideshow at a circus; nor was I there to perform tricks. I'd been in the long wood most of those two days, coming back to the house for hurried meals. Time away from my task was wasted, so my day was full. At night I slept heavily.

The phone, when it rang like this, was startling. A reminder of another world. I was in two minds about answering it, I had the morning's work planned and the tools were under my arm. But I picked it up.

'Hello. Nicholas Morell speaking.'

'Nick! Great! Glad I caught you. I phoned all yesterday.' It was Freddie, sounding as buoyant as ever.

'Sorry about that. I was out.'

'I got your letter.'

What letter, I wondered?

'God, man; it's wonderful! We had an office session. Everyone thinks it's the best thing you've come up with in a long time.'

Freddie was the only person who told me clearly when I had made a mistake, so that when he said something was right I knew it was his honest opinion. And he was a good advertising man.

'Oh, the notes I sent you?'

'Too bloody true. We've done what we can to work them into the current assignments, but can't see exactly where it all fits. The thing is, Nick, we need you at this juncture. Sorry about it, and all that. I know this is your break time. But if you could just get here for the day, and put the new stuff on a firm basis, I'm sure we could handle it from there.'

He was right: I couldn't hang about at Longwood indefinitely.

'I'll be up,' I said.

'Good man,' said Freddie. 'I knew you'd say that. Shaw is on his way.' Shaw was the company driver. He'd been my chauffeur for years, on the occasions when I didn't drive myself. 'Shouldn't be long now,' Freddie went on. 'Left over an hour ago.'

I had just time to change out of my labouring clothes when Shaw pulled up outside the house.

'Nice place, sir.' He viewed it sceptically, as he did most things. 'Bit big?'

'We shan't use all of it. Not at first.'

'Not ever, by the look of it,' said Shaw.

We drove off. It was the first time I had been out of the house, except to go to the village, for some time, and it was pleasant to see the busy world going about its affairs, an eternal oyster. London was a shock of pleasure: the very squalor of the city stirred me; the noise, confusion, traffic, hubbub, made the blood tingle and run a little faster.

Freddie welcomed me with a wide grin, and his uninhibited embrace. 'It's the boy wonder,' he shouted. 'Ex-boy! The dynamic management! Everyone else has gone out to the pub. I thought we'd have a quiet chat . . . Put me in the picture, and I'll look as though I know what I'm talking about.'

We had drinks in the office and discussed the notes. It was a couple of hours before we made sense of everything – that is, before we discarded those aspects that wouldn't work. But I was surprised to see how effective the total picture had become.

'Golly, we can do a bit with this,' said Freddie. 'Pity you haven't a spot more time.'

'I have all the time you think we need,' I told him.

'You're staying in town?'

'I'll go back to the apartment tonight.'

'But I thought . . .'

'What?'

'Sarah said you had to get back to Longwood again. I thought she meant tonight?'

'Good Lord, no. There's nothing urgent. Work comes first.'

He hesitated, unsure of himself. 'What about the arrangements, and all that? You? Sarah? The plans?'

'Good heavens, that's going to work out okay. At least, I hope so.'

He looked relieved – back was the enormous smile. 'Great! We'll make use of that.'

The rest of the team had been drifting back into the office over the last hour. I was glad to see them; they were old friends, reassuring, relaxed, and real – very real.

'Where's Sarah?'

'With the chloride people. She's got something going, and said she might not be back till late.'

She hadn't turned up in the office by the time the rest of us called it a day.

'She'll be at the flat,' said Freddie, 'but God knows when. Why don't you come and have a bite with Rosie and me?' Rosie was the latest and loveliest in a long line of Freddie's partners.

'I'll be all right, I've got things to do. But thanks.'

I wanted to be alone anyhow, to take stock. The day had been abrupt and unexpected. I had not once thought of the pagoda, the flight pond, the wood. I had switched momentarily, but completely. I wondered how I felt about that; I wondered what Sarah would say. I was very anxious to see her.

The apartment was cold, dank, and empty. I got the impression there had been no one in it for a long time. I went round the place switching on lights, turning up the heating, checking things for the night. I would wait there until Sarah turned up. The fridge was empty so we would have to go out. And I noticed there was nothing of hers in the place. Her clothes – her ludicrously extravagant collection of shoes – her makeup – they had all gone.

I sat in the apartment a long time, surprised I didn't feel more upset. It didn't even seem very unexpected. I had behaved so distantly, I knew I had, that of course she would react like this. Sarah would never ask twice, nor put pressure on me: she was deeply proud. If I showed signs of doubt or hesitancy, she would be quick to sense it and to walk out. It was pretty obvious that was what she had done.

Our apartment felt alien. We had been together ever since we moved here, and it was a depressing place without her. Much later, I went out to eat by myself.

Sarah didn't turn up at the office next morning.

'You know what she's like,' said Freddie. 'Once she gets her teeth into something, she doesn't like to let go. She got these new accounts. I'll bet she comes in with a fat contract.'

'Of course. I'll be around for a day or two, so we're bound to meet.'

He thought that was very funny.

But the rest of the staff were all on tap and we had a session that galvanized us all. There was some hysterical laughter; it was suggested I went back to the country and stayed there a bit longer, for life was unnecessarily hectic with me around. It was a mood of contained excitement, with everyone glad to be back at work.

'It's a fallacy,' I told Freddie. 'You don't need me – look at the load of work you got through while I was away.'

'I know.' He was suddenly serious. 'I just think they're pleased to see you. Everyone seemed to have the impression you weren't too well.'

'What?'

'Or that something had gone wrong. You and Sarah.'

'Oh . . . Do you know where she is?'

'She phoned in an hour ago.'

'Could you get a message to her . . . say I'll meet her for lunch, usual place, usual time?'

We often used to eat in a restaurant off Charlotte Street. It

75

was sufficiently far from the office for us to be on our own.

She was there, on the first floor by the window, when I arrived.

'Hello, love.'

I kissed her, and she smiled, happy to see me.

'They told me you looked very well,' she said. 'You really do. Country air agrees with you.'

'It would be nicer if you were there.'

She gave a gentle smile, resigned, but tender. 'We'll have to see,' she said.

I ordered the meal and a bottle of wine.

'A bottle of wine?' We didn't generally drink in the middle of the day.

'It's nice to see you. It's a celebration.'

'A celebration?'

'Something like that.'

But we both knew it wasn't.

'I was surprised you were here today,' she said. 'I thought you would be going back.'

'I'm a working man, you know. Too young to retire. Besides there's no rush to get back. I have nothing urgent to do at Longwood.'

'How is it? The house? the garden? Now the place is furnished?'

'It's just as we expected. Even nicer . . .'' I hesitated, then continued, 'What's the matter, Sarah? You weren't in the apartment, and you've taken your things.'

'I'm staying with friends,' she said simply.

'For long?'

'I don't know. You were away, so there was no point. You aren't coming back to stay, are you?'

I had to shake my head. 'No . . . What friends?'

'You don't know them.' She began to eat, then stopped. 'Things aren't quite as we arranged, are they?'

'They could be, couldn't they?'

'Not that we had worked out the details.' I knew she was talking about the honeymoon.

'Near enough,' I said. 'We were going to take the car across to

76

the Continent, and drive around for three or four weeks just as the spirit moved us.'

'I think we have to be sure the spirit *does* move us,' she said.

'What do you mean?'

'We mustn't do anything just because it's expected of us.'

'Expected by whom?'

'By anyone. By each other. What I expect, what you expect, that's not reason enough for doing anything. Not reason enough for committing ourselves.'

I felt my heart sink. I had tried not to look at things so clearly, but she always did. It wasn't possible to pretend.

'Don't you want to go?' I asked.

'It wasn't just any holiday,' she said. Again the smile, as tender but perhaps with a hint of accusation. 'It was a few weeks together, a honeymoon. Your idea, Nicky, your gesture.'

'Are you against it?'

'I wasn't. Now I don't know. As I say, and I know you think like this, we are neither of us going to do anything we don't honestly want.'

'You don't want to go ahead with it?'

'Yes Nicky, if *you* do.'

She had put me against a wall, before a firing squad. She was making me speak what I felt. I had to look at the inexplicable, explain the impossible! How could I speak about creatures in a dream? Do you tell someone passion has gone out of your love because of some pretty fantasy? An unreality? Three unrealities? Because of a senseless, inexplicable infatuation, a reversion to childhood, where playing a game is more important than life? I couldn't tell her anything, because I couldn't say I was bewitched by a dead girl.

'When is this honeymoon due to start? When did we arrange it with the office?' I always left the practicalities to her.

'On Monday of next week.'

'So they don't expect us to turn up then?'

She looked amused. 'They'd be surprised if we did.'

'What shall we do?'

'That's the answer, isn't it, Nick? We aren't so sure now. And we have *never* been unsure about each other.'

'That means?'

'We should wait until we're sure again. Don't you think?'

I had to nod, slowly . . . I couldn't understand why it gave me such pain. I was turning my back on what I wanted out of life, being deliberately perverse. But I couldn't help myself. For I wanted to be quit of this beloved, endearing entanglement with her, God knew why!

She went on. 'I think I'm going to take this holiday. I'd like it. Anyhow, I think I need it, and I'll have this new account tied up by the end of the week. We don't need to say anything to anyone. Things might work out . . . one way or another . . . during that time. It will be easier to tell them – if we have to – later.'

I was glad I had ordered the wine.

'What will you do?' she asked.

I knew what I would do, but I told her something different. 'I think I'll do as we said. I'll make the trip. Just take the car across to France . . . Spain, Italy . . . anywhere.' She nodded, non-committal.

'Where will you be?' I asked. 'Do you have an address if we need to get in touch?'

She hesitated. 'I don't have one,' she said. 'I can't be sure.'

So, it ends on this note, I thought: if not with deception, with less than honesty on both sides. I felt very sad. But we had at least said something to each other, and what we hadn't said, we had both understood.

'Shall I run you to the office?' I asked.

'No thanks, I'm not going back. I have another appointment.' She glanced at her watch. 'I have to go now.'

'Can't I drop you anywhere?' It seemed a mundane, flat, ending to such happiness. Surely we could permit ourselves a proper parting?

She shook her head. 'Someone is picking me up.'

I couldn't bring myself to ask, was this business or pleasure? In so short a time, had she switched affections? It should have pained me, but I think it was only hurt pride that stung.

'You don't mind if I don't wait?' she said. She gave me a cheek to kiss, and hurried away, busy, preoccupied, anxious.

She didn't look back or wave as she went down the stairs. I delayed over the last of the wine. I never smoke, but the smell of a nearby cigar was comforting. I was surprised to find my hands trembling slightly, and I thought my heart beat faster. One doesn't realize what one's feeling sometimes – until one's body tells one.

I paid the bill and went back to the office.

Freddie had lined up a meeting of our 'inner cabinet', our copy-writers. We spent the afternoon briefing them, listening to suggestions, extending the programmes, drawing up budgets, campaigns, the whole pattern of our work. Freddie had already chatted to special accounts, and reactions were good. We had a promising prospect. But the afternoon passed tediously. I said my piece, but the essence had gone out of me. Was this a reaction to lunchtime with Sarah? Or to something else? Was it time to get back to Longwood? What shocks, what silences, were being suffered there?

'You here again tomorrow?' asked Freddie, cock-a-hoop at the way things were going.

'Of course . . . Well, the morning certainly.'

We had a drink together in the pub across the road.

'How was Sarah?' He was pleased that everything was back to normal – I knew that was how he saw it.

'Splendid,' I said. 'Her darling self.'

'Work things out?' he asked. 'I mean what about Monday? It is *this* Monday, isn't it?'

I gave a dishonest grin. 'We won't be around on Monday, if that's what you mean. In fact, if you check on the books, you'll see we won't be around till the end of the month. Neither of us.'

He gave me a bear-hug, spilling my whisky.

'Have a great time. There were never two people . . . Well, forget about that. Just have a great time, both of you.'

Rosie, or someone, appeared in the doorway. 'Got to go, old man. Domesticity calls.' He ambled away, large, bulky, good-humoured, through the unwinding crowd. I noted that he waved before he led the girl out.

I finished my drink and had another. I had thought of driving back to Longwood that night, but after another couple of drinks

I decided against it. I had no special reason to be drinking: I just wanted to keep my mind blank for the rest of my time in London. The apartment was even chillier and more unfamiliar. I ate, then went to bed.

I saw Freddie in the office next day and hung around until lunch. 'I have people to see,' he told me.

'Okay. Let me know what happens about the new projects. I'll give you a call, from wherever we are.' I was keeping up the pretence to the end . . . I couldn't bring myself to disappoint him.

Later, I drove myself down to Sussex, taking my time since it was going to be too late to work in the wood that afternoon. But when I arrived I made use of the last of the light to stroll to the flight pond, to the pagoda. There was no indication of anything out of the way, but I knew perfectly well that behind the darkening curtain of green, a sigh of relief had gone up.

7

I have called it a pagoda, but it may have been part of a Chinese fishing-temple; the simple structure outside such a building, with an up-curving roof at three levels, and a balustrade in many colours. It was made of wood and metal, painted yellow, light-blue, and a pale ochre. The spaces between the wooden pillars were fretted with geometrical designs of diamonds, squares, and struts, painted the same colours. Most of the balustrade had fallen away and the pieces were scattered in the bushes. I gradually collected them.

The search took me the best part of the morning after I got back. At first I didn't have much idea what I was looking for, but gradually the design began to take shape. I drew a plan of how it might have looked, then for no reason tore it up, and drew it again with assurance. Suddenly I knew exactly what it should look like. I couldn't explain this abrupt insight.

Most of the pieces lay where they had fallen, the ends rotted, the long thick nails rusted, layers of dirt and dead leaves covering them. Some sections I could just pick up and slot back into place, but a few had been used as stakes for plants, and I didn't find them until later in the day. The job of patching them together was painstakingly slow and I hadn't finished when the sun dropped out of sight. There was no point going on after that; matching the colours was impossible.

I sat in the kitchen having my meal, summarizing the day. I had spent it gradually putting a jigsaw puzzle together. It had seemed an imperative task; I hadn't questioned it. But now I asked myself why it was so important? Did I have to do this? What did it mean? Why should it fascinate me as it did? Was it just that I loved this house and garden, was fortunate enough to have bought it, and had the chance to restore it? If that was all I was doing, there was no harm in that.

But the other experience, the visions? They needed some explanation, but, oddly, it didn't seem important. After all, what I was doing seemed fairly innocent. I was not harming another soul – for once I was not even competing. Nobody stood to lose. When I remembered Sarah, I thought that even she probably didn't consider she had lost anything. But that was the one thought I pushed quickly out of mind, because I was uneasily aware that each morning I went down to the long wood as though I were returning to someone I loved. I couldn't think who it might be, but it gave me a sense of guilt.

Time passed obliviously, as if childhood had returned. The game went on, a secret game, a private game, a form of solitaire, for although I never saw the shadows in the wood I knew that by my presence and their dependence, I was their mechanism, feeding their awakened appetites.

The pagoda took shape: it had been more lost in the thicket than destroyed. The job was to strip away the creepers that had got into every cranny of the fretwork; once the little temple was free it was easy to cut back the rest of the accumulated rubbish.

It took nearly a week to clear it, but then it stood there, a little jewel set in greenery. I was very proud as I admired the now clearly seen, rubble-free structure.

I hadn't looked for any other reward for the task I had so

enjoyed doing. In fact, I'd forgotten my associates in the pleasure of viewing. But a reward was given. It was very unexpected, proving that they too could be caught off guard, as relaxed in my presence as I in theirs.

There were two shadows, just out of sight, as I turned from my pagoda . . . on the fringe of vision, that area I had learned to hold; two shadows that thickened, cleared, and substantiated a little, came and went. This was the first occasion that two images had come to me simultaneously. Not the man this time, not his wife or daughter. Two different images, new to me.

They were both men. One rotund, plump-faced, balding, about forty-five, dressed in a dark jacket and trousers; what hair he had was a frizzy fringe round his pate, reminding me of a priest. He was very much the scholar, glasses perched on his nose, peering forward at the pagoda, inspecting, very intent. The other man was younger, not yet thirty; tall, straight, good-looking; a striking young man, eager, a little fierce. All this was probably exaggerated by his uniform, his sword-belt, the flash of ribbons and braid, for he was dressed in bright colours as an officer of the Hussars. I was so taken aback that I looked straight at them, and of course they were gone.

Bridges came three times a week, but it was about ten days after I had been back at Longwood that I first saw him. He was wheeling barrowloads of compost into the walled garden. 'Keeping busy in the wood, then, sir?' He managed to make most comments sound ironic, though there was never a trace of expression on his dry, leathery face.

'Not been touched for a long time down there, has it?' I asked.

'Don't have to be,' he said. 'Not much there, is there? Long as the path's kept clear.'

'What about the stuff they built down there?'

'What stuff?' He was genuinely surprised.

'There used to be a sort of summer-house.'

'Where was that then?'

'Beyond the pond.'

He shrugged. 'Don't bother to go down there,' he said.

'It's behind the yew hedge.'

'Oh, yes?' I don't know if he took that as a criticism. 'I've got enough on me hands,' he said grimly, and went off, pushing the wheelbarrow. To my knowledge he never went to see what I had been doing. Anything not in the walled garden or the orchard he seemed to consider a waste of time.

For those two weeks Bridges was the only person I saw. I got him to bring in some things from the village store, but there was enough produce from the garden to live on very well. The weather was dry and warm for the month; autumn was a slow-dying Indian summer. Time evaporated like a dream; it was an idyllic sequence of days, cut off from the world, cut off in fact from parts of my own life, a blissful suspension.

I didn't try to exploit it; I didn't try to will my visions to materialize; I didn't drive myself to complete the work. I merely spent my waking hours recreating a minor work of art. I'm not sure how long I could have gone on like this, or how long I would have. I had not answered the telephone on the few occasions it had rung, and after a few days I had taken it off the hook so I couldn't even hear it.

I had put the pagoda together; though it was still shaky and frail, I wanted very much to paint it. But I wasn't sure I could match the delicate colours, and I was undecided what to do. It was as though there was a difference of opinion in the atmosphere around me, one voice suggesting I painted it, another hesitating. As though two telephone lines had crossed, and I was hearing both conversations. I left it as it was and the uncertainty died down.

The pagoda, standing behind the yews, could not be seen by anyone coming down the path from the house, and came as a shock of delight as one circled the water. It faced the pond and there were signs that a little bridge had once led to the edge of the water. I could find no parts for this. They must have been lost a long time ago.

I still had to join the struts together properly. They had been nailed in places, and jointed in others. I would have to nail them

83

all, I thought, or could I use glue? I spent quite a bit of time sitting on the little platform, the up-curving roofs above shading me from the mild sun. I knew that I had only to take time, and the answers would come to me. Sometimes it was as if a voice spoke, or several voices.

I was sitting in the pagoda when I heard the sound of a car horn. You could sometimes hear a car in the distance as it went to the village, but this was different. It began playing a short tattoo, was silent for a moment, then played it again. With a stab of anxiety I recognized the signal.

It had to be Sarah.

I went up to the house slowly, trying to catch up on these last few weeks, trying to orientate myself. I was about to be pulled back into the doubtful pleasures of the other world. Sarah was walking round the house, trying the door handle and looking in the windows, when she saw me.

She was delighted, running to kiss me. 'God, darling, you are dirty!'

I hadn't noticed I was covered with mud. 'I'm working,' I grinned at her. 'This place has to be perfect, otherwise it isn't good enough for us.'

'It's all locked. Where's the gardener?'

'He doesn't come today.' I had the key in my pocket, and gave it to her.

'Darling, have you got any food in the house? Can we make tea or something? I've brought a friend.'

I saw a man watching us from the other side of the car. The first thing I noticed was how quiet he was, almost passive. Even when he smiled and shook hands it was in a distant fashion. I wondered if it was my imagination: perhaps two weeks of solitude made everyone from beyond Longwood appear a little remote.

'This is Robert Everett. I suppose you've heard me talk about him? He's an old friend.'

I couldn't remember her ever mentioning the name.

'Come in,' I said. 'Of course I've got stacks of food. Anyhow, it's nearly sundown: we could have something to drink.'

'We won't, darling. Bobby is driving.'

It was Sarah's car. I wondered why 'Bobby' was doing the driving.

'Well, I've earned a whisky,' I said. 'Remember where the things are? If you get something together, I'll wash off the mud.'

There was a table set in the dining-room by the time I got down. It was the first time I had used the room, and it looked very pleasant. The light outside was dying, and the banks of bushes darkened across the lawn. Everett was by the window.

'What do you think?' I asked. 'How do you like the place?'

He nodded slowly. 'It's very elegant,' he said. 'Lovely rooms. You must be very happy to have found it.'

'Yes. The more one lives in it, the more enjoyable it is.'

'What about France?' asked Sarah. She had taken over, cutting cake, pouring tea.

'France?'

'You were going to Europe. I thought you were going to drive about . . . you know, everywhere.'

'I changed my mind. I stopped off here, and there was so much to do.'

She nodded.

'What made you think I'd be here?'

'I didn't,' she said. 'It was just the off-chance. We were going past, more or less. In the district. Bobby has to go and see some people not far from here.'

'How far? I mean, would you like to stay?'

'Thanks, that isn't possible,' he said.

'He has to go to Lewes,' added Sarah.

'That's not far.'

'Arrangements have already been made there,' said Bobby.

'Another time,' I said.

He nodded his thanks gravely.

'You haven't broken the contract?' I asked Sarah. She looked puzzled. 'You haven't been back to the office?'

'No,' she smiled. 'When I've got this chance of a break I'm not going to waste it!'

'Where have you been?'

She looked blank for a second, and gave an indeterminate

shrug. 'Nowhere special. Lots of places, in fact. Mostly with friends.' There was a fraction of a pause. 'Would you like to show Bobby the house?' she asked.

'By all means.'

We all got up and went round the rest of the rooms. He nodded appreciatively at each one, but I got the impression he was watching me most of the time. Perhaps he wanted to say something and didn't quite know the moment when.

But he didn't say anything, at least nothing significant, nothing on the subject that must have been preying on his mind. Sarah was much more adept than he was: one would never have guessed from her easy manner what had happened in these last two or three weeks. But it was clear to me. I got the message in an interrupted glance between the two of them, a split second when they were not aware I was watching, one brief look across the corridor, but full of meaning. Something very important was being said, one to the other. And I absorbed the message instantly, absorbed its implication. It was nothing they did or said, but I knew Sarah had taken a new lover, and for some strange reason that was why they had come to see me.

They didn't leave for another hour. I think Sarah tried to give him a chance to say something – she made a point of leaving us, and went through to the kitchen. 'I'd better clear up the mess.'

'You'll find everything in order,' I told her.

'I don't suppose you've been eating properly.'

'Of course I have. Don't I look fit?'

She stopped in the doorway and looked at me with a sudden thoughtfulness. 'You look very fit. I haven't seen you look better for a long time.' She was almost resentful, I thought. Then she took the tea dishes out noisily, and we heard her rearranging things in the kitchen. I played the polite host to my uninvited guest.

'Are you going to be long in these parts?'

He was doubtful. 'That depends on what happens.'

'Oh? Business?'

'In a way. I'll have a better idea in the next few days.'

It was the first time I had taken a good look at him; the way he dressed, his looks, his age. He had been so passive that one didn't really notice these things. He was a little taller than me – about six foot, dark, with black hair; smart, quietly dressed. He was powerfully built, with broad shoulders, and moved slowly, giving the impression that he was a hard man to surprise. He spoke quietly, listening to what one had to say, nodding, seeming to give thought even to flippant remarks – nodding appreciation when I made jokes, but not really smiling. He had a round face, almost expressionless, even bland. I wondered what it was that had attracted Sarah: she wasn't usually impressed by the strong, silent man. Nevertheless I was pretty sure what had charmed her. His eyes. Large, dark eyes that moved slowly, and were deeply hooded, giving a warm feeling, friendly, almost gentle. He was sitting in my house waiting, about to tell me how he was disrupting my life, but I couldn't summon up any dislike for the man.

Even when we joined Sarah in the kitchen and I saw her, busy, domestic, amongst our familiar things, all I felt was a sense of loss; I still had no anger.

'Now you're here you can both give me a hand. Bobby, you dry. Nick, I think you should throw that rubbish out. It's going bad.'

We did as we were told. Bobby showed himself to be no better than I was in the kitchen. He stacked dishes beside her, and they worked together, both preoccupied. She gave him a quick look, but he didn't respond. Whatever had to be said, still had to be said when they left.

He got into the car. My final guess about him was that he was a couple of years older than I. Then Sarah kissed me, gently, tenderly, and I wondered if it was a way of saying good-bye.

I stood outside in the dark for a long time once they had gone.

8

'You won't get much done down there this morning,' said Bridges.

I was just about to leave the house. 'Why not?'

'Look over there, then.' He had a grim satisfaction in his voice. 'Weather's going to break.' A huge black cloud hung over the fields at the back.

'That's gone past,' I said. 'It's missed us.'

'Not it,' said Bridges.

'The wind's blowing in that direction.' The wind was a light south-westerly, and the clouds were to the north-east.

'You'll see.' Bridges nodded sharply. 'You'll get wet.'

I was half-way down the wood when the rain came. For a few minutes it was torrential. I ran for the stables, where I stood at a window and watched water pour down the glass. After five minutes it eased off, but the drive was running like a stream. He was right: it didn't look as though I was going to get much done that morning.

I had sheltered in the tack room. In a corner was the bundle of papers I had found there previously. I thumbed through them – receipts, plans, and all. At the bottom of the pile was a batch sticking together. I eased the top papers apart and saw that they included a number of drawings. Some of them were plans of the house and grounds, but a separate sheet of drawings was headed Longwood Pagoda, with a sketch of a pagoda very similar to the one in the wood. On the next two sheets were faint drawings of sections of the structure, and a detailed sketch of the pagoda roofs with its upturned corners. There were notes to indicate measurements, and other instructions, but as I tried to separate the pages the lettering began to strip off on to the damp sheet below. I collected the bundle together and carried it back to the house.

The rain had stopped and Bridges was working by the front door, but he didn't say anything.

I took the pages to the boiler room in the cellars. The best chance of saving them was to dry them out. Behind the boiler was a wooden bench, and I put the bundle on it, spreading out those papers that came apart easily. I decided to add the other papers I had found earlier in the house, and then sat down to sort them out.

The cellar windows extended a foot or two above ground-level, protected by an iron grating and wire mesh through which filtered a grey light, sufficient to allow me to examine the more legible pages. This time I recognized references to old stories that I'd only half understood, half guessed-at, when I had previously glanced through them. Now I felt I was getting a clearer impression of incidents that had puzzled me. One thing was certain – well, almost certain: the property had been built by a young and prosperous couple, newly married, on the site of an older building. They had raised their family here, continuing in prosperity, influential in the district, merchants who had grown wealthier as they grew older. But they had rivals and enemies, if I understood these documents correctly. There had been some litigation, first threatened, then subsided, then to the fore again, over many years. I couldn't make out the cause of the trouble. The papers were not in order, not all equally possible to read; but they confirmed a long, bitter quarrel involving a relative, or a partner – I couldn't find out who it was, for some pages were missing – but whoever it was, he had been deeply hated.

I didn't notice time slip by; I was transported into this other age, this other world, which seemed so close that I suffered – and hated too – on their behalf, identified with those who had lived in this house before me. And as I read, pages slipping to the floor, as I searched for continuity in this history, I began to fear the worst; feared it as the diaries showed *they* had feared it. As legal documents piled up against them, threatening dispossession – God! the panic and alarm that shook their world! They were to lose the house they had built! Pride couldn't have been more humbled, mocked, degraded. The case had gone to law, as another batch of documents showed; everything was against them. A life's work was going to nought. Letters between them suggested they might choose to set the place ablaze rather than let it fall into the hands of a family they detested. But how could they burn down a house built in the shape of their soul? Better to fight on, keep protesting their case, though a fortune was being eaten away.

My heart went out to them as I searched through page after page, some almost indecipherable, so yellowed, aged, destroyed, that I began guessing, filling in the blanks, imagining, sensing the crises about to engulf them finally. I nearly said 'engulf us', I was so partisan. Scrambling through a heap of papers for some continuity, dismissing sheets that cracked as they unrolled, sheets decorated with ornate handwriting which I could no longer take time to translate, I was lost to my own century as I put scraps of domestic history in some order – at least in an order that made sense to my own mind. The moment came when I searched for a further batch of papers, convinced that I was about to find evidence of new owners – but such papers were not there. I could hardly believe it . . . The litigation had been dropped. But why? What had happened? Had I missed some vital pages? I checked back. No, that was not likely. Events had come to a critical session, the case was drawing to a close, letters within the family showed they had given up hope. And then – the case was over! Without judgement? Impossible! There had to be some other evidence, some explanation . . . I was down on my hands and knees searching through documents on the stone floor. Perhaps – as there was nothing to be understood from the legal correspondence – perhaps in the private letters? The diaries?

The confusion was not just of dates, years, a mixture of childish and adult memoirs . . . but also a hotch-potch of material from those away from home, those who had married, were in foreign countries, in armies, in wars. But out of it grew an accumulation of whispers and hints that began to collect in the very air around me, a crystallization, a stalactite gradually shaping itself beside me. And a frightening shape it was, at that!

I had the power of hindsight for there were later documents, later letters, within the family, looking back to these fraught years . . . and they seemed to be saying something . . . something about a dog? Their dog, the guard dog of their precious home, Longwood, a dog about which there was an outcry. A beloved dog they had had destroyed.

What had happened? What had the dog done? The incident . . . the accident . . . became clearer in retrospect. That long, legal attack on their rights to this property had come to a sudden tragic end with the death of their persecutor. At the critical moment he had died. But later diaries hinted that his death had been no accident, for when this new owner (as he was about to become, with judgement on the point of going in his favour), when this new owner had unwisely jumped the gun and taken it upon himself to view his coveted property, parading, no doubt, around the precincts, someone – who knows who? – someone had . . . Or let us say, as one letter said, '*Somehow* the leash was slipped . . . later the metal-studded collar was retrieved'. Someone had indeed unleashed a dog of war, and he had gone with a howl reminiscent of his forest ancestors, an avenging long-fanged brute taking up an alien scent and going in a fury through orchard and gardens, losing scent, recovering it, whipping backwards and forwards across the lawns, into bushes, from stables to woods, back to walled gardens, baying in frustration until the note in its throat had changed. A sudden certainty! Animal triumph!

He was gone like the wind, down the long wood, along the path under the trees and the rhododendron bushes, heading for the flight pond where the smell of the intruder was all pervasive, saturated with the smell of his fear, of his terror . . . All pride of victory and possession had gone with those first sounds – the distant snarl of an animal on the hunt. The strength had gone from him, his waving arms, vainly protecting his stricken face, failing before the onrush of the baying, leaping hound that went once . . . twice . . . for his throat. Waving arms were torn aside, blood gushed over the fashionable jacket, shirt and cravat were torn to shreds . . . And with the third wild rush, leaping the height of a man's shoulder, teeth sinking deep, trained to kill, trained to protect its own small human pack – which indeed it did. Scream after scream – heard but unattended, heard without pity at partially open windows by those who waited until that last scream choked into silence . . .

Later there were doctors; more than one, as letters pointed out . . . statements to magistrates and those in authority. All that could be done was, of course, done. But the moment was over. The threat had vanished. No litigation, no threat of dispossession.

Of course there was scandal, that was to be expected. But nothing was said in their presence. God knows what was suggested behind their backs, but suspicion could not mount a case, especially against people of proper worth and standing. As far as I could see, Longwood had remained with them to the last of these documents. The incident was summed up in a sober black line from a newspaper – 'A Tragic Accident'. And in the margin, in ink now blotted out of certain recognition, the comment . . . what did it say? I held it to the light, frowning over it. *What* had someone written: '*The price to pay*'? Was that what it was? Who had written that?

I sat in the silence of the cellar, documents at my feet, by my side, in my hands. How much of this had I truly made out from these papers? How much had I read? What had I supplied myself? Guessed at? Half understood? Was this history all in these papers, this collection of diaries, letters, documents, over a lifetime? Would someone else interpret them differently? It seemed to me more real than my own life, those bits and pieces of a nightmare.

I was brought back forcibly to my own century by the sound of a car pulling up a few feet away from me on the drive outside the cellar window. A moment later I heard Bridges shout, 'You there, sir? Someone to see you.' I was still deep under the weight of years, and could hardly respond. I think I was shaking; my hand trembled. Perhaps in the chill of the cellars I had caught cold.

I had not quite recovered as I went upstairs, puzzling to think who might have come to see me. Only Sarah knew I was here. I went out to the front. It was Bobby Everett.

'Hope it's all right to drop in like this,' he said.

'Of course. Why not?' I was looking towards the car. It was a different car, and Sarah wasn't there.

'Sarah not here?' I asked.

He looked a little surprised. 'Were you expecting her?'

'No, not really. I just thought . . . Come on in.'

He came into the house with me.

'How are things in Lewes?' I asked.

'That's just it,' he said. 'They're a little confused. The people I'm going to see haven't turned up; they're expected tomorrow or the next day.'

'What are you going to do?'

'I shall have to hang around, and I can't really afford the time.'

I hadn't quite cleared my mind. 'What about Sarah?'

'Sarah?' He didn't seem to follow my train of thought. 'She dropped me off. She went back.'

Something didn't click into place, and I guessed he was telling a lie. It was pretty clear to me why he had come back: Sarah had sent him. What he had not had the courage to tell me the day before, he had to summon up courage to tell me now. And he was on his own until he did this, I guessed.

'Where are you staying?' I asked.

'Oh, they arranged that all right. I'm in Lewes. An attractive little place.'

'I know it. Where are you?'

'Just off the High Street. Down the slope. Georgian. Very pleasant.'

'You're welcome to stay here.'

'That's kind, but it wouldn't be practical.'

My guess was that Sarah was in Lewes, waiting for him to come back to report on progress.

'Sarah and I went into Lewes once or twice for meals.'

'Really?' He didn't seem particularly interested. He was looking up at the house. 'I didn't really take all this in yesterday.' He waved vaguely at the building. 'It's even more charming than I thought. No wonder you spend your time here.'

'Sarah must have told you that.'

He didn't deny it. 'Oh yes, she said that since you found the place – well, shortly after – you have been hard to prise out of it.'

'It must seem like that.'

'Isn't it true?' He looked at me questioningly.

'Well, yes, there's been a lot to do. The last owners let it go a bit. It needed repainting for a start.'

'She told me about that. About the painters.'

'They were very professional.'

'About their alarm.'

'Oh, that.'

We moved slowly round outside the house as though by mutual consent.

'How long have you known her?' I asked.

'Sarah? A long time. All my life, in fact. Well, all *her* life, to be exact.'

He had the capacity to surprise me. 'All her life?'

'We knew each other as children. Not very well, of course, I was that much older, too old to pay her any attention. But we lived quite close.'

'In Suffolk?' I asked, knowing Sarah had lived in Norfolk.

'In Norfolk,' he said. 'We're related. Distantly. An uncle of hers and an aunt of mine were cousins.'

It was just possible. He was sauntering round the house admiringly as he continued, 'Of course, you know how it is. Families break up, grow apart. She went to live in London, and I was abroad for a year or two.'

'Whereabouts?' I was now doubtful that *all* he had said was a lie. It could have been partly true.

'The States,' he said. He seemed to be giving me only a fraction of his attention, not really concerned what impression his words might make. It was a disconcerting technique.

'I hope I'm not keeping you from something?'

'Not at all,' I said. 'It's still too wet to do anything in the garden.'

'Does that take up much time?'

'It does at present.' He had changed the conversation. If he had anything to tell me about Sarah, I'd give him the chance. 'Sarah and I have known each other for five years, and we've

94

been living together for three. I've never heard her talk about you.'

'I'm not surprised. We've been in touch again only recently.'

'Did you know we intended to get married?'

'Of course. I think she said you had both expected to be abroad on a honeymoon this month.'

'That was the idea. Things got a little delayed. I think she needed a little extra time.'

He nodded thoughtfully. 'Your marriage was the reason for buying the house, I understand?'

He made everything sound like a question. I didn't feel obliged to answer, but I did. 'It seemed the right thing to do. If we were changing things you know, settling down, growing older in a way, then it was best to do it properly.'

'You mean, if one is accepting the traditional role, then one makes the total sacrifice?'

I shot a quick glance at him. There wasn't the least hint of a smile on his face. 'I didn't think of it like that. And I don't think Sarah did . . . Do you think she did?'

'I don't know her that well now she's grown up.'

I wondered why the hell he was beating about the bush like this. All he had to do was come into the open and say he'd stolen the girl.

'She tells me you've been remarkably successful with your business.'

Good Lord! Was he trying to find out how he matched up to me in that world? 'We've done quite well. It's an interesting job: publicity, advertising. What are you involved in?'

'Research, mostly. At the present moment.'

'In what business?'

He seemed to be giving it some thought. 'I'm at a crossroads, I think. It's been rather academic so far. My work in the States was lecturing. Still, I'll see how things go in the next few months.'

I began to wonder if he was out of a job, but he looked much too affluent for that – much too successful. 'Are you back in England to stay?'

'I believe so,' he said.

We had been walking around the house and now arrived back at the front door.

'Come in,' I invited him. 'Like some coffee?'

'Thanks.'

We went into the kitchen and I made coffee.

'Do you have any help?' he asked.

'Running the place? There's the gardener, and a couple of women come from the village once a week, just to see things aren't going to pieces.'

He nodded, and I wondered what he was leading up to. I went on, 'It will be a lot easier from that point of view when we get settled in.' He looked puzzled. 'When Sarah is here,' I explained.

'Is that what you are arranging?'

I poured out the coffee, feeling that I had to be careful what I said. 'Not exactly. It's not scheduled. I mean there's no date.'

'Oh?'

'There was a date, more or less. But perhaps we were rushing things.' For some reason he appeared to want to understand. Perhaps it was important to him: perhaps he needed to know before he committed himself. I couldn't help liking him; he was treading so carefully, as though it was important not to hurt my feelings. For two pins I'd have said, *Why the hell don't you tell me what's going on between you and Sarah?* But he was so placid, so calm, that I didn't have the heart.

We sat and drank coffee in the kitchen.

'I understand you're going back to work in a couple of weeks,' he said. Was he going to ask me for a job?

'Yes. In two or three weeks, something like that.'

'Sarah told me she would be returning to town then.'

'Where is she now?'

'I'm not sure. I think she's with friends.'

'What friends?' I made it sound casual. There was no point telling him I thought he was a poor liar.

'She did tell me. Back in Norfolk, I think; friends, or family.'

'Isn't she coming back to Lewes?'

'I hope so. I'll let you know if she gets in touch.' He seemed so genuinely friendly I couldn't say anything.

96

'So you are going to be at a loose end for a couple of days?' I suggested.

'One, anyhow. I think it won't be more.'

'Do you go back to London after that?'

'It's possible. Do *you* look forward to going back?'

I was about to say I did, but I hesitated. 'I suppose so. In one way. In another, I feel I have to settle one or two other things first.'

He nodded as though he understood. 'You usually live in London, don't you?'

'That's right.'

'It must have been a full-time undertaking, getting your company going. It's a very competitive field.'

'It was fun.'

'Did you have much time for anything else?'

'I took time off, all right. You know, the usual young man's race against time. Packing in all the action before it's too late. Seems hectic when you look back. We were setting the business up. I've got one or two good associates, friends really, and we loved the pressure. Loved the fight, actually. Especially when things went well.'

'And they did?'

'Mostly. One chum, Freddie, he was with me more or less from the start. We worked out of one room at the back of a squalid office near Wardour Street. Everyone has to start that way. One good account, a bit of pressure, a bit of luck . . . I don't pretend it wasn't hard graft. And the time off bit . . . we'd knock off some Thursday nights late, lock-up till the Monday, drive to Dover, take the car through France, mostly to the snow. Ski, girls, the same old routine. Spend money we didn't have. A big con, but it generally worked. And it was good at the time. Even with Sarah, we kept it up for quite a bit. Didn't realize we weren't still in the first flush. But it sank in.'

I don't think I've ever spoken so much about myself before. Certainly not all in an unbroken spiel like that.

'Until what sunk in?'

'That we weren't still at that stage any more. You know, it

had all gone very well up till then. I don't suppose we were very keen to change.'

'Sarah as well?'

'Not so much Sarah, I suppose. Mostly me.' I stopped. I couldn't think why the devil I had told him all this. It couldn't possibly interest him, and it was none of his business. 'I'm sorry, I'm being a bloody bore.'

'Why should you think that?' he asked. He wasn't being polite; he really wanted to know.

'Look, it's an old story. I suppose most people go through it. Men, anyhow. I threw a lot into the work, because I wanted to. And the games? That was the same thing, I suppose. Just so long as things moved fast enough and far enough, that was satisfactory.'

'Was?'

'God! It's a stage you grow out of, isn't it?' That rather annoyed me. I took the cups and put them in the sink. Dishes tended to accumulate there during the week until the two women came to clean up.

Whatever I had said appeared to impress him. I couldn't think why, it was nothing original, I had thrown no new lights on the process of maturing. If he thought I had, then he must be more of an innocent than I had taken him to be. I began to wonder if Sarah realized what he was like. He had patiently absorbed what I said as if it were unique. He didn't appear to pass any judgement either, just listened, nodded occasionally, didn't even smile – which might have been a relief. In one sense it was like talking to a child – but a wise and perceptive child. I was uneasy however; it was unlike me to give so much away, even so much trivia. But I quickly reviewed what I'd said, and there was nothing harmful, nothing he might pass on to Sarah; nothing she didn't already know.

'You're a very young man to have achieved what you have,' he said thoughtfully.

'Oh come on! This generation you have to do it while you're under forty. The first time it's been possible in this country. You could do it in the States since the turn of the century. Now we're catching on, catching up.'

'Not so many have managed this.' He lifted a hand to indicate the room. We were still in the confusion of the kitchen, but I knew what he meant.

'It's a house,' I said. 'Just a house.'

'That sometimes represents a lot. It's pretty tangible, isn't it? I mean, a house is an extension of some people's personalities, isn't it?'

'In a way,' I nodded.

'You choose where you live. What it's going to be like. You make it as you want.'

I remembered something, and wondered if I'd risk saying it. 'It isn't just you, is it? A house? There were people before, people who owned it, people who built it.'

He sat silent for a few moments. 'Yes, that's true. I suppose it means more to some people than others?' There was the question in his voice again.

I wasn't sure whether to say this, but I did. 'It means a lot to me.'

He nodded over that, as though agreeing. 'Sarah tells me you are concerned to get the place into its original state. To restore it where possible.'

'Sarah seems to have told you quite a lot about me,' I said sharply.

He looked at me in surprise. 'She talks about you all the time. Does that seem strange? She is very concerned about you.'

'Concerned?'

'Well, you're going to get married.' Obviously that was explanation enough for him.

'That's correct.'

'And that you want the house to be perfect. She said that was the reason you had agreed to delay things.'

'She said that?'

'Yes. Isn't that the case?'

She had been very loyal. That was putting my procrastinations in their best light. It made it seem that what I was doing, I was doing for her. I hoped she believed it; I doubted it myself.

'Yes. That's right,' I said.

'I think she thinks she's very lucky,' he said. He got up. The sun was shining outside. 'I mustn't keep you.'

'That's all right. Have a look round the garden.'

We walked towards the wood. I remembered the chimney-piece in the stables. 'Have a look at Sarah's favourite item.' I took him up to the room in the stables and he stood looking at the fireplace. 'Very fine.' He seemed a bit doubtful. 'A little out of place, isn't it? Out of period?'

'Completely out,' I grinned. 'That's what she likes, I think. Anyhow, it's wonderful in its own right.'

'Yes, I suppose so. A little modern for me.'

We went round the walled garden, along the drive, into the orchard, and had a word with Bridges. I noticed that I carefully did not take him into the wood, nor did I speak about the pagoda. I wondered why afterwards. He was so obviously interested in what I had been doing that I would have liked to discuss it with him . . . But I was very careful not to. I mused over that. Now there's ambivalence for you, I thought.

He prepared to leave soon after that.

'Drop in again,' I invited him.

'That's very kind, but it won't be possible.'

I wondered what he would report back – that was, if he was making the report I suspected. I didn't think I had given anything away, but it was hard to know what was going on behind those large, placid, seemingly sympathetic eyes.

I had lost a lot of time that morning – what with the rain and my guest. As soon as he'd gone, I got back to work.

9

I couldn't be quite sure what it was that Everett had said that stuck in my mind, but for the rest of the day I didn't give full attention to what I was doing. He had somehow implied that I was delaying our plans, my plans for marriage to Sarah, through an infatuation with this house. He hadn't exactly said that; and I couldn't pinpoint what it was that left me with this impression, for he hadn't been in any way critical. He hadn't seemed to make judgements about anything, merely nodded receptively over the fact that I had got side-tracked.

I was carefully scraping clean the fretwork round the pagoda, but I had to stop to think. Was that what I was really doing? Had *I* caused the delay? For one thing was obvious, there had been no marriage; Sarah was no longer around, God knows where she was! Perhaps I ought to be looking for her! I moved away from the pagoda; but still there was this hesitation. I had to complete the work, make it as beautiful, as charming as it once had been, and as it was again becoming.

The afternoon passed, and I gradually forgot the visit, but I half expected Robert Everett to turn up again next morning. There was no sign of him, nor of Bridges either, for that matter, so the house and garden were unusually silent. It was indeed a solitary day. I was lackadaisical, and had to push myself to stay interested in what I was doing. I went to the village for a meal in the evening, feeling an isolation I hadn't sensed before.

But I did a lot of work the next day, and the next. The whole outer structure of the pagoda was in place, and it was a most attractive shell. I began once more to feel I was not alone, as though we had all been down in a trough and had only now climbed out of it. The old enthusiasm returned. Whatever the obstacle had been, it had passed. If I had done something to offend – and oddly enough that was what occurred to me – I had been forgiven. We began making headway again.

Bobby Everett had obviously become involved with his work, or with the people he had come to Sussex to see. Or perhaps he had gone back to London.

I had got into the habit of keeping the phone off the hook, but I put it back on during the evenings when I was in the house, and I hadn't taken it off one morning as I left the house. It started to ring. Bridges was there.

'Phone, sir,' he shouted. So I went back.

It was Sarah.

'Darling, are you all right? How's everything going? Isn't it about time we both thought of getting back to work? I'm in town myself – as a matter of fact, that's what I'm ringing about. I wondered if you'd be back? I mean, will you be using the flat? I've got a friend who's come up to London, and I wondered if you'd mind if we stayed there?'

'Good Lord, no! It's your flat too. You use it. I don't think I'll be up in town for a day or two, anyhow.'

'Sure you don't mind?'

'Of course not. Have a nice time.'

'It's boring without you, darling.'

'Won't be long now,' I said cheerfully 'I've got this place almost finished.' I kept the sharp and sudden suspicion out of my voice. Did she think I was so gullible? It gave me a sick feeling that she thought it necessary to use this deception. She was free to do as she pleased and give her love and confidence to whomsoever she chose. There was no need to spin out an old happiness if she felt it was dead.

And I was sure who the friend was, and understood why he had not been back to Longwood.

I think it was the very ordinariness of this deception that hurt me. Much better to shake hands and say good-bye – we had loved deeply and for many years; in fact, I knew that I loved her still. That it should degenerate in such a conventional way, was not her style. Nor mine. The phone call took the heart out of me. I sat in the house for a long time.

'Not working then?' asked Bridges at the kitchen door.

'Later.'

But I didn't think I would do anything. One thing had to be cleared up first: everything should be ended cleanly. I had to let them both understand that I knew what had happened. The best thing to do – the only thing – was to tell them to love each other without subterfuge and guilt. It was my fault that Sarah had lost the feeling she'd had for me.

I changed into city clothes. I would drive to the flat: they would be there now, and if not, I would wait. Better to get the unpleasant details over.

Bridges was surprised to see me back the car out of the garage.

'Didn't know it was you, sir. Not in them clothes.'

As I turned towards the front drive I saw another car coming in. There wasn't room for us both to pass. The other driver pulled up and got out.

'Sorry,' he said, 'I should have phoned. You going out?'

It took me a split second to realize it was Everett.

'Are you still here?' It was a senseless question, but I couldn't quite put my thoughts in order.

'Yes. I got a bit tied up, and the work took longer than I thought. It's not finished in fact. I'll back out of your way. Let you pass.'

'No, no, that's all right. I'm not going anywhere.'

I reversed into the wide sweep of the drive in front of the house, and he pulled up his car just ahead of me.

If he noticed I was dressed in a dark grey suit, hardly my working clothes, he didn't remark on it.

We had a drink in my study; I felt I needed it. I was very pleased to see him, surprisingly so. A weight had suddenly lifted. Whoever it was, it wasn't Everett who was sharing my flat with Sarah.

'Then I found I had this time off . . . I thought I'd take up your invitation. Drop in and see you.'

'I'm glad you did.'

We strolled round the lawn. I couldn't very well say: if *you* aren't staying with Sarah in London, who the hell is? And for some reason I didn't care very much. It had been the thought of the deception that had depressed me. I began to think I might be wrong – completely wrong – about the two of them.

'I thought you'd gone back to London.'

'I don't see how I can for a few days.'

'Sarah phoned me. She's back in the flat.'

'Yes, I know.'

'You know?'

'She phoned me as well. She's there with some cousin, someone she's been staying with. She seemed to think I should remember her, but I don't.'

'Oh.' None of my assumptions were making sense.

Bridges came out of the walled garden, saw us, and gave a passing nod.

'You seem to have got everything under control,' said Everett. He looked with approval round the garden and up to the house. 'You've got it in pretty good order.'

'It's coming along.'

'Sarah said you would really put it back on its feet.'

'She said that?'

He nodded 'Yes, weeks ago. When we first got in touch again.'

'That was a coincidence, wasn't it? How did it happen?'

'Meeting Sarah? Let me think.' He frowned. 'Oh yes, I was back in London. This aunt told me about her, and suggested I get in touch.'

'*You* got in touch?'

He hesitated. 'Yes. But I think Sarah had phoned this aunt first; to see if I was around.'

'I see.'

He managed to make it very indeterminate. But at some stage Sarah had inquired in the family about him, and he had responded. Well, if they were cousins – and they were, of a sort – why not?

'What else are you doing?' He was peering up at the house, inspecting the roof.

I gave him a quick look. It seemed a loaded question. But he was casually inspecting slates and guttering. Perhaps he was making conversation. 'I'm taking things slowly now. It's ready to live in. The rest is . . . well, decoration. Restoring. That sort of thing.'

He nodded, still looking up at the roof. 'Quite an undertaking,' he said thoughtfully. 'No wonder things got delayed. Did you think it would take so long?'

'I never thought about it.'

It struck me that this was a continuation of the conversation we had had on his previous visit; he had led it back on to the same track. There had to be a reason for that.

'Are you concerned about Sarah?'

He looked at me blankly. 'What do you mean?'

'Are you concerned about her? Worried about her? Do you think . . . as one of her family . . . that you have to look after her? Something like that?'

He couldn't hide his amusement. 'I think Sarah can look after herself, don't you?'

'Look, let me put things straight. We were going to get married. It was my idea.'

'She told me that.'

'We both saw this house, and agreed to let things wait until we had it as a home. As I told you, Sarah needs a little more time.'

'Did she say that?'

'I'm not sure if she said it, but it's how she's acting. It's only a delay. We've known each other a long time. Nothing will go wrong.'

'You think she doesn't want to get tied up . . . irrevocably, so to speak?'

'I don't know.' I didn't need to discuss anything with him, but the suggestion that Sarah was delaying things had sounded cheap. 'It's not just Sarah. I'm after something, I'm trying to do something . . . I'm not sure what. I'd like it to be perfect.'

'What exactly?'

'The house. Everything.'

We walked the length of the lawn without speaking. Then he said, 'Perfection is a tough goal, a terrible thing to saddle yourself with. It takes some achieving.'

'Perfection.' I shrugged. 'You know what I mean.'

'What exactly?'

Anyone else I would have fobbed off; but he had a puzzled air of concern, an interest in what I was doing, that was hard to brush aside. 'I don't know. It's just . . . up to now, things have gone right. We've come along together on the crest of a wave. I'd like it to stay that way.'

'Is she like that, then?'

'What?'

'Attracted by success?'

'I didn't say that.'

'It sounded that way. As if she couldn't accept things except in top gear.'

'I don't think she's like that.'

'As the song goes, would she be happy with you in a tumbledown shack by an old railroad track?'

I laughed. 'My guess is it would depend on how noisy the trains were.'

I saw a car come in at the drive and remembered that Doreen and Fay . . . I knew their names now . . . were due from the village. They waved, and went into the house. They had a routine, and I didn't interfere. A moment later the phone rang.

'Won't you answer that?' asked Everett.

'They will.'

Doreen threw up a window. 'It's for the doctor.'

'What doctor?'

'That's all right,' said Everett. 'I hope you don't mind, I gave your number in case of developments.' He began walking towards the house. Afterwards, he came out of my study. 'Sorry about that. I'll have to nip along. Thanks for the drink.'

'I didn't know you were a doctor.' I don't know why I felt offended.

He was getting into his car, preoccupied. 'Didn't Sarah say?' He appeared to attach no importance to it. 'If I give you a ring, think you'll have time off? Care to come for a meal? One or two nice places in Lewes. I'll phone.'

When I went back into the house, Doreen and Fay were going from room to room, tidying, cleaning, putting things in order. Always together. I hadn't minded at first, but I was finding it a little irritating now.

'Your friend a doctor, then?'

'So it seems. You still working as a double act?'

They both giggled and winked at each other. 'Get through things a lot quicker that way,' they said.

I left them, and went down to the garage. It was a matter of no significance, I told myself, that Robert Everett was a doctor. But, again, I couldn't settle to my work. Something was preying on my mind. This was the first time I had ever felt uneasy as I walked through the wood; yet I couldn't say what I was uneasy about. The pagoda stood, dappled light through the trees picking out its charm, but I didn't respond; and I was unwilling to start work again fiddling with various tools, testing them, cleaning them, scraping rust from a bracket, without interest, without enthusiasm.

I sat in the pagoda wondering why I was ill at ease, looking round the pond, peering into shadows. It was all unduly still, or, more accurately, lifeless. That disturbed me. Perhaps it *was* really lifeless. Perhaps the energy had drained away. Perhaps I was alone in a way I hadn't been before, for I had become part of a group. A family haunted me, and I was happy to be haunted by it. What if they were no longer there, if I was no longer in touch. I was sick with the thought.

Leaving the tools, I stood at the edge of the pond. Usually I had some indication that I was not alone before I was able to focus on my images. This time I had nothing. I tried to summon them, and it was a very difficult thing to do – there were no rules for it, no way in which I could channel or concentrate the necessary energy. Every time I merely sensed a grey space – a cold, blank emptiness, not exactly hostile, but disinterested, as though the magic had gone, as if it had all been an illusion and there had never been anyone or anything there.

I couldn't get quit of this melancholy. Suddenly, the pagoda, the long wood, my work, even the house itself, seemed purposeless. I tried to throw off the feeling, walking round the pond, along the path, stopping, starting again, turning slowly, quickly, trying to coax something out of my imagination. But I knew that wasn't the way. What I had experienced in the past few weeks was not of my doing. Those five beings who had come and gone, had watched, waited, appeared, disappeared, had not come from effort on my part. They had presented themselves of their own accord. Perhaps they were like people in a dream, with an existence of their own. The dreamer is not able to manipulate the beings in his dream. They have their own logic.

I knew it was useless to try to invent them. They were either with me in the darkening wood, or they weren't. It was the thought of being without them, deserted, that upset me. And then I realized what it was that was making me feel uneasy. It was I who had broken the link, who had destroyed the fragile communication. My uneasiness was a sense of guilt. I had done something of which they disapproved, which made them feel threatened. They had retreated in order to protect themselves. And I guessed where this 'guilt' lay. It was with strangers – the coming and going of other people; people who intruded into my life, and therefore into theirs. It had to do with human contact. Perhaps all human contact, even with Bridges, and the women working in the house; but more so, far more so, with anyone who concerned me closely. Sarah, for example; and now Everett. He had intruded, taken up my time. I guessed that I was like a heart pumping in a body. If I were not there, then the essence of life would be missing, the shadows would be shadows again. And the longer I was away, the more I was distracted by other things, the more likely it was that the life I had roused would die.

For a moment I felt like calling, 'I'm here, I'm back.' But that wouldn't work. It would have to be done slowly, patiently, and even then I couldn't be sure – the spirit might have gone out of them. Father, mother, soldier with the multi-coloured uniform, busy, balding scholar. Perhaps the spirit was already gone from the girl in dancing-pumps, lace-dressed, beribboned, a wraith again.

I knew there was no point staying in the wood after night fell. The place went cold, I had never sensed any presence except by day. Unlike the evil spirits of old wives' tales, my phantoms appeared by sunlight. But I stayed where I was, restless, blaming myself for losing something magical and precious.

I was about to leave, had picked up the tools and stepped from the pagoda. A high moon, white, was coming and going behind clouds. I had given up any thoughts, any – but I stopped dead. No sound! no vision! Nothing to trigger off senses. Nothing I could explain, and yet. . . .

I could have laughed in the dark. As it was, I went back to the house singing. I suppose they were like bulbs below the ground in winter. There had been a frost, but then something I had done – perhaps just the passion of my wishing – had been sufficient. There was new life. I had suddenly felt it, and I knew they were there.

10

I'd made a good start in restoring the pagoda, but there were several struts missing from the little balcony round it. It was supported by delicately shaped wooden pillars connected to a balustrade. Some sections were almost complete, so it was possible to see how it had once been; but between other pillars there were empty gaps where diamonds making up the diagonal patterns had vanished. It still had a charm as it was. Even the worn colours, pale blue, light yellow and a dusty flaking ochre, were charming. Looking across at it from the other side of the pond I could see its reflection in the water. Perhaps that was why it had been built there in the first place, to create this mirror pattern. And I saw that the picture would be infinitely improved if only the missing pieces hadn't been lost. New strips of wood wouldn't do. How could they be made to match? Who could carve them so delicately? Besides, I didn't want to involve anyone else.

Ripples on the pond blurred the reflection, sending the colours into a pale confusion, and I saw a dark shape under accumulated ages of leaves and mud. Something lay a few steps from the edge of the water, and I somehow knew exactly what it was before I waded in. The mud was inches deep, and my feet sank, but I was so elated I hardly noticed. The problem was to clear away the muck – leaves mostly – before trying to lift what was clearly a piece of the wooden framework. A great suction of foul air held it like a limpet. There was a noise like a drain being unblocked as I shifted it. A little wave spread across the pond, and I let it ease back.

I realized I'd have to take it carefully, washing the mess away, feeling along the frame in the slimy mud until I could tell it was safe to lift again. By this time I was soaking and covered in filth. I was getting a bit clumsy as my feet and hands grew numb. I slipped in the mud, unsteady, a little dazed, caught up in the excitement of my discovery – a gold-digger striking lucky. I was determined to get this treasure out of the water safely in one piece. But the frame came out of the water with unexpected ease at the next attempt, and I went clambering up the little bank with my prize.

It was a square of wood, exactly as I had imagined; a section of balustrade, almost complete, the paint patchy, but the wood in better condition than the pagoda itself. Could the mud and slime have helped to preserve it? It was sodden with the icy water, as I was myself, and covered in black slime. I was shivering, but I went back into the water to splash the frame clean. The dirt streaked off, ochres and blues came to life. And there – a diagonal of pure lemon yellow.

I stood it against the pagoda and could see where it fitted; this was the most miraculous jigsaw puzzle, and it was coming together! I clapped my hands in a sort of triumph. Birds flew up in a startled flutter. The horses in the field galloped off noisily. And there was another noise . . . I wasn't sure what it was at first – in fact, I wasn't sure if I had really heard it. Mingled with the wheeling birds and the trampling horses, it sounded like applause.

It was almost as though the rules had been broken. The sound stopped abruptly, before I could locate it. Only the thud of the hoofs remained; the horses completed their circuit of the field, coming back to watch me, tossing heads, switching tails, eyes big. The birds resettled. Pigeons swooped over the field, and soft clouds veiled the sun. Everything was back to normal. I must have been mistaken about that other sound. Nothing could be heard through such a barrier of time.

I examined the newly discovered pieces of the balustrade for my pagoda, and ran my fingers over the soaked wood, feeling for cracks or rot, amazed at how the whole thing held together. I would have stayed there admiringly but my teeth were chattering and I was beginning to shake. I went up to the house, unsteadily.

Bridges saw me as I reached the back door. I didn't know he was there; I was never sure which three days of the week he worked for me.

'Fall into something, did you, sir?' He was very matter-of-fact, as if every day of his life people ran past him soaked to the skin and shaking with cold.

'Be all right,' I managed to say.

I thawed out in a hot bath, then I took my time dressing, luxuriating in the thought that the pagoda might be completely restored. There could be further pieces of that lost balustrade – or other parts – in the pond. I would work out a way to drag the bottom. If the mud at the edge was anything to go by, then the middle would be thick with it. I would get the sort of waders that were used for fishing. I could use rakes, nets. It wouldn't be difficult. I wanted to take another look at my discovery.

Bridges was on the lookout for me. 'You want to be careful down there, sir,' he nodded warningly. 'That pond, under them trees, no knowing how deep it goes.'

I guessed he was right.

The new section was every bit as beautiful as I had thought, a rectangle with diagonal struts from corner to corner – all coloured – and another, smaller, rectangle in the centre. One end was diamond-shaped, and I thought at first I had found a complete section that would slot in between two pillars; but it was a foot or so short. Obviously there had been another such diamond shape at the other end: that would balance the design.

I hadn't come down to work, but I looked around to see if there were any signs of this other piece. It would be made of four strips of wood, moulded and painted. There wasn't much chance of it surviving if it had fallen in the bracken. But perhaps . . . I went back to the edge of the pond.

Once or twice before when working, I had noticed a special sort of quiet fall over the place. I was aware of it now. Even the birds were silent. The feeling was strong as I reached the water on the far side. The path here wasn't even cleared. If this was the children's game of 'You're hot . . . You're cold', then I was very hot. The indications were strong – an increase in the intensity of that silence. It was hard to understand how silence could become more intense, but it did.

I heard the phone ring from the house. I had left it switched on with the garden bell, and now it sounded across the field, but there was no point going back to answer it. Even at a run, it would take a good four minutes. After a moment the bell stopped. The pressure round me was still there, but it had fluctuated at the sound of that bell. I was still being urged to finish this search. I hesitated.

'You there, sir?' Bridges shouted from the top of the path.

'What's that?'

'For you,' shouted Bridges. I noticed he didn't come down the path, he had stopped at the top, where the rhododendron bushes started. 'I answered. Knew you'd never get there.'

'Thanks.'

'That there doctor,' called Bridges, 'Everett whatsit. I said you'd be around, sir. Said he'd call back in ten minutes.'

'Oh, thanks.'

'Right, sir.' Bridges was moving off.

The spell had gone; though the wood was still silent it was now a ragged silence. Well, there was no urgency to continue this search. What was lost had been lost a long time. It would stay until the next day. Besides, I was intrigued by Everett: perhaps Sarah had been in touch with him. I wondered what he wanted.

As I turned to go I found my limbs unexpectedly heavy; a lethargy had settled on me, a weakness. Walking was laboured, an unusual feeling. Even the bushes, the bracken, made heavy going. I wondered if I had caught a chill when I was in the water. I was sweating. Perhaps it was going to thunder – the day *had* seemed warm. It didn't occur to me that anything else could be hampering me. That would have been too fantastic.

I realized Bridges was calling again. 'I'll be going now, sir,' he shouted. ' 'Less you want me to wait and answer that phone?'

'You go,' I called. 'I'm coming.'

'Night,' shouted Bridges.

I was breathing with more effort than usual. My heart hammered as if I had been running. If I wasn't well, the sooner I got back to the house the better. I'd tell Everett when he phoned. His call might be very opportune. The path swam as I made my way back. Something I had eaten? Too long without food? I didn't know the answer, but I knew I could use a stiff drink.

I had taken about a dozen steps away from the pond when the atmosphere seemed to change. The oppressive feeling lifted; I breathed easily again, and I knew there was nothing to stop me getting back to the house as quickly as I wanted.

But I didn't move, I came to a stop, in mid-flight, so to speak, in the very moment of taking a quicker step. A second later, and I would have been out of sight of the pond. But something seemed to brush past me . . . causing me to catch my breath, to make my mouth turn dry, to make my skin prickle, to bewilder, to dazzle! I only half believed what I saw . . . what I *thought* I saw. I had to turn slowly, go back on my tracks, take a step back. I was being coaxed to return . . . being mesmerized, unable to help myself. Ahead of me, between me and the pond, not doing anything, nothing blatant, nothing so crude as trying to influence me, but just being . . . just existing, was a faint, uncertain shadow, the wraith that I had expected her to be. The shape, the outline, and almost . . . almost . . . the colour. The frail reality of the girl, the flutter of her dress, the flow of fair hair in the dark, was there; or the promise of her was there. All I had to do was go closer, go back to where I had stood. . . . But I was still unmoving. Perhaps I was about to follow, perhaps I wasn't – I don't know . . .

The phone went again. I knew, as before, that there was no chance of answering it. But the magic was broken. I was listening to the bell ringing, listening and watching her. I didn't see her face, not clearly. But I sensed her dismay, and that dismay echoed within me. Still, I couldn't move. I couldn't follow her. Something stopped me. I didn't know at the time what it was; all I felt was a sense of sadness, heartbreak. And another emotion, no stronger than a question at that moment. A doubt. Then even that was gone, as the wraith had gone, and the phone stopped ringing, and the long wood fell silent. But now it was the silence of all natural things. Of the birds shuffling in the first moments of night, of horses padding past over grass. Silence. Ordinary silence.

I went back to the house, trying to make sense of my life in this place. I sat by the phone, pouring myself a drink. Several drinks. I think I was there for about an hour. Everett didn't phone.

But the following morning he called, while I was dressing.

'Sorry to ring you so early,' he said. 'But I tried to get in touch with you yesterday. It looks like I've got a rare evening free today, and I wondered if you'd care for a meal? That's if you have nothing better to do.'

Something at the back of my mind nagged away suspiciously; Robert Everett and Sarah. Sharing some secret, treading carefully, watching me – that's what he was doing certainly, watching me.

'I'd like that very much,' I said.

'Good. I'm at the White Hart. It's on the High Street.'

'I know it.'

'Seven?'

'I'll be there.'

I didn't know exactly what I suspected; I'd discarded the idea they were having an affair, but now it swept back into my mind. I couldn't really believe it, and was angry with myself for reconsidering it. But it kept coming back.

Everett was waiting outside the hotel. 'You can park here,' he said. 'I've arranged to have a meal in Brighton. I hope you don't mind. We'll go on from here in my car. Some friends might join us for a drink later.'

He chatted cheerfully as he drove. His friends were a young doctor and his wife with whom he was working. I gathered they were attached to the University on the outskirts of the town.

It was out of season in Brighton, but the place managed to keep a bright, busy face long after summer crowds had gone. Street lights sparkled on roads as a squall blew in from the sea, washing blackly against its beaches. The hotels along the front,

standing out white in the darkness, were as excellent a statement of the good life as one could find this side of the Channel,
their showy splendour hard to resist.

The dining-room was large, high-roofed and peopled by a
mixed crew, all ages, all styles. The meal was good. How little I
had been out since I had been in Longwood! And how little I
had missed it. For years I had hardly been in one place for any
length of time. Work would have taken me restlessly to a dozen
cities during the time I had been building my pagoda. I would
have been caught up in a flow of projects. Now one, fictitious
and inexplicable, filled my time.

'Sorry? What did you say?' I was giving Everett only part of
my attention.

'He's a doctor, as you'd expect in that job. I don't think she
does anything.'

I'd missed the beginning of the story, and listened until he
made sense. 'What did you say his name was?'

A quick look of surprise. 'Andrew Delmar. And Ruth. Must
be in their mid-thirties. Quite good fun. I gather from Sarah
you don't know many people in the district, but Brighton isn't
too far.'

I grinned. So this was an exercise in looking after me. It
would be difficult for Everett to understand, that being alone in
Longwood was a hectic and crowded experience.

'I was surprised to learn you were a doctor.'

'Oh? Why was that?'

'I don't know. Perhaps I expected Sarah to say Doctor Robert
Everett, not Mister.'

'Did she say Mister?'

'Come to think of it, I don't suppose she did.'

'Perhaps I should have mentioned it.'

'Of course not. Do you specialize?'

He nodded. 'I studied neurology.'

'What exactly? The nervous system?'

'The brain and nervous system. Organic diseases. Abnormalities.'

'I see.' I wasn't sure that I did see. It was so unexpected that
this bland, sombre-eyed man with the impassive expression and

the broad shoulders should be involved with such responsibilities. At most he was a year or two older than me but his occupation seemed that of a far older man.

'Where do you practise?'

'I worked in the States, but I've also spent some time in London. I qualified here.'

I had a pang of mixed envy and admiration: his contribution seemed much more valuable than mine. But the feeling passed quickly. 'Are you working here now?'

He hesitated. 'I'm involved with some research. That's why I'm in touch with Delmar.'

'He's into neurology, too?'

He grinned. 'Well in. He's written quite a bit.'

'What about?'

'Nervous disorders, for the most part.'

I was becoming very interested. I didn't realize why at first; my instincts were away ahead of my intellect. Something suddenly was very important in what he was saying, but I couldn't quite identify what it was.

'You deal in these disorders? I mean, a neurologist is concerned about the way people understand things? Or don't understand them?'

'I'm not sure I follow.'

'Do you – or this friend, Delmar – do you cure, or analyse, or investigate, the way we respond to life?' I didn't want to come right out in the open and explain anything too accurately. 'Do you understand what makes the brain tick?'

'We try to understand.'

'I mean, like the nerves . . . no, the senses, picking up information from the outside world and passing it back to the brain, and the brain making sense of it?'

'You should have taken it up professionally,' he smiled.

'Is that what happens?'

'Briefly, yes. In a way. Information reaches the brain by way of one set of nerves and the brain sends out its instructions along another set. The spinal cord is the main nerve trunk, with nerves leading from there to all parts of the body.'

'Everything is experienced by the brain?'

'You could put it like that. It is the control centre for all nervous activity.'

The most important questions seemed to me to be about sight and sound. After all, I had seen, and I had heard. I didn't think it possible that I should ever touch. Not in the long wood. Not that beloved family. 'So when we see things . . . ?'

'See things?' He didn't seem quite sure what I meant.

'People or things. If we see them . . . what's happening?'

'The optic nerve contains fibres from the retina in the eye. When we see something, information is transmitted along these nerves to the visual centre in the brain.'

'So what we see must be actually *there*?'

'I don't get the point.'

I pushed back my plate. It was very important. The questions had not occurred to me before, but now, as if by miraculous coincidence, someone with answers, with reassurance, had turned up. 'It's not actually possible to see things that aren't there, is it?'

'Not if the system is functioning properly. But as I said, there are abnormalities.'

'What does that mean?'

'Coffee?'

'What? Oh, thanks.'

'Well a common experience, I suppose we've all gone through it once, something that shows we can *think* we see something and it either isn't as we think or it isn't there at all, is when we've had too much to drink.'

'You mean a drunk man sees something that isn't there?'

'It happens. A person who suffers from delirium tremens has the most alarming hallucinations.'

'But he's not actually *seeing* things.'

'He thinks he is. As far as he's concerned, those snakes and rats crawling over him are there.'

He wasn't answering the point that concerned me. I had to put it more exactly. 'In a case like that, suppose he recovers a bit, and then suppose he has another attack next day, the things he sees wouldn't have the same continuity, would they?'

'You mean, if he saw a grey rat coming out of the wall in one place, would it be the same rat in the same place next day?'

'Something like that.'

'I don't suppose there'd be a continuity like that. After all, there isn't an object in reality that's giving rise to what he sees. It's registered in his brain only because there's a breakdown in his nervous system.' He looked at me drily. 'The poisonous effects of alcohol are formidable. I was going to offer you a brandy with your coffee, but perhaps you'd rather not?'

'I'll risk it,' I said.

I drank it with a sense of relief, with light-heartedness almost. I must have been worried about my state of mind, a worry which I had not allowed to surface. Now Everett seemed to be saying that the visions I had seen, because they had continuity, were not just figments of my mind. They were not something I had concocted. To come and go as they did presupposed a logic, a reality, of their own. It was no abnormality on my part to see them; unlike a drunk man or a lunatic, I was reacting to something outside myself. Perhaps that was why I was suddenly light-hearted, light-headed. That family, all five of them, lived and shared life with me in Longwood. It was an odd quirk that it should be a cousin of Sarah's who should tell me that the causes of my infatuation were really there.

'I imagine this is all because of the painters?' said Everett.

'The painters?' I looked at him blankly.

'I gather they thought they saw things when they were working in your house.'

'Sarah told you that?'

He nodded. 'She said you had a lot of trouble convincing them.'

'Yes, they did think they heard footsteps. They didn't see anything.'

'I guess it's the same principle,' suggested Everett.

'I explained it was the wood in the floorboards, contracting.'

'That convinced them?'

'I don't think it did. Sarah told you this?'

He nodded. 'I think she was impressed that the painters . . . three of them, weren't there? . . . got scared, but you didn't think twice about being there on your own.'

'They were all Londoners; I don't think they'd spent a night out of a big city. That first night, when one of them was by himself, he was really upset. It took a lot of guts for him to stick at the job.'

'Well, there you have it. The brain getting the right information, but giving a wrong interpretation. Imagination can scare the hell out of a grown man.'

I remembered being alone in Longwood myself the night I had heard the steps outside my door – the dancing steps. I hadn't been scared. But then, it hadn't been imagination.

I glanced at Everett, who was tapping his coffee cup thoughtfully. I had a feeling that he, if anyone, might understand. He went on. 'Interesting that they should believe in those footsteps, after you'd shown them the real cause. You demonstrate the floorboards, they choose to believe something much less realistic.'

'I don't think they actually chose. That's not the right word.'

He shrugged. 'It was a choice, the most exciting choice, which had the effect of keeping things interesting. Generating energy, dispelling boredom.'

'They didn't do it deliberately.'

'You're right. Not deliberately, or it would have failed. Their ghost was created with another part of the mind – subconscious, irrational.'

I knew he was right off the mark, and I had the evidence to prove it. 'You mean that even though they didn't realize what they were doing, they really invented that sound?'

'Not the sound, the cause . . . the ghost. You don't believe in ghosts?'

'No.' I certainly did not believe in ghosts. But then I had never thought about 'them' as ghosts. He was demeaning them by using the word.

'I'd like to bet the painters didn't believe in ghosts,' said Everett thoughtfully. 'Trouble is, people's beliefs don't all come together in one compact and logical philosophy. It's generally a confusion, little bits and pieces picked up in childhood, never examined, seldom acknowledged.'

'And that's neurology?'

He smiled. 'Not really. Though there's an overlap here and there.'

A very pretty girl was heading towards us from the door, smiling and waving. She was followed by a fair man, a little older than Everett.

'Here they are,' said Everett and rose to greet them.

As he had said, the Delmars, doctor and wife, were very amusing. We were on 'Andy', 'Ruth' and 'Nicky' terms immediately. With Everett there had previously been a slight formality. Now he too was 'Bobby'. We chatted at the table, then went into the bar. The two doctors had a professional matter to arrange, but apart from that it seemed as if they were going out of their way to be welcoming to me.

'We were talking about the workers at Nicky's house,' said Everett.

'Those famous painters!' Delmar laughed.

'Good Lord, don't say you know about them as well!'

'I told them,' said Everett.

'The men who heard those people in the night?' asked Ruth. She was quite alarmed.

I played it down. 'It's not much of a story.'

'Have *you* heard anything?' she asked.

I hesitated. 'There *are* noises. It's an old house, and fairly big.'

'Very big,' said Everett.

'What do you hear?' She was intent on frightening herself.

'I suppose I heard what they heard.'

'Talking? Whispering?'

'No, just movement. What sounds like movement.'

'Blimey! And you're in the place alone?'

'Come and join me,' I invited her.

She gave an exaggerated shiver. 'I don't know how you can . . . Anything else? Just noises, or have you seen anything?'

It was just chatter, but it took me by surprise. I hesitated. 'It's the sort of place you could think anything – if you wanted to. Bobby thinks my painters made it up to keep from getting bored. My trouble is I don't get bored, so I don't need to invent anything. I see only what is actually there.'

'What a pity,' she said. She wrinkled her nose. 'How dull.'

I issued a vague invitation. 'You must come over and see the house. I'll find out when Sarah'll be down next.' They all thought it was a great idea.

A little later we split up, and Everett drove me back to Lewes to pick up my car. 'Keep in touch with them,' he said. 'If you're at a loose end, give them a call.'

He was disarmingly considerate. The whole outing had been arranged to involve me with other people. I thanked him, and was just leaving him in the hallway of his hotel when the night porter joined us.

'The lady's arrived, sir. I said you'd be late. I put her in room four seven.' He had a hoarse but audible whisper.

'Thanks.' Everett shook hands with me on the step, suddenly in a hurry to be on his own.

I drove back to Longwood, trying to shut my mind to the possibilities, to one possibility in particular. Something in Everett's manner, something in his look, in the way he was anxious to be quit of me, convinced me that the lady who had arrived at his hotel had to be Sarah.

It was late when I got home, too late to do anything about it. But I fidgeted about for ten minutes and then put through a call to the flat. A girl's voice answered, sleepily.

'Sarah?' I wasn't quite sure.

'Sorry, she isn't in just now.' It was a young voice, pleasant, but I didn't recognize it.

'When do you expect her back?' There was a moment's hesitation. 'This is Nick Morell.'

'Oh, I see.' There was still the hesitation. 'I'm not sure, I think she might be late. This is Angela Rose. I'm staying with Sarah.'

'Yes, I'd heard,' I said. 'Could you give me any idea when she'll be home?'

'She left a note. It might be very late. It might be tomorrow.'

'Oh, right.' I was non-committal. 'I'll call another time.'

'Any message?'

'Nothing special.' I left it at that.

I told myself I had already been through all this meaningless suspicion. Sarah was entitled to live her own life; I wasn't offering her anything. The vacuum, where there had once been so much deep feeling, had never been openly and honestly acknowledged; perhaps we had been hoping that if we didn't talk about it it would vanish. But it was there all right. And in a way it was a vacuum which I'd welcomed – until now. Now I felt betrayed. Was this all a careful ploy? And what did it add up to?

Bobby takes me to dinner, to meet friends, plays a part, so that my guard is lowered, my suspicions lulled: then he and Sarah carry on this hole-in-corner affair? There was no need for such secrecy. I had no claims on Sarah nor she on me. All ties can be broken if the will to hold them breaks. Sarah had only to kiss me good-bye, with thanks on both sides for so much past love and happiness. That was the only gesture needed, then she and Bobby could enjoy each other to their hearts' content. It was the deception I could not forgive. That was what was demeaning, and I wasn't going to tolerate it. But it took many sleepless hours before I decided what to do.

I was awake early. As I got the car out, I saw Bridges. 'London, sir?' he said cheerfully.

I shook my head. 'Won't be long,' I told him.

I was in Lewes shortly before ten o'clock. I parked the car a short distance from the hotel, as I had an idea it might be recognized. This had to be done swiftly and without warning, without much regard for convention.

I walked along the main street and into the hotel. There were several people with the attendant at the desk. I went past quickly. The number of the room had stuck in my head: 'Four seven'. I went up the stairs and along the first landing. The room was at the end of a short corridor, and I was outside it before I had time to have second thoughts. I gave a brief knock and tried the handle.

A voice called, 'Who's there?' but I was already in the room. A girl was at the dressing-table in the act of lifting up her hair, her fingers holding dark tresses above her head, half turned towards the door, her négligé partly covering her bare shoulders, a little startled, eyes wide, looking at me. She was the only person there, and I'd never seen her in my life.

'I'm sorry,' I said. 'I beg your pardon. Wrong room. I'm looking for Bobby Everett.'

'He's gone,' she said. 'If you'd like to leave a message . . .'

'I'm sorry, I will.' I was in a hurry to go, trying to think fast, but my mind had gone blank.

I stopped at the desk. 'Please tell Mr Everett that Nick Morell called.' I couldn't think of anything to cover my intrusion, nothing momentous enough to explain the morning call. 'Could you ask him to phone?' That at least would give me time. I was out of the hotel quickly in case they asked for details.

11

The phone was ringing in the house as I pulled up outside Longwood. 'Been going like that off and on,' said Bridges, grimly pleased, 'ever since you left this morning.'

It was still ringing when I went in.

'Hello, darling.' It was Sarah. 'I got this message, that you called.'

'Lovely to hear you, Sarah. It was nothing, just a crazy idea.' It was coming to me as I talked. 'I thought we might give a little party. A dinner party. You know, while your cousin Bobby's in these parts. If you could manage it.'

'You mean, there? At Longwood?'

'Yes.'

'Darling . . .' She hestiated. 'How splendid. Is Bobby still down there?'

'Yes, I saw him last night. And a couple of his friends. They'd like to see the house. And I think his girl friend's just turned up.'

'His girl friend?'

'I think it's his girl friend. Just caught a glimpse of her in her nightie. Very nice.'

'I didn't think he could stay there so long.'

'Apparently he had to. But I think he goes soon. That's why I thought if we could arrange it at speed – like for tomorrow evening . . . ?'

'Darling, I think that's out. We've got Hans coming.'

'Hans? Our favourite German millionaire?'

Hans wasn't his name but we all called him that in the office, first to annoy him, then, as he took it in such good part, as a much-prized nickname. He was a valuable client who had made a fortune distributing films in Europe.

'He's here tonight for two days' non-stop talking. You know what he's like.'

'Bring him down, darling. He'd enjoy that.'

She gave it a moment's thought. When she spoke the old amusement was back in her voice. 'He might at that. I'll call you later. I'll phone him, and see what I can do.'

I seemed to be in limbo the rest of the morning. The idea of a party had bubbled up from nowhere; it wouldn't be difficult to organize at short notice if Sarah could manage to get down. I asked Bridges if there was likely to be any help in the village.

'The George do that kind of thing,' he said. 'Not too good, I hear. But you can get things in the village all right. Got some good enough shops. Them two will come in and help.'

'Fay and Doreen?'

'Shouldn't wonder.'

But I was aware the whole episode was taking a slice out of my life. In order to cover up my stupidity, I had got myself into this charade. I looked with anxiety down the long wood path a couple of times during the day, but I felt I had to stay close to the house to take calls from Sarah or Bobby.

They rang within a few minutes of each other. 'I called Hans at his office,' said Sarah. 'He's looking forward to it. Flying in tomorrow morning . . .'

'Look, Sarah,' I said, 'can you get down as soon as possible? There'll be things to organize.'

'It means bringing Hans.'

'That's all right.'

'What are we going to have, apart from alcohol?' she asked.

'I'll fix it.'

124

Then Bobby phoned. 'Everything all right?' he asked. 'I hear you were in very early.'

'Sorry about that. I got carried away. We're trying to fix a party at short notice, here at Longwood.'

'We?'

'Sarah's coming down.'

'Splendid,' said Bobby.

'I wondered if you and the two Delmars could make it? And, having walked in on that attractive lady, perhaps she's free tomorrow evening?'

'A party? At Longwood? We must certainly try for that.' He sounded as though he were thinking fast. 'And Sarah? That *would* be nice.'

After that I thought I'd get a chance to get back to work, and collected a rake from the garage. I meant to drag the edges of the pond, but I guessed it would be a broken session. The phone went again before I had left and I went back to hear Sarah.

'Darling, I think it would be nice if Freddie came along. We'll have to make use of the time anyhow. Hans will talk business, and Freddie should be there.'

'Good idea.'

'And this friend of mine, Angela. The one you spoke to on the phone. I'll bring her.'

'Right.'

'And Freddie will want to bring Rosie.'

I was almost beginning to look forward to this function.

I told Bridges. 'About ten of them?' he said thoughtfully. 'I'll be around, sir. Show them where to put their cars.'

'Can't think there'll be many of those,' I said.

'Best be around.' Bridges was quite dogged. 'That's what I always used to do with them do's. Don't want them driving over the grass, do we?' He came back to me a little later. 'You'd better phone that Fay. Tell them what's up. She can pop round the village and do that shopping for you.'

I did that, then took the rake and went down to the pond. It seemed a long time since I had been there, though it was only a little more than twenty-four hours, and that last visit had been uneventful. I reminded myself that it was the time before that I had been in such close touch – when I had seen her, had even resisted her. I wondered if I would have cause to regret that. I was being sidetracked now, meeting people, arranging a dinner, picking up pieces that would lead nowhere.

I took a little debris from the black water. Ripples ran across the oily surface, giving no promise. I sat in the pagoda, my eyes closed, very sad about something. The place must be making me morbid. *'In a world of genuine ills there is no room for a rich man with self-pity,'* – a text from a Puritan past, but true. I went back to the house, mouthing some form of prayer, or something like a prayer. I was saying 'Next time . . . next time . . .' They would understand me.

Perhaps because I had expected nothing, the party at Longwood stood out like a beacon in those days of silence and twilight. For a start, every light in the house appeared to be on and the building was etched like a castle in the night. For various complicated reasons, hard to follow and not worth unravelling, guests arrived in cars by themselves. Bobby was in one car, his beautiful girl friend in another. Oh yes, she was going to drive on to London that night, and he was going back to Lewes. The Delmars were in another car. Freddie and Rosie arrived first, noisy and delighted to be there.

'Had to come and see you were all in order.' Freddie clapped me heartily on the shoulders.

Earlier the two women from the village had arrived, having done all the shopping, and set about cooking. One husband came in tow. 'He's looking after drinks,' Fay informed me. 'He's very good at that. And he'll be handy.' I wondered what to pay him. 'Good Lord, nothing! He'll just have a little of what's going.' But they brought two cars. I was glad Bridges was there. He had everyone neatly parked by the stables, noses pointing to the exit. 'Important, that,' he informed me.

He had also helped in the house; it was the first time I had seen Bridges in the house. He seemed to know it well. The husband got some of my sound equipment going, and music was spilling from the front door as the cars arrived.

'It is wonderful. Magnificent, Nicky! You devil, you are richer than me!' Hans stood outside in admiration, having been brought down in a chauffeur-driven car.

'Why didn't Sarah bring you? Where is she?'

'She is coming later. Nicky, what a place! It's a palace!'

They crowded into the hall.

'Meet Eveline,' Bobby introduced us. She was as beautiful as I had thought, her dress slipping over one shoulder.

'I'd have recognized you anywhere,' I told her. I'd been having a few drinks as I waited for people to arrive. The time ahead had promised to be tedious; now it seemed as though it would be anything but. In the noise and good will I had been transformed from one role to another. The hall, sparkling in bright lights from a single chandelier, was unrecognizable as the dark and gentle place in which I had heard those soft feet dancing.

Carpets had been pulled aside. 'You never know,' said Fay, 'some of them might fancy dancing.'

The last car to arrive was Sarah's. She had a very pretty passenger, and she kissed me at the door. 'Darling, this is our non-paying guest, Angela.'

Freddie cheered as they arrived. 'Now Hans can go and bother some other girls. Rosie is not used to his methods.'

'God, this is too much.' Hans threw arms round the new arrivals. 'Such women! I will take our company's business from him. He has too much.' Someone turned up the music. The husband came in with drinks. 'A butler!' shouted Hans. 'An English butler!'

The noise was persistent from then on.

'What a splendid idea, darling. What made you think of it?' I didn't know whether to tell Sarah. What could I say? I was jealous, thinking she was having an affair? Or that I was not as jealous as I ought to have been?

Or should I joke? 'I just thought . . . Well, breaks the pattern, I suppose.'

She looked up quickly; a searching look; then the disappointed smile, defensive, superficial, as she realized the pattern had *not* been broken. 'Lovely, anyhow. Better see Hans is okay.' She went to look after her special guest.

'We have to talk business,' he shouted across the room to me. But no one spoke business that night.

It was the early hours of the morning before anyone showed signs of leaving. Previously Fay and Doreen had gone off with Fay's husband, head rolling helplessly, in the back seat. ' 'Course he can take anything,' Fay said loyally as just about everybody helped him into the car. 'Trouble is, he mixed it.' She drove off, fair hair and rose-coloured cheeks, peasant remnant of some Saxon court.

Bridges cycled away in the dark. 'Don't bother to come in the morning,' I shouted.

'I don't work here tomorrow, do I?' he called back scathingly.

'I have a staff like this at home,' said Hans. 'We give parties like this in Germany.'

'Started boasting have we, Hans? Time to go home?'

'Oh God,' Hans was dejected. 'And I try to speak only understatements!'

But it was time for the cars to come cautiously up the drive, time for waving and kissing, for tail-lights vanishing down the road.

'Do you have to go?' I asked Sarah. Perhaps it was just a formality.

'You know I do. I have to take Angela. And we've got Hans for the return journey.'

There was a splutter of gravel on the driveway, and everyone seemed to be gone. Bobby gave his girl friend directions, then watched anxiously as she disappeared towards London. 'Looks like I'm last, Nicky,' he said. 'That was a really nice party. A nice idea.'

I had a feeling he wanted to add something, but he didn't.

The house was very silent after he had gone. I walked round, turning off lights. Bottles and dishes lay everywhere. 'We'll be in sometime tomorrow to tidy up,' Fay had said. 'Don't worry.'

In the darkness it began to feel more like the house I knew. White, high-flying clouds suggested morning long before dawn arrived. I didn't go to bed; it was too late. As if a great stone had been dropped into water, something within the place was in turmoil, and waves swept outwards, with a criss-cross of currents in the dark washing back to take the place of the noise, life, light and laughter that had filled rooms, that had left no space for whatever else lived there. A busy world had crowded out a frail one.

A breeze picked up as the morning chill passed over the earth. Whatever had retreated would always return . . . if one knew how to conjure it.

12

The days that followed were unexpected and disappointing. I had hoped to return to that idyllic period of the weeks before; but there were calls from the office next day, and the day after. Business with Hans had run into snags. It was a valuable account, and I could not ignore it. A note came from Bobby Everett, old-fashioned style, thanking me for the evening. He was leaving Lewes the next day unexpectedly, but hoped to be working with Delmar again later. I went up to the office and had a day with Hans and his chairman, who had flown in that morning. We sorted out most of the snags.

'Okay?' Freddie saw me at the end of the day, concealing anxieties.

'They have some problems but it should be okay.'

'It's reassurance they need,' said Freddie. 'Fairly constantly. Like having one of us in Munich all the time.'

Freddie was right: Hans and his partners needed someone in close contact for a week or two.

'Think you should go?' Freddie looked at me thoughtfully.

'I can't.' But I couldn't give any reason as he raised an eyebrow.

The problem solved itself.

'Sarah is going,' Freddie told me. He looked a little accusingly. 'She's flying out tonight with them and she'll be staying a couple of weeks.'

I was very aware of the burden she had taken on herself.

'Can you manage? I mean, on your own?'

'Don't be silly,' she said lightly. But she added, 'Someone has to keep the firm ticking over.' It was the first time she had said anything that sounded like criticism.

'Look, I'll go.'

'I said don't be silly, darling.' She pecked my cheek. Hans came in, delighted: 'We have stolen your best man.' He pumped my hand.

The taxi was there and they were gone. She left a message telling me the apartment was empty: Angela too had moved on.

I stayed there the next few nights. We were constantly on the phone to Munich, and it became obvious that Sarah was coping.

'We are keeping her,' Hans was loud and clear over the phone. 'We offer her far more salary. We are making her chief director.'

I guessed what we owed to her, but Freddie wouldn't let it pass. 'She's been covering a lot for all of us,' he said. 'Especially lately.' I knew what he meant, but then there was nothing I could do about it.

Next day I packed a case with papers, took copies of work in progress, and made an excuse of a meeting in Southampton. 'I can go there from Longwood,' I told Freddie. 'It will be easier.'

He was in good spirits, but he said, 'Maybe you should open an office in the country. Lots of firms are moving out of town. It would cut the rates.'

I had this sense of escape as I drove out of London, as though I had an assignation with a lover. The guilt of it disturbed me, a mirror of the guilt I had projected on to Sarah and Bobby . . . But I was the guilty one, hurrying to a rendezvous with shadows. Sweat broke out on my forehead. I drove on, hoping for what? What, I asked? In this fragmented dream?

It was a homecoming to walk down the path between the azalea and rhododendron bushes, each turn of the path so familiar. Happiness seemed to billow up inside me, it was almost an effort to breathe. And when I got to the end of the path, I stopped to savour my pleasure. The pond rippled in the breeze as I walked round it slowly, reminding myself of each shadowy corner. Then I turned to the yew hedge sheltering the pagoda.

The balustrade and strips of wood lying against the walls where I had left them, had quite dried out. The rotted ends were stronger than I had expected; they could be treated and restored, and with re-painting they would be perfectly adequate. A labour of much love became possible. It was a heady feeling, ecstatic. The little glade basked in an autumnal warmth, with sunshine that hardly touched the ground, dappled, flickering, like a smile that came and went. The genius of the place was amused by my obvious pleasure. I was certain then that I had been accepted back, even welcomed back, though there was no sign of those who welcomed me. I didn't need them to appear, like a stage-trick in a puff of smoke. It was enough to feel the secret embrace. I knew now that I could come and go, could visit London, be involved with associates, and that I could come back, pick up the threads of this other life. They would be waiting. So we had taken a step forward in our relationship: it would not be so desperate if I were to leave them again. There was now some understanding.

I sat in the pagoda and the realization came to me that they too had done some heart-searching. They had made compromises. They understood that only on such terms could I continue to work with them; it was a compromise we had all accepted. All of us, I thought to myself. For we needed one another.

With a much easier mind I went back to the house that evening. The rules of the game had been worked out. From now on, I could live in both worlds.

The thought that Sarah was out of the country seemed to lift a weight from my mind. It was a disloyal thought, and I regretted it, but I couldn't help it. Even more comforting was the fact Everett was no longer on my doorstep. He had meant well, but he had been an intrusion, making me wary in case I was revealing more than I intended. Now he was gone, and Sarah was in Munich, shackles had been struck off, the fantasy could be explored. I had no one to answer to.

The following morning there was a letter from Freddie in the form of an office memo, brief and to the point. It noted the last quarter's returns, the cash flow, and by implication, my own lack of time spent on company affairs. Freddie was a minority partner, but a partner, entitled to make these comments. The question was, What income did I see myself contributing over the next few weeks?

I couldn't have received the letter at a better time. I was on the crest of a wave. Nothing was difficult, nothing was beyond accomplishment. I was about to phone him and put his mind at ease, but instead I phoned my contacts in Southampton and brought the meeting forward to that afternoon. I told them I had an opportunity to offer something very special. As I drove out of Longwood I had no idea what this special offer might be, but I was unconcerned. Something would turn up, an inspiration, without a doubt. I couldn't think why I was so confident and assured. Adrenalin was racing through my bloodstream (had Bobby been around, I would have checked if that was how adrenalin functioned). I was gambling, leaving things to chance. The feeling that had overcome me in the pagoda had lingered. I guessed it wasn't rational, this expectation of great things, this sharp enjoyment of life, with everything in a holiday mood. My subconscious was working at top speed, and I was confident nothing could go wrong. By the time I reached Southampton I had a campaign format ready to discuss.

I spent the rest of the day with a trio of managers who listened, criticized, and argued until close on midnight. By the time we got to the whisky-and-water stage, they were cautiously happy. I didn't push it any further. We agreed to sleep on it.

I drove back to Longwood at about three in the morning, just wanting to be there. I had earned the right to be back.

The phone woke me. Sunshine was coming in at my window, and it was nearly noon. There was a message from the office to say Sarah would have to stay in Germany an extra week. Did I approve? I told them anything Sarah decided didn't require my authority.

After that I dressed in my working clothes, taking my time, eating a late breakfast, savouring everything. I had cleared the decks; now I was going to reap a reward . . . half-seen, half-guessed, much-beloved, a desired prize.

On one previous occasion I had worked myself to the point of exhaustion, but this time I did so with a manic enthusiasm that felt no fatigue. I seemed to be getting directions in an endless and accurate flow. I cleared scrub from behind the pagoda and found scraps of a fretwork, a pelmet, rusting metals, long thick nails. I stored them in the pagoda for sorting, then I dragged one end of the pond and brought out more of the balustrade. I felt as though I could go on forever. Icy water and thick mud didn't register: I climbed in and out of the pond with the precious discoveries, slipping down the bank, stumbling through the bushes, surprised to see the scratches, and the blood on my mudcaked slacks. The pitch of the pond dropped steeply; even a couple of steps from the bank and it was deep. What sobered me up was one moment of helplessness as my feet sank; a fine silt offered no support, closing over my shoes, holding them like limpets, with a suction of pounds per inch that sent panic through my nervous system, and had me struggling, puffing, striking out, as I floundered to the side. I fell on the bank, gaining breath and realizing that my body was chilled to the bone. My trophies lay round me, bits and pieces of the pagoda, some fragments of a vase, other ornaments that must once have decorated the inside of the building. I started to shiver with an overwhelming numbness. I couldn't stand up, I was too cold to use my hands. But I got up gradually, and took a few steps towards the path.

I don't know if it was my weak state or something else that hampered me, but I found it harder and harder to make headway. I was shaking uncontrollably now, cursing myself for having gone on so long; I could hardly walk; my teeth chattered. I was shaking, shaking! What the devil had I done to myself? I turned to the pagoda and found I could walk in that direction: it was moving the other way that was difficult. I knew I had to get back up to the house; I needed warmth, a drink, a hot bath. I steadied myself, and moved forward. This time the pressure was greater. I was frozen! I called out aloud, 'For God's sake! I can't do any more!' The pressure seemed to ease, hesitate, then evaporate. I went tottering on my ice-cold limbs round the pond, up the path, back to the house.

I lay in hot water for hours, and then I drank whisky. I had a lot to think about, I told myself, but it boiled down to the realization that I had to parcel out this work like I would any other. If I went on like this, like a madman, I would be treated as a madman. It needed time and strength. No one else could supply that. The ecstasy that went to my head and drove me on was dangerous, and I had to watch out for it.

Another letter from Freddie came in the morning, containing a second office memo. I hoped this wasn't going to become a habit. It read: 'You bastard. Southampton fantastic. Am working out a contract for them. Will be in touch when the project gets down to details. F.'

That should have meant a lot to me. It must seem to those in the office that I was really pulling my weight, and it was also an excellent account for the company as a whole. But I felt little as I read it. Nevertheless, I was pleased to think that Freddie would now be off my back for a few days.

I put on fresh clothes, and took a towel and a coat to the woods.

'What you doing down there then?' said Bridges.

'Needs cleaning out,' I told him.

'Don't wonder at it.' It was clear he thought whatever I was doing was a waste of effort.

I took my time this morning before I started work, and I didn't stay in the water as I had done the previous day. I made sure my clothes were dry, rolling up my slacks, and going into the pond in bare feet. The feeling of mud disgusted me, and I had to force myself to stay in. Even so, I came out after about ten minutes, dried myself and sat in the one patch of sunlight that shone through the trees.

The weather was changing. The late mild days that had lingered into autumn were beginning to go. All that was left were pale skies, still blue, with high cloud, white, fleecy, but with a cold wind blowing.

I had been very clear-thinking, much more rational in my attitude to this work. I was pacing myself, planning it. And all morning I stuck to the formula. I would work for a time, then dry myself and rest, collect the bits and pieces, examine them, stack them in the pagoda, and only then go back to the water to go on searching.

I don't know when it was the rhythm changed. I don't remember becoming so absorbed that I deliberately kept going, but I suddenly realized that the light was fading and I was moving slowly with fatigue. It was late in the afternoon and I hadn't broken to eat; I guessed I'd been in action for many hours. I came out of the water, dazed, puzzled, feeling as though I had been in a trance. Of course I'd known what I was doing, but the restrictions I'd put on myself had been forgotten. I had been working like a robot! I looked round the wood as if trying to find someone to blame. There was no one there but myself. Could I have been so self-destructive?

I dried slowly, thoroughly. Certainly I wasn't in the exhausted condition I had been in the day before. But I did have to be careful: there was a point beyond which I shouldn't go. I had become oblivious of everything; it was a little like being drunk.

I finished work long before the sun went down, long before the unseen watchers usually vanished. Perhaps they would see this as a warning of the way I was going to operate. I would be more valuable to them if they didn't abuse the powers they had. I was the tool; if the tool were blunted, the work would be ruined. When I left the wood there were no problems; no attempts to delay me or make me change my mind. The system was working.

And it worked better next day; and the next. I found I was thinking of nothing but our progress, mulling over each tiny scrap dredged up from the mud. I was eating little, sleeping less and less, seemingly never tired nor hungry. A little sleep, a little food, and I was back at work for long hours, sometimes hearing the phone ringing in the house, sometimes leaving it off the hook. I went on like this for days, dodging Bridges in case he thought it odd.

Gradually I was aware that I was back in the rhythm I had

tried to break, working obsessively, overjoyed by each discovery no matter how small, even another rusty nail or a fragment of broken pottery in the pool. Some were beautiful; some were rough Victorian fairground pieces. But amongst them there was a model of country lovers. I found the central part, a shepherdess and her swain, but flowers and sheep were broken. I went scrabbling about in the silt for hours looking for them, cursing my stupidity, warning myself as the chill crept through me; but it was only exhaustion that brought me out of the water. I had worked out a way of cleaning mud from the things I found, rinsing them in a basin as a gold-digger washes the sand from his tray. It was a good system. Out of the basin I picked tiny bits of wood and china, and I took them to the house in the evening, poring over them, trying to fit them together. It was late, once or twice nearly morning, before I put the endless games away.

The change had been slow, for I had thought of myself as dealing rationally with the work. I'm not sure what made me see the folly of how I was behaving.

I was in the act of starting to dredge a new section of the pond bed (I had been doing this systematically, square by square, so that nothing would be missed) and was taking a step further from the bank, testing the depths as I neared the middle of the pond. The bottom was softer than I expected, giving way under my feet like quicksand. I got away just in time. A bubble of foul-smelling air rose to the surface and burst; silt spread out. I didn't like the look of it and headed for the bank. For the first time for several days I had the old feeling of making my way against some resistance. There was the same breathlessness I had known before; I had to fight for air; I had to fight to reach the bank. The effort to move was enormous. I had a stab of panic: I could be suffocating, losing consciousness; I could be pushed back under water! A sudden fear helped me, and I scrambled out and broke into a run. I had to get away as fast as possible. But when I had gone only a few steps, had just reached the path and wasn't looking where I was going, I was suddenly very afraid. In my unfocused vision, in a blur of bushes and shadows, I saw someone blocking my way.

The soldier was only a step ahead of me. I'd never seen him so clearly. He barred the path, facing me, tall, erect, seemingly towering above me. He was in uniform, a bright blaze of colour, sword catching the light, shining, jangling, clanking at his side, even in twilight. Did I really hear that sound?

He was standing across the path, puffed up in fury, mouth wide, shouting the orders I could never hear, a terrifying image. And I was terrified. I knew what he was ordering me to do – my work was not yet finished, I was on the verge of some important discovery, I had to get back, like a man, like a soldier, on duty. I was under threat – what threat I didn't know, but it was awesome! I backed off. He seemed to be on top of me still. There was nothing else for it but to get back into the water; to search the area as he commanded. That was the message conveyed by that soundless shouting! I went back. I had no choice: it had never been so clear what my function was. Here, now, at this moment of great importance, I had to dive, dredge, plunge into that stinking pool. I went backwards until I felt the water round my ankles, then I turned and began to walk in.

Again, I can give no reason why my mood changed. Perhaps because the vision was out of sight, was behind me; and I was about to accept defeat. The painted devil had momentarily vanished. Courage of a sort welled up inside me. I would not be so abused! I would not go another step into this foul muck! I was my own man. I did what I did from choice! From love and not from fear!

I spun round. He was there, bloated face up against my face, pride, power and arrogance in his purple colouring, his blue, white, yellow, red, mottled and resplendent uniform, like a burst of fire, a burst of something beyond the vision. He was an explosion, a firework, a cannon in action!

I shouted! God knows where I got the strength from, or the courage, but I shouted. I damned him for his impudence: that was a phrase he would know from his own time. 'Get out of my way, you meaningless, unreal, long-dead thing! You vain, stupid, bullying fool! You aren't here! This place belongs to *me*!'

My voice was a screech in the stillness, and I was shaking, but standing facing him, seeing the vision, the incredulous shattered face, fading slowly with a horrified realization. Gone was the explosive bluster, gone the bursting splash of colour. All gone. All silent in the evening wood . . . With only birds rustling in bushes and the wind picking up and blowing the dry leaves. And, as I moved, the wild flutter of wings. A bird rose from the bush ahead, the bush that had seemed to bar my path. Colourful, squawking, a big jay. Up above me . . . up into the darkening sky.

13

Of course there had to be reparations. We couldn't live without each other. My whole function had vanished next day as I hung about the house, unwilling to brave the stricken atmosphere around the pond. I felt sick. Life had evaporated as I had shouted my anger, and the figure had disintegrated. I delayed . . . but I had to go back.

The wood was hushed. A churchyard.

I stood a long time, allowing the world around me to creep from under cover, to reassemble a shattered faith. Yes, something was still there, still existed, breathing its own form of life. I waited. It seemed to take a very long time, and then the grove began to be peopled. I counted the uncertain outlines . . . one . . . two . . . three . . . And a moment later . . . four. Insubstantial, but certainly four. And that was all. No proud, tall, multi-coloured shadow. No crimson-splashed soldier.

Nevertheless we made our amends. Without words. A silent acceptance that things would go on as before, but on different terms. On my terms, at my pace, within the limits of my human and fallible powers. And to prove the point I sat toying with pieces of broken porcelain, and then I left and strolled back towards the house.

No obstacles were put in my way. No pressures. First one shadow and then another vanished in dusty, speckled sunlight. I dragged my heels, in two minds about going back to the house.

The spell of the place was hard to break, but I had to prove I would do things in my fashion, as I pleased, no longer dancing attendance – moved no longer by their subtleties nor by their force.

It was as well I did go back to the house. A car was parked outside, and Bobby Everett greeted me. 'Hello.'

I was surprised but pleased to see him. 'I thought you were going to be away a week.'

'It's eleven days.'

I could hardly believe him. 'Come in, come in. Have you driven far?'

'Only from Lewes this morning.'

'I thought you'd left Lewes?'

'I had to go back, for a day or two at least.'

We didn't go into the house, but strolled about on the lawn.

'It's a bit sooner than I expected,' he explained. 'Andy has this case, and I'm very interested.'

'Andy Delmar? The doctor?'

He nodded. He was very thoughtful, wrapped up in himself. When he did speak it was almost as though he was talking to himself, and I was merely a sounding-board. I kept in step. It was a pleasant relief to be talking to, to be listening to, another human being. 'The lady in question – the patient – is a woman who is confined to a wheelchair. She's been so, on and off, for a year or two. Some times she's more incapacitated than others. He did the usual tests, assumed the usual hypotheses. Paralysis can have many causes. He's very thorough, Andy. Very thorough.'

I listened for the pleasure of another person's voice; I had no interest in his case.

He went on thoughtfully, counting on mental fingers. 'Brain, spinal cord, nervous system. Injury or disease. Where and how extensive. General, or a stroke. With her – the legs and lower parts. Paraplegia.'

From where we were walking I could see the long wood, and I wondered what was happening there. But I tried to show an intelligent interest.

'Really a question for a neurologist?'

'What? Oh yes . . . Certainly at first.'

He didn't explain that, but ambled on, talking as he went. There could be many causes, it was a wide field to sift through. The backbone cannot protect the spine from accidents of a violent nature. Blood clots may rupture an artery. Hard patches may grow on the nerve covering. Tumours . . . infections . . . He let his voice tail off vaguely. It was just as well, since I was in no mood for a lecture. I wondered, as I looked towards the woods, why there had been four shadows only. What had happened to the fifth, my enemy, the soldier?

'Not that paralysis results only from physical causes.' He was speaking even more softly, musing to himself.

'From what else?' I asked. Time to go into the house, I thought, and began to head him that way.

'There can be mental factors. Emotions can affect the automatic nervous system.'

I nodded casually; I knew the power of feelings, of mental life. But I caught myself frowning at the thought. 'Confined to a wheelchair. Paralysed by her feelings?'

'Does that surprise you?'

'Not really. It's just . . . when you think about it.'

He nodded. 'Yes, of course.'

Something, someone, was trying to catch my attention from the wood. I don't know why I thought that, perhaps a light, a reflection, a movement . . . It was like a distraction. I glanced towards it.

Everett was saying, 'She might need to be ill.'

I looked back from the trees. I couldn't think what the hell was making me feel uneasy. 'You mean she might have some reason to be ill, so she manages to lose the use of her legs?' I didn't intend it, but there was a scoffing note in my voice.

'You don't think that likely?'

I shrugged. The light, or the movement, flickered just out of sight. 'It's possible, I suppose, but how does she kid a lot of qualified doctors?'

'She doesn't kid them.' He glanced towards me. I guessed he hadn't noticed the distant movement across the field, though the disturbance amongst the trees seemed quite distinct to me, bushes agitated, like a wind getting up . . . but only in one small concentrated area. Sooner or later he would have to notice it, and it would be hard to explain.

'It's possible for it to be so important to her to have the advantages of paralysis that she achieves that state without being aware of what she is doing.'

I thought there was some sort of sound coming from the wood; not loud, something that could be mistaken for the hum of insects . . . if one didn't know otherwise.

'A lot of what we do is unconscious,' he was saying.

I turned my back on the wood. 'Why would anyone want to be confined to a wheelchair?'

'The alternatives may be worse,' said Everett. 'Or she might think they are worse. She may achieve something by being ill.'

'Like what?'

'Lots of things. She may claim attention, or she might be protecting herself from something.'

The noise in the wood was louder. If it was going to build up like this . . . I suddenly realized what it reminded me of: a child trying to interrupt a conversation, or like someone threatening. I had already shown what I thought of their threats. I turned angrily towards the woods. There was no sound . . . no movement.

'Anything the matter?' He followed my gaze across the lawn.

'I thought I heard something.'

He listened. 'Then you have better hearing than me.' He stood looking round in admiration. 'My, my, you're working wonders with this garden. Looks better every time I see it.'

But he hadn't seen it. No one had seen that silent wood. What would he make of that, I wondered?

We walked back into the house.

'How's Sarah?' he wanted to know.

'She's still in Germany,' I told him, and then I wondered if this was the case. I hadn't been in touch with my office for days.

'That was a great party,' he said looking round the hall.

'If you're staying in Lewes, drop in,' I said.

'Thanks, but from now on that won't be so easy.'

'Are you working with Andy?'

'Most of the time.'

'On his case? This woman?' I don't know why it came back into my mind.

'Amongst other things.' It didn't seem deliberate, but Everett never appeared to give very much away.

When he'd gone I was still thinking about the woman in the wheelchair. I walked about the house, made a snack, tidied up a few things, then went to the garage to pick myself some tools; but all the time the image of a paralysed woman kept obtruding into my mind. I was annoyed to be so caught up with his story. There was nothing particularly special about it. It wasn't the first case of psychosomatic disease I'd heard of, if that was indeed what it was.

I headed for the long wood with a rake which could reach areas of the pond I had not yet explored. But as I walked down the path I stopped. I seemed to have forgotten something, and I tried to think what it was. Something in the stables? I retraced my steps. It wasn't until I got there that I realized what was on my mind . . . The woman who had a reason not to walk, and therefore went about in a wheelchair.

I tossed the rake aside and cursed Everett. Why the hell had he told me that ludicrous story? The oddity of it stuck in my mind; like a jingle, a scrap of a tune, it kept recurring. I visualized the woman sitting in a wickerwork chair quite clearly, greying hair, dark clothes, about fifty, round-faced, slightly plump . . . Good God! There was no such person. This was a figment of my imagination. She probably wasn't remotely like that, so why did I have to have such a clear and detailed picture? But I had to finish the description, because there was something familiar about the eyes. They were shrouded a little. Brave, grey eyes, but shrouded. Defensive. Looking out, not seeing everything. The look of someone intent on seeing part and cutting out part. Perhaps she was afraid of what she might see if she relaxed and let reality present itself.

What was I trying to do, I asked myself? Carry out a diagnosis on someone I had never seen? Whose name I didn't know? I marvelled – perhaps I'd been on my own too long! I went into the house and had a drink. It was early afternoon; I don't drink before evening, but I was so angry at this imposition Everett had unloaded on to me. I wondered what significance it could have: was a ghost raised?

My drink did the trick. Whisky was a medicine that went back a thousand years – dissolving the wheelchair, woman and all. I didn't need a second glass. Bobby Everett, grave-faced, speculative, was gone, evaporated in a bright afternoon. I collected the rake again.

Everett's visit had delayed me and I was anxious to get back to work. I made up my mind to continue as I had done that morning, remembering the phrases that had run through my head then. *'At my own pace.' 'On my terms.'* Things were going to be like that.

But my mind wasn't on the task. I scraped through the water, stirring up black mud, doing more harm than good. Then I stood at the edge of the pond, leaning on the rake, disinterested. I didn't bother to look towards the shadows. That afternoon the family were hardly in my thoughts. I went and sat in the pagoda, insects humming, the sun thinly shining; I was uneasy, threatened, though I could think of no reason for it.

And I was angry for being so easily sidetracked. Angry with Everett for arriving on my doorstep as he did, constantly intruding, distracting, disturbing. With snippets from his case-book. Did he not realize I had no interest in his clients? It was as though he had deliberately intended to delay me. I sat up with a start. It was deliberate! Everett had concocted the whole thing! He had invented this story. There was no woman in a wheel-chair, no such case! Perhaps he didn't even work with Delmar! Why was he doing this? It didn't make sense, but whatever the reason, two could play these foolish games.

I thought of phoning Delmar, but he too would be part of the charade. Everett would have arranged things with his friend. The pieces would be fixed, and Delmar would confirm every-thing. An elaborate web must have been spun. The very innocence of those involved quite startled me. Delmar's wife? I could easily find out. I had only to check that she would be alone.

I phoned the number Everett had given me for their research

department. Yes, Dr Delmar was in the clinic, but wouldn't be available for an hour. I promised to call back, and left immediately for Brighton.

The Delmars had a converted farmhouse outside Lewes. As I arrived Ruth Delmar was parking her car. She was surprised, but pleased, to see me. 'If you've come to see Andy, you're unlucky. He's going to be late.'

'I was just passing the village, and remembered you lived here.'

'Come in!' She poured drinks. 'Nice to see you.' She was very welcoming, as though we were old friends. Perhaps she wasn't in the conspiracy, perhaps it was only Everett and Delmar.

'Andy will be too late to eat. We can have a snack.'

'No, no, don't bother.'

'A sandwich with the drinks.' She was on her way to the kitchen. 'Chat to me while I make them.'

It was simple to bring the conversation round to Andy and Bobby.

'They're as thick as thieves,' she said. 'Ever since Bobby came back from the States.'

'Do they work together?'

'Not actually. Bobby is in London most of the time. I think he does research for his American people. He's only recently been in touch with Andy.'

'Only recently?' That was exactly what I had thought.

'About three months,' she said. 'Andy had this phone call. They'd been out of touch for years. It's only recently Bobby has got interested in this side of the business . . . it was something he did when he was in New York.'

'What is Andy working on?'

'They give him all the difficult cases.' She tried not to show how pleased she was. 'He's got theories about them. This famous paper he's writing – did he tell you he was writing a paper?'

'No.'

'But he's taking so long about it.'

'Is Bobby involved?'

'He is now, at least part of the time. He consults Andy. It's

144

not exactly a collaboration. Without being big-headed, Andy knows more about this area than most consultants. Bobby seems to be working alongside him, at some of his cases. But Andy is the specialist, and Bobby is learning things.'

'Does that mean he's changed direction?'

'Maybe, just a bit.' She looked thoughtful. 'But after all, he *is* a neurologist. I don't think it can be that much of a change.' She was uncertain, she probably didn't know much more than I did myself. 'It's really just a change of emphasis,' she said. That sounded like something she'd overheard. 'From the physical to the mental.'

There was one important question.

'When he drops in, he chats to me about his latest problem. This time it's an old woman in a wheelchair. She can't walk, but apparently there's nothing really wrong with her. That must be one of Andy's cases.'

She shook her head. 'I know them all. There's no old woman in a wheelchair.'

I felt a grim excitement. He'd been lying to me. But I would double-check. 'Bobby seemed absolutely absorbed,' I persisted.

She was still shaking her head. 'I would have known . . .' Then she looked at me sharply. 'Are you sure she's an *old* woman? How old?'

I couldn't think what had made me suppose Everett had been talking about an old woman. 'I don't know.'

'Mrs Palmer?'

'Who?'

'You don't mean Mrs Palmer?'

'I don't remember a name . . .'

'The magnificent Mrs Palmer! *She's* in a wheelchair. For life! Puzzled the best brains in many a teaching hospital. But I could cure her – I'd shoot the husband!'

I must have been looking blank, for she started laughing.

'Mrs Palmer is twenty-eight; a figure like a film-star, a face to match. *Mr* Palmer is revolting, uncouth, forty-odd. No wonder she's paralysed, who wouldn't be? I'd stick in the chair forever, if I were her.'

My grey-haired, grey-eyed, shrouded, defensive, old lady: could this be the same person? I had felt so close to solving the problem, but Everett had been telling the truth, and it left me where I started . . . trying to understand why he had told me this story. Was it just his obsession with it himself, or had he some other reason? I had this uneasy feeling – it still persisted – that I was being manipulated.

I couldn't solve anything while keeping up a façade of friendly conversation.

'Why don't you wait? Andy won't be long now. He might have Bobby with him.'

'I really must go.'

'Okay, we'll fix a date. Come to dinner? One evening when I know Andy will be back at a reasonable hour.'

'Love to.'

'Bring Sarah.'

'Great.'

On the way home I felt I'd closed an escape hatch. But escape from what? I had nothing to fear. Nothing to escape from.

14

It was hard to understand why the incident seemed so important. After all, what had happened? Everett had paid another of his casual visits, using me as audience while he mulled over one of his patients' problems; I had suspected the story to be a fiction; now I was convinced it was true. Surely there was nothing particularly significant about that?

But the next morning, it *did* seem important, and I couldn't fathom why. It was one of those days that Bridges didn't put in an appearance and I had the place to myself. It was an ideal opportunity to get on with my work, but that sense of uneasiness still hung over me. In the back of my mind was a vague suspicion, hard to pin-point, but concerning Everett. Not just that last visit, but the man himself, everything about him. Ever since he had turned up, he had been a source of anxiety. Bland eyes, smiling, even his friendliness a disguise. Nothing was genuine; all was a means to an end. And the end was intrusive, to say the least.

I pushed him out of my mind. I was giving him too much importance. Everett was an awkward fool, an intellectual without much feeling or sensitivity, and even less instinct. He had butted into an alien world – a fragile, unsuspected world – bruising it, disturbing it, dismaying it. He had no conception that there could be such a dimension as the one that engulfed me here. *His* universe was materialistic, his interpretations were scientific. The woman in the wheelchair was explicable in terms that made sense to himself and Andy Delmar. Rationally.

I had gravitated to the flight pond, and the sight of it calmed me. I was surprised to realize how angry I had felt. Surely Everett wasn't *that* much of a threat? I could brush him aside; I would be busy next time he called. He wasn't a friend of mine, he was Sarah's problem.

It was comforting to stand in that isolated little clearing, slowly taking in the familiar background of bushes, trees, the faintly rippling water. Peace of mind flooded back. The air was warmer and the breeze had eased round to the south. Perhaps such sensations could be explained in Everett's scientific terms.

But the whiff of perfume was another matter. There was no explanation for that perfume, the scent of lavender, rich, strong, as it came from behind me. From in front! All round! I was being surrounded and embraced . . . well, almost embraced . . . by senses that lacked touch. And yet, at that moment, it was *almost* as if . . . almost as if there were the faintest suggestion, a slight delicate pressure in passing . . . a touch of warmth, welcome, affection. Even of love. It was brief, fragmentary . . . gone! But the perfume stayed.

There was still one question that required an answer, and I had been skirting round it for weeks. In one form or another I had been considering it, or more often backing away. Now I had a new-found confidence: I could ask any question this morning – even one about my own sanity, for I knew how things would look to the outside world. I had a catalogue of the evidence against myself: the manner in which I had grown solitary; obsessed by Longwood; neglecting my business; more significant, my wife . . . that is, the girl who should have been my wife by now. I had cut myself off. Without knowing the reasons for this it must look paranoiac. But what was the alternative? Should I give my reasons, describe the people at Longwood? Would I then appear more credible or more sane?

I had no doubts in my own mind about my sanity, but I realized the way it might look to an outsider. What I needed was substantiation; experiences that would back mine; voices to confirm what I was saying; eyes and ears that had seen and heard what I had. That would be evidence. And to find it wouldn't be a hard task, for there *was* such impersonal evidence, neither biased nor subjective. Numbers counted for something in such matters, and there had been three of the painters.

'That you, guv?'

I was surprised that he recognized my voice over the phone immediately.

'Hello, Mac. How's it going?'

'Don't complain,' said the painter. 'How're you, then? Settled in?'

'More or less.'

'Got the missus there?'

It was an odd question.

'We're not *that* settled.'

Then he said, 'You down there by yourself?' And I realized what he had been asking.

'For the time being. The place needed more than painting, you know.'

There was a pause, then he said, 'What's it about then, guv?'

'Remember the noises you heard?'

There was another pause. 'That's right,' he said.

'Wasn't just you, Mac, was it? The other two heard them as well?'

'Both of them, guv.'

'The same sounds as you, Mac? I mean, what they heard wasn't different?'

148

'We told you, at the time. We was all there together, we heard the same thing. Like the bloke walking through the house. That time you said it was you on the stairs – we knew it wasn't you. We'd heard that one before, heard it at the same time, like I said. All in the same room. Then Joe, you know, Joe – he said, "Bloody hell. Listen to him! I'm getting out." But he stayed put.'

'I believe you.'

'You all right, then?'

'I'm fine.' I realized he was anxious: that was something that hadn't occurred to me. 'I'm okay. I just wanted to check on what had happened.'

'You still hearing him?'

I wondered why the painter thought the footsteps were a man's.

'I'm hearing something,' I told him.

'Not just that boiler, then?'

I was cautious. 'Well, that's still the only explanation I can think of. That's why I phoned. I wondered if anything else had happened?'

He was equally cautious. 'Like what?'

'Like voices? Music? Anything?' I didn't want to come out in the open and ask a leading question.

'Nothing like that, guv. God, no – no bloody music. Don't say you've heard bloody music.'

'No, I'm just investigating. I mean, noises can be explained away. The creaking boards, and things like that. I'm trying to find something that can't be explained.'

I don't know if he was convinced. 'I don't see what you mean,' he said. 'What sort of things? I mean, all that stamping about was bad enough. That needed some explaining.'

'For example, did any of you see anything?'

Again there was the split-second pause. Maybe it was a question he had not expected. 'We didn't see anything, guv.' He seemed a little quieter.

'You didn't smell anything?'

That surprised him. 'What sort of smell? I mean, you often get smells.'

149

'Anything. Like perfume . . . a perfume you wouldn't expect.'

'Like what?'

'Like . . . rose-petals?'

'There's roses under the windows.'

I remembered the rich fragrance in the wood. I could almost imagine it in the room as I held the phone. Very close. Just behind me. Should I say 'lavender'? Better not to be too exact.

'Like dead leaves? Dead flowers? Dried dead flowers, herbs, that sort of thing? You know those old-fashioned flower-bags, with crushed petals? Women used to carry them in the old days.'

'I know them,' said the painter. 'Nothing like that.'

He wasn't quite giving me the confirmation I needed. Almost by omission he was denying something.

'What about outside?' I asked him. 'What about the garden?'

'We didn't go in the garden, did we, guv?'

'And you never actually saw anything?'

'No, guv.'

'How's the new job going?'

'Very nice.'

'Seen anything of the others?'

'Seen a bit of Joe. He's done a few things for me. Haven't seen anything of Alf.'

The smell of the perfume was still in the room as I put down the phone. An encroachment? Had some barrier crumbled?

It amazed me how everything had changed in so short a time, and yet nothing had altered, nothing you could put your finger on. Nevertheless I guessed what had turned the key. It was my realization that Everett was dangerous, my determination to guard against him. That was all. Merely a resolution. I had seen the two sides of this battle, at last, and I had made a decision.

The house was bathed with this faint trace of sweet-smelling lavender. It was odd that I had conjured up the thought of music when I had spoken to the painter, for I had never heard music. Never thought of it. But now, although I didn't hear anything one could definitely call music, there was a suggestion

. . . just a suggestion, of something harmonic, of a melody I couldn't quite catch – somewhere in the distance. Certainly not in the house, perhaps not even in the garden. But I couldn't be sure . . . It might have come from the wood. I listened at the open window, determined to be convinced, to accept nothing that didn't stand up to a proper examination. None of my experience had been imaginary. I did not intend to let it become so now.

I opened a window. There *was* a sound, but it could have been bees; a late sortie from the hive. A cleansing flight. Or the hum of insects – it was sunny enough to have brought a cloud of them to life.

I headed back to the wood in a state of unreasonable happiness; the perfume had gone to my head; I was relaxed, at ease, much loved, an object of approval. I was reminded of astrologers who speak of the influence of planets – Jupiter sweeps across the heavens, and our lives move in and out of shadows. Spirits beyond our control make or break us. I felt that now. A star had started to shine, I was being given a reward!

Good resolutions inspired me. I would put the last few bits of my pagoda together, paint it, clear round it, I would . . . I stopped in my tracks. This was the wrong direction! I had turned unwittingly and was heading out of the wood. I tried to go down the path again.

There was no great power to delay me, no force holding me back . . . but a gentle resistance, a light breeze, persuasive as a sigh. I stopped. Why was this? Was I no longer needed? I went on to the pond – very much on my own. With an ordinary man's step, and an ordinary man's vision. The pagoda was almost complete, missing a few scraps; but *they* had vanished completely. Perhaps I had done all that was possible. Perhaps work was finished.

Anyhow, the woods were empty, and I walked away.

What followed was the child's game of 'hot or cold' we had played before. No one gave me directions, but I had discovered a sense these last few weeks that responded to unseen companions and to soundless voices. It wasn't an inner ear; I didn't exactly hear anything, but I knew what was meant. If I tried to analyse this sense, all I can say is that it felt like pressure, making me first hot, then cold. The heat was sticky, hands damp, face flushed. And a sudden panic-stricken struggle to breathe. And when it was cold a clammy, icy air swirled round me.

This was the way they played, not with malice but of necessity. They had no other way of guiding me, of directing me to where they were waiting. And although I could not see them, I knew when I had arrived. The heat, the cold, vanished. I was in their shelter again.

It was an eerie way of moving out of the wood. An erratic journey, keeping faith, following blindly. For in their world I *was* blind, with no idea where I was going. Yet it was my own familiar world, garden at Longwood, with nothing to alarm or startle, while the perfume stayed with me. Very close.

I took for granted that we were heading for the house, but the way was blocked by the chill air. I was being moved like a pawn, away from the walled garden . . . away from the lawns . . . away from the orchard.

I was glad that Bridges wasn't there to see that unsteady progress as I was shuttled about, gradually moving towards the stables. I wondered if this was our goal. Or were we going to stop and start, stop and start, in our passage past it? It also occurred to me that the day had been carefully chosen, that this journey had taken place precisely because Bridges was not here. My guess was that if another person had turned up, the spell would have evaporated and I would have been left standing, a little dazed, on my own driveway.

No one came, and I began walking quite quickly towards the stables. I was now sure that was where I was going. There was a flutter of something alongside me. Out of the corner of my eye – being careful not to turn or look – I caught a glimpse, just a glimpse, of a white dress. Muslin? Ribbons? Tied at the waist. The waist? How could I be sure? Someone was running beside me – a white dress to her ankles, being held up . . . running over the loose stones, keeping pace with me. I headed for the stable-door. There were feet coming, going, the faster I went, exactly like dancing . . . in fact, dancing! It was a moment of joy, a shared joy. She was as ecstatic as I. As bewildered probably, as ephemeral. Perhaps the mist that curtained her from me also cut me off from her; perhaps she too was only *partly* aware of me, only partly able to see or sense me. So did she also share this intolerable need to burst through whatever it was that divided us? At that moment it seemed possible. Something like passion made it seem possible.

The door to the stables was in two parts. The top section hung open. I caught it, stumbling over the cobbles, breathless. I had run twenty or thirty yards, and I was holding on for dear life, exhausted. The world swam. I held on, panting, and the world righted itself. The stables were silent. But this was, I had no doubt, where they wanted me to be.

I looked round for directions, but I knew they had gone. Everyone had gone, and I understood. They would be as depleted as I. To have got this far was enough; the effort had been enormous. The rest could wait. I didn't even go into the stables. Whatever I had to do would be shown to me later. I went back to the house.

The phone started ringing as I came in.

'Hello, Nick.' It was Everett. He sounded unusually cheerful. 'We're going to be in your part of the world later today, Andy and I. We thought it might be a good idea to take you out for a meal?'

'That's very kind, I would have enjoyed that. I'm afraid I can't. I'm absolutely up to my eyes in work.'

'You can't spare a couple of hours?'

'I'd like to, but I've let things pile up. This is the crunch. I'm shutting myself in until it's finished.'

'Still busy with the house?'

'Lord, no, that's been the trouble. I let it take up too much of my time. This is business . . . before my partners ask me to resign.'

'Any idea how long it will take?'

'A couple of days. Maybe three or four.'

'What about after that? Any chance we'll get together?'

His was the chill hand that had frosted so many blooms each time he came to Longwood.

'Fine, that might work out nicely. Perhaps when I get back from London.'

'You're going to London?'

'Good Lord, I have to. That's where we have the office.'

There was a pause. Then he went on, 'What's the news? Is Sarah there?'

My mind seemed to go blank for a second. 'What's that?'

'Is Sarah back?'

I could hear myself sounding cheerful, almost hearty. 'Of course. She must be. Or can't be long now.' I had no idea where she was. How long had she been in Germany?

Another brief pause. Something came through in that silence. There was something he wanted to say.

'Oh, by the way, I hear you were asking about Mrs Palmer?'

I was baffled. 'Who?'

'Mrs Palmer. I understand you're interested.'

Was Everett trying to be funny?

'I don't know who you're talking about, old man.'

'Mrs Palmer . . . you were asking Ruth about her. This patient of Andy's. Actually there's some development in her case, and that was one of the things we wanted to tell you about.'

The woman in the wheelchair! '*That* Mrs Palmer. I'm way out of my depth there, chum. I'll have to leave that sort of thing to the experts, you and Andy. I've got my time cut out just trying to run my own business. I'll give you a call. Let's try to meet when I come back.'

'Oh, right. Give my regards to Sarah.'

I was pretty sure he had got the message. I had to make sure I had the seclusion I was going to need. As far as I was concerned, Everett was expendable.

15

Several times on previous occasions when our encounters had been successful, I had been left exhausted, and there didn't seem to be any reason for it. It was the same on this occasion. I slept most of the rest of the day. I woke once; the phone was ringing.

'I hear you're coming in to the office?' It was Freddie.

I was hardly awake. 'What's that?'

'We had your friend Everett on the blower saying he was coming up to town and he wondered what day you were going to be in.'

'Yes, I'll be up. I've got some stuff to finish.' Then I realized how odd it was of Everett to make that call. 'Did he say what he wanted?'

'He seems to think he owes you a dinner.'

I was scarcely awake. 'I'll phone you,' I said. I was very angry. What the hell did Everett think he was up to? I was on the point of calling him and telling him to mind his own affairs, but I was overcome by sleep. I don't think I moved all night.

I woke feeling I had been unconscious rather than asleep. There were low clouds over the fields, a sharp wind keeping them on the move. Rain threatened but held off. I got up early and quickly made myself some coffee. I caught sight of myself in a mirror, doing everything at speed, and pulled up. In this sort of mood I had worked myself to a collapse once before. I would not do it again.

I didn't have any doubts about picking up the threads of the day before. Somewhere by the stables they would be waiting for me. Or perhaps they would materialize as I arrived. Perhaps *that* was how it worked: their existence depended on me.

Bridges was in the walled garden. From the garden door he could see the stables. I had forgotten about him; this might be awkward. I called 'Good morning' to him, but he was already on his way with a wheelbarrow, and didn't pay me the slightest attention.

I sensed an atmosphere of anticipation outside the stable block. There were three doors: double doors opened into the garage which had once held the carriage; a second door, the proper stable-door with the top section that opened for the long-departed horses, was in the middle of the block; and there was a separate door into the tack room.

I wasn't sure which way to go in, but it was as if I were being conducted by a guide. We entered by the stable-door. I closed it behind me, and felt cut off immediately. Then I remembered that I had never made contact in a building, so I opened the door again and at once the atmosphere was easier.

At the end of the stables, in what was now the garage, a narrow staircase led to the groom's quarters above. I felt no urgent inclination to cross to the bottom of the stairs, suddenly doubtful about my purpose. Maybe I was supposed to be heading in another direction? I turned away. It was like stopping a flow of water which was not powerful in itself but the moment one tried to hold it back the weight built up. No doubt then that I was being directed towards the stairs.

There was a door at the bottom which I opened. In the chill morning light the plaster was seen peeling away. That was something to repair anyhow. I began to go upstairs. Once again I ran into a soft resistance, each step being more difficult to take. The message was obvious. I backed to the bottom step and peered around. There was silence . . . the place was cold and clammy.

'Come on then? What's the job?'

The whole place seemed to vibrate. I stood for a minute, and was about to go when I found myself looking at the plaster again.

I didn't believe it! Could such mysterious and unearthly effort be directed to such a mundane job? Patching up plaster? I would have got round to this anyhow, or brought in a plasterer. It didn't seem worth coming back a hundred-odd years to get me to repair the wall. I had a spasm of disbelief: perhaps everything I had been doing was equally futile, pagoda and all.

I picked at a chunk of plaster hanging from the wall, which came away, dry and crumbly. Behind it were the marks of four or five balusters. I picked another bit. It was rotten and decaying. More broke off; then a big piece came down in a shower of dust. The outline of other balusters could be seen above: someone had plastered a handrail into the wall. I wasn't very excited by the discovery – it didn't match finding the pagoda – but I was intrigued.

I began to dig into the plaster with my fingers, but it became too solid to shift. There was a knife in the garage, and I used it to gouge plaster from between the railings. The more I worked, the more absorbed I became. Clearly a layer of plaster had been added, so that the wall was now about two inches thicker than it had been originally. The balusters had vanished into those two inches. They were wrought iron. I had seen similar work on balconies in parts of London, in Notting Hill Gate, in Islington, probably of the same date, the first half of the nineteenth century. Nothing remarkable, but pleasant, very much of their time.

I worked patiently, thoughtfully. There seemed an ambiguity in what I was doing. Yesterday I had been raced to this stable block; this morning the impetus was much less . . . very much less . . . as though there had been second thoughts. Maybe there was a priority in these things. One task before another.

Bridges went past several times that morning. Once he stopped. 'Still there, Mr Morell?'

'Still here,' I shouted.

'Off for dinner.'

'Right.'

A few moments later he stuck his head through the door. 'What's that, then? Wall come down?'

'Bits of it. It could be dangerous.'

He had a good look at it. Whatever I was doing might be odd in his eyes, but it wasn't without logic.

'Right, then, I'll be going.'

He was still mulling it over as he cycled off. I went up to the house and washed the dust out of my hair. I collected brushes,

157

tools, a hammer, chisel, had something to eat, then went back to the stables. I continued chopping back the wall, cleaning the iron sections, getting rid of a mass of dusty rubble. The smell of decaying plaster hung in the air, and I tied a handkerchief over my face to keep out the dust.

I was absorbed by my task, but in the late afternoon I became aware that the interest had evaporated from around me. I thought at first this sense of being alone had to do with being indoors; I supposed the building round me acted as an insulation. So I made sure the stable-doors were left open. This helped to clear the air, but there was no longer any scent of lavender, no indication that they were there. The feeling of being on my own grew stronger. I began to have doubts. Was this what they had brought me here to do? What else was there?

The windows on the staircase were filthy. I had to use the same handkerchief to clean the grime away – cobwebs, dead flies, dust. I managed to clear one corner of the glass beside me. The window looked out over a small orchard – untended apple-trees, overgrown, propped up with rotting supports, a few uprooted, several dying. I pressed my eye to the one clear patch of window. The orchard sloped away towards the wood, facing south-west, catching the dying sun.

Under the leafless tree nearest the stables I saw the tall figure of the man. He was motionless, greyer and gaunter than I had remembered him, looking up at the stables, at the flat above me. I couldn't see what held him so static, so absorbed. I knew there was another window in the end room which would also look over the orchard, but there was nobody in there. Another figure was standing further down the orchard – indistinct, in shadow as the sun set behind the trees, but I thought it was the woman. Beyond that was a third shape, even more in shadow, then a fourth. I couldn't be sure, but if there was a fifth then that would account for them all. Who were they all looking at? Who could possibly be at the window of that upper room?

I didn't often have a sense of fear, and it wasn't really fear that I felt now. But a prickle of anxiety ran up my spine. An unpleasant sensation.

The room they were staring at lay at the end of the corridor, just above me, in the groom's quarters. There was nothing else for it; I had to see if there was someone there.

My feet on the stairs made a noise to waken the dead. Wooden boards cracked, and the sound echoed through the building. I was suddenly very loath to go any further. I kicked a heap of old plaster off the steps. It fell in a cloud of white dust. No one moved in the flat above.

I gave them a moment to react, then I shouted, 'Hello there.' No answer.

I went up the rest of the stairs and along the corridor. The room was silent, the door half shut. I had the oddest sensation of being in two places at once, of being split, of being two people – one somewhere above, looking down on this scene. I pushed open the door. The window that overlooked the orchard was the first thing I saw. It was as grimy as the one I had just left.

I gently eased the door right back until it was flat against the wall. Another window looked out to the front, to the walled garden where Bridges could be seen working. It was all so ordinary and mundane. There was no one there. And yet . . . who had they been looking up at? Who had been in the room?

I crossed to the back window. The glass was streaked with dirt, and I pressed my face against it to look out.

It took me a few seconds to make out the orchard in the lengthening shadows. But gradually it fell into place, and then I saw the picture as I had already seen it: the man under the near tree, the other shapes further and further away; all motionless, all rigid. The man, grey-faced, ashen; the woman, whom I could see more clearly from this angle, equally strained and gaunt. And beyond her the other figures, suggesting a chill, fearful doubt. All peering up towards this window as though they could still see whoever it was who had been here . . . And then it was as though the sun came out again. Perhaps it really did. A cold shaft of light between low branches picked out the figures in their hiding-places, as if they had all seen something at the same moment. They all moved, appearing to be in light for a brief second; perhaps they all stepped from cover. She did, she must have done, for I saw her distinctly in the white dress I had glimpsed the day before, stepping into the light: no longer

159

hiding, but smiling, waving a long, outstretched arm, something white in her hand. A handkerchief? Long hair was tossed back as she waved, very happy, overjoyed about something. What? What had they all seen? I was alone at this window, behind the filth and grime . . .. peering down.

I had the feeling I should wave back. The man was looking up, a faint smile of approval. The woman bowed her head, a regal gesture. Of the others, I hardly saw the two men, but furthest away, now melting back into the gnarled apple-trees, the girl was merging into quickly falling shadows. Suddenly they had gone. Not abruptly, but seemingly unwilling. For them it had been a moment to be savoured.

I stood by the window in the growing chill. It was so clearly a triumph.

It took me some time to realize who they had been waiting for at this window.

Bridges shouted, 'Night, then,' and when I didn't answer he called, 'All right?'

'Oh, good-night, Bridges. See you tomorrow.'

'Day after,' he called back as he cycled away.

I looked out at the orchard as the stunted trees at the foot of the slope vanished in the evening light. The world tasted of the cold of coming winter. The moon was a silvery white, faintly bright. An owl hooted very close, perhaps in the trees over the stable roof. At the window I tried to locate the big bird. It fell silent and I thought it had gone; then it called again – startling in its nearness – and I heard the sound of wings, a slow beat, as it took off and flapped through the orchard. It was so much at home, so relaxed – like the fox I remembered seeing. Foxes and owls possessed this place by virtue of the ages they had lived and died here, whereas I was a stranger. No ancestors of mine had marked this patch of earth as theirs had done. That was why I was the interloper. The figures in the orchard had more right here than I. They remained proprietors of Longwood – land, house, and outbuildings. Come to think of it, they were still managing the estate, giving orders. Was it that I felt I justified my transitory claim by serving them, by devoting my time and energy to them? That was a partial truth; I was possessed myself, at least by one of them. It was a matter of choice, I knew. A folly, but my own doing.

It was dark before I moved from the window, stiff and cold. I'd been there perhaps an hour, passive, barely thinking, absorbing the gloom and silence, animal-like in a way; ruminating; growing aware of what was next for me. For I realized that the work I had been given on the stairs was merely a ploy to coax me here. For some reason they had feared to bring me directly to this room. Why, I wondered? It was so dark that I couldn't see the chimneypiece, but I could trace it with my hands, the four naked bodies standing out in all their exaggeration. Even in the dark I could sense the mastery of those figures – the assurance with which they had been cut. They indicated a squat power, had a modern feel about them – nothing elegant nor delicate, but something of our own time. It was a constant surprise to find them here; even in the dark they were out of keeping. Yet they were a work of art. As Sarah had said, this was the finest single thing in the whole place.

I don't know what attracted me to the fireplace in the first place, but it became more and more disturbing. There was no electricity in the flat but I stayed, tracing the flat faces with my fingers as though trying to memorize them, and the four other figures which held up the lintel, the panels which they framed, the sculptured flowers. What a labour of love this must have been! Some artist, trapped by a war, watching a world destroy itself, had poured out his frustration in this unlikely billet. A burst of energy had exploded here.

I had to pull myself away from the room and grope along the corridor. Plaster crumbled underfoot on the stairs but I was no longer interested in the balusters. I went back to the house and began searching for a bundle of papers I had previously brought from the stables to dry. I don't know what I expected to find in them, but I knew I would find something.

I couldn't remember where I'd put the papers. I remembered the photograph amongst them, yellowed and faded, of the gardening party. That, too, seemed to have been mislaid. Had I given them to Sarah? I was sure they were still in the house.

Next to my bedroom I found the box in which I had first

discovered the plans and documents concerning Longwood. Some of the papers were there, though not all, and on top was a sketch of the stables. The next sheet showed the layout of the first floor. Copybook handwriting could just be deciphered, '*Living quarters for Samuels (Groom)*'.

I had become quite used to interpreting these architects' sketches, and had a good look at the area of the fireplace, but it was hard to tell what it would have been like in its original state.

I went through the rest of the papers; there was nothing else about the end room.

I usually slept well but this night I lay awake. A pattern was becoming clearer. For instance, I now understood the vacillating fashion in which I had been brought to the stables. I was sure I had been coaxed into the buildling, first to the staircase and then further on. The figures in the orchard had not concealed their object, nor their joy: it was that end room that obsessed them. I puzzled over the thought that for some reason they felt I had to be persuaded there, to be led there in easy stages. *That* had been their triumph: my face seen at the dirt-stained window.

And now that I had been in that room I had the same impetuous need to get back to it. I was certain the whole picture would reveal itself, as it had done before, and I would know exactly what to do. A growing passion preyed on my mind, so that I could hardly sleep. I could feel my hands on the stone figure in the dark. I had a dream; frightening and confused, of alternately smashing and restoring the figures. Once before at Longwood I had awakened with a telephone bell ringing. This time it was Freddie.

'Hello Nick. I wondered if it was today you were coming into the office.'

'Don't say Everett's been on to you again?'

'What's that? Oh, no, that's not it.' He sounded very subdued.

'Something wrong?'

'It might be a good plan if you could make it.'

I could see the stable block from my bedroom window. The sun glinted on the end window.

'Of all times, Freddie, this is not the best.'

'I think you have to,' said Freddie. He was unusually firm.

My heart sank. 'What's the problem?'

'Didn't you get my letter?'

'What letter?' I remembered with a stab of guilt that a stack of mail lay on the hall table. As it arrived day by day I had put it there to be dealt with when I could get round to it. I wondered how many letters there were – and how long had I been collecting them. Time vanished in this place.

'I've written to you twice,' said Freddie, the friendly warmth absent from his voice.

'I'm sorry,' I said. 'I mislaid a lot of things.'

'I think you'd better get here,' he cut in. 'I'll be around till lunch. You'll have to make it before then.' He was really upset.

'I'll be there,' I told him.

A chill seemed to fall over the place, but it must have been my imagination. I projected these feelings, for nothing could come from the stables, nor the wood; they were inanimate. But it seemed otherwise.

I hoped Freddie would be alone in the office. That was odd for me; I was usually delighted to see the rest of our team. As I drove I realized I didn't even know if Sarah would be there. Was she back from Germany yet? How had that project gone? Perhaps one of the many letters on the hall table could have told me about that. I tried to be interested, but I wasn't. All I could feel was an uncomfortable sense that something had gone wrong and I would have to waste precious time sorting it out. If Sarah was back from Germany, it was going to be embarrassing to have this meeting in public.

The office was busy and crowded when I went in. I don't think anyone other than Freddie expected me, for they all looked a little taken aback as I walked through. I called 'Howdy folks' as I passed the reception hall and the outer office. One or two answered, but they gave me an impression of uneasiness, almost as though a stranger was being too familiar.

Freddie was in our joint room, rather wan and a little tired, I thought.

'Glad you could make it.' I noticed he didn't thump my arm

as he usually did. He had a couple of files which he put on my desk. 'Did you find my letters?'

'Actually no, I . . .'

'Look through these.' He was pretty exhausted.

'You want me to read them now?'

He nodded. 'It would be as well.'

He went out to let me read in peace.

The first was a simple picture of the loss of business in the last few weeks. The job I'd put together in Southampton, for example, had gone to pieces, and it seemed the clients had tried to get clarification from me, either at the office, or at Longwood. There had been no great crisis, merely a loss of interest when questions weren't answered. Other projects had run into trouble, and it was easy to see why. Freddie had been trying to do the work of three people: I was not there, and Sarah was in Germany. A letter ended the file, one from Freddie's assistant. Well, more than an assistant – he had been with us for years, flogging himself to death in the early days when we were trying to get going. Now he was resigning. He didn't say why, but between the lines was the suggestion that the firm didn't exist any more and that Freddie was a fool not to be off on his own, and that he wasn't going on like this. He had a face-saving excuse – he'd been offered something better by one of the international agencies – but to my knowledge he'd been offered such a position a dozen times before.

The second file contained only a few pages. Some cables from Sarah, a report from Hans. It looked as though at least one project had gone well for us. But the last page again had a sting. It was a dual message from both Hans and Sarah, with pencilled notes to soften the formality. Sarah was staying on to help them with a promising situation that she had been responsible for creating. There was no definite time-schedule: they would let us know when the picture was clearer. The financial side of Sarah's term with them was up to us. Hans expected it to be high, since she was worth a lot to any firm.

I read it slowly. The details weren't all there, but it was clear in essentials. Sarah was staying in Munich.

I don't know what I felt. I tried to summon up anxiety on

both scores – over both files – but all I felt was a distant concern. I was expected to be shocked – to be desolated; but I sat fiddling with a pencil, trying to work out dates. How long since I had been regularly at work: two months? Three? When had Sarah gone to Germany? I didn't seem able to concentrate. I wondered what was happening in the stables. I remembered the dark, the cold, the filthy windows. I could see it all, feel it. It was more real than this office.

Freddie came back, thought I was still reading the files, and sat at his desk and waited. I looked up after a bit. I couldn't think what to say . . . what he would expect me to say.

'Sorry,' said Freddie. 'I did all I could.'

'None of this is your fault, Freddie.' I looked back at the files.

'And God knows about Sarah,' he said.

'It might turn out quite well,' I indicated the last sheet, 'this new project of theirs.'

He looked at me as if I were mad. A moment later he said, 'Maybe we should go for a drink.'

We went to the pub we used across the road and had a couple of whiskies. I thought he looked very pale. 'You all right?'

He shrugged his shoulders. 'It's been a rough few weeks.'

'You should have told me.'

'I did.' He wasn't smiling. He ordered another round.

'Sorry about those letters.' It sounded very inadequate. 'I think I know where they are.'

'Doesn't matter,' said Freddie. 'The damage is done.' Then he went on without looking at me, 'What happens now, Nick? How do you see things?'

'We've been in worse spots before, Freddie. Much worse. Remember the time they stole the Jaggers account?'

'That was different. We were all in it together.'

'So we are,' I said.

'I think we've lost Sarah.'

'She'll be back.'

'Why should she? What's in it for her?' He gave me a cold look. I'd never seen him like this.

'What's such a problem?' I asked. 'In a few weeks . . .'

'What about you, Nick? What are you doing?'

165

'I'm just telling you. In a few weeks – two at the most – I'll be back at work. We'll pull the show together, Freddie, we've done it many times. I just needed the break. Now it's your turn. Can't you take some time off? You disappear for the next two weeks as well. We'll make an appointment now. Here. Two weeks from today.'

'What will there be to come back to?'

'That's a bit of an overstatement, isn't it? We can pay staff for a couple of weeks . . . Things can tick over, can't they?'

'You don't just drop clients and pick them up as it suits you.' Freddie was dismissive. 'The trouble is, Nick, you've changed. You've let just about everyone down, and that's something you've never done in your life before. Now – everyone! Where the hell have you been, anyhow? *What have you been doing?*'

'Look, Freddie, if you think I've let you down . . .'

'Bugger that!' he said. 'It doesn't matter about me; it doesn't mean that much. But don't tell me you didn't foul it up for Sarah!'

I couldn't understand him at first. 'It was her own choice. She wanted to go and fix this job. We're old friends with Hans . . .'

'Are you being deliberately dumb? What happened about this marriage business? What do you think that did to her?'

'I don't see that's your business . . .'

'Well, it is. It's part of the cock-up.'

'But it was her decision.'

'Sarah called it off?'

'More or less. The last time I was up – the time before – she was having doubts. She told me something had gone out of things for us . . .'

'I believe you! It probably had. But that was you, old chum, not Sarah. After all, it wasn't Sarah hanging around in that big house, skulking away from people. She tried to cover for you, to keep things going. What's the matter with you Nick. *She* said you weren't, but I think you're ill.'

I caught sight of myself in the big mirror behind the bar. I was looking at Freddie, incredulity all over my face. I wanted to say something, but my mind went blank. 'Ill? What in God's name . . . ? Of course I'm not ill!'

'Then what the devil's going on? You know what you've done? Not just to Sarah? You've chucked away years of work, and a lot of good friends.'

'You amongst them?' It was a poor defence and he treated it as such.

'Cut it out, Nick, you know better than that. But that's the measure of the change in you. Nothing you do or say is on the level now. You seem to be covering up for something all the time. You aren't honest. Not even with me. There's a constant deception going on. What the hell is it? If I didn't know you better, I'd think you had some woman there.'

I don't know why that shocked me. I went cold suddenly. What would he say if I told him? For a split second I was on the point of saying something . . . I had a longing to ask Freddie for help . . . but help for what? I didn't need help.

'Let's keep this to business, Freddie,' I said quietly. 'You're entitled to complain about my failure there. We're in this together. You have a big stake in this company and I've lost you some cash.'

'Oh, shut up.' He signalled to the barman.

'Take this as a guarantee,' I went on. 'You will be compensated in full for anything you've lost. I accept responsibility. You get them to cost the losses in accounts . . .'

He went out without saying another word. I was left there as the barman brought the two drinks.

There didn't seem a lot I could do about the situation as long as Freddie was in this mood. I didn't fancy going back to the office. For the first time I felt alien there. Almost their enemy.

I wasn't happy driving to Longwood, but at the same time I was anxious to get back. A whole day had been lost. I thought about my promise, and was sure I could keep it. I could finish most of what I wanted to do in the next two weeks. Probably I would then be back at work, back in the office, picking up the strands of life again, my ordinary, mundane existence. This interlude of magic would not last forever: it was a dream to be snatched at while it was there. It was a treasure that could never be repeated. Nothing else would even measure up to it in future. *Nothing* could match it. It wasn't that I had broken faith with anyone, as Freddie seemed to think. It wasn't possible to make comparisons, to make judgements. There were no ethics involved. I *had* to do what I was doing, it was a compulsion. And if I felt any guilt, it was soon gone.

16

The closer I got to Longwood, the faster I drove. I was back before the light started to go. Apart from those drinks with Freddie I'd had nothing all day, but I was too anxious to get down to the stables to stop for anything to eat.

I had the feeling I was being watched again, but that was something I was used to. Perhaps they were in the orchard, as they had been the day before. I hurried up the stairs. It was darker inside the building. There was an old carriage lamp on the wall of the garage – I would try to make that work.

I went softly along the corridor. I don't know why. There was nobody I could disturb. One couldn't disturb the dead. The room was gloomy as before, but it didn't seem so chilly. It was as though someone had had a fire. I glanced at the grate; the ashes were a waxy mass of many years ago.

But the idea, once born, persisted. I would have a fire. It would make the place more cheerful, and bring a little warmth to the accumulated cold of all those solitary winters.

I found paper in the garage, and a few bits of a wooden box. An oily rag and some cardboard made a fair heap in the grate. I set light to it and it smouldered away, then burst into flames. I fed it more pieces of wood. Flames flickered and jumped; my shadow danced on the walls.

I sat on what was left of the wooden box and warmed myself. This wasn't what I had raced home to do, but it was an hour of restitution. Besides I needed time, to get an inkling of what was required of me.

As the fire died down I began to examine the way the chimneypiece had been constructed, the way it had been built into the wall, taking a careful look round the edges of the cement. Clearly the whole new section had been stuck in, in one piece – and it could probably be taken out in the same way. But there was no way of knowing for sure without chipping away some plaster. This would take time, but I was getting quite skilful at it. I collected the knife I'd used on the staircase, built up the fire again, and got down to work. Outside, the moon hung over the orchard.

The plaster round the stonework was much firmer than that which had rotted round the balusters, but a bit of it finally chipped away. I worked along behind it with my knife, painfully slowly as the blade was rusty. It would be more sensible to wait until morning and to use proper tools. I had a crowbar in the house; the job would be done in a fraction of the time. I was torn between an urge to keep going, and a voice telling me to collect proper tools, do it effectively, take my time.

The decision was taken for me when the knife snapped and I was left holding the stub of a blade, a couple of inches long. I wasn't going to get far with that.

The fire was now low, but I didn't want to take any risks. A spark could do a lot of damage in this old building. I pressed my foot on the ashes until all that was left was a dying glow, and turned to go.

I think I'd taken only a couple of steps – I hadn't reached the door – when I froze in the dark! For a moment the power went out of me. It was a moment of terror. In the distance there was the most eerie sound, a wail, a frightening, drawn-out howl. I'd never heard anything like it. I couldn't move. Then the blood seemed to start flowing back into my veins.

'What in God's name?' I whispered to myself. And then I remembered the owl, and I cursed myself for being such a child. Such a fool! What did I suppose it was? It had to be the owl. To allow myself to be alarmed by something as ordinary as a barn owl! I was angry at such stupidity as I felt for the door.

The second time the howl echoed in the moonlit garden I couldn't tell how far away it was, but my instincts told me it was a lot nearer. A lot nearer, in a few appalling seconds.

And it was no owl.

I could hardly move to the window, but I forced myself to look out. The stunted trees were motionless. No breeze stirred. Hardly a leaf trembled. There was just the faintest movement in the long grass at the foot of the slope, where the apple-trees merged with the pines of the long wood. Dry grasses bent slightly. Must be the wind picking up. Less protection there . . .

But that was no owl.

Again my head came up with the answer. It was obvious! On a night like this . . . in such moonlight . . . foxes! A vixen calling her mate! I should have recognized that unearthly sound. After all, foxes patrolled this patch of ground with impunity, and one of them was warning aliens of his own species. Nevertheless, that bark in the night had awakened apprehensions, and I walked cautiously along the corridor to the head of the stairs.

A split second before I heard it, I knew it was going to happen, and the sound seemed to go off in my head.

God! From so close! From just outside the window? No, not so near . . . but somewhere . . . where? Perhaps I could see. I had my face against the glass, the filthy, cobwebbed glass, wide-eyed. I *knew* I was wide-eyed, I could feel myself staring, eyes popping with shock . . . searching the orchard. The moon was coming and going. Something under the trees? No, shadows . . . But the noise! That long, drawn-out, terrifying howl. It was an animal all right – but a fox? Could it really be a fox?

The orchard was silent . . . empty . . . My heart pounded. I was aware of it, like a hammer, thumping. Gradually I began to breathe again.

So . . . dark shadows and nothing more, as high clouds raced over the sky. No matter what leapt into the mind, it must have been a fox.

But I stopped on the stairs, another thought sweeping over me, bewilderingly. The noise had come from a long way off when I heard it the first time; then it had been somewhere close; and now, the third time, was right outside. Nothing could travel that fast, no fox, no owl . . .

Well . . . I stood there a long time, no sign or sound in the night. Perhaps I had exaggerated the further distance. And perhaps it had not been so near.

Anyhow, it had gone.

I went down the rest of the stairs on tiptoes, cursing the plaster that crumbled under my feet. When I got to the bottom I realized how tightly I was gripping the handle of my knife – with its two inches of rusted blade.

I hesitated at the stair door. It occurred to me I'd be safe if I stayed where I was. I could close this door; there was a heavy latch on it. I could go back upstairs. The fire could be coaxed to life; the room was warm. I could stay there until morning, and sleep on the floor. Or get on with what I was doing . . . At least, until it was light and I could see what was in the shadows, under the bushes, beside the path back to the house. That was the thing to do, for I would have a short distance to go. Fifty yards, perhaps. Or sixty? Sixty, with sudden moonlight and then blind in the dark. If I opened the door, I might be stepping out into God knew what!

I nearly went back. The warmth coaxed me, the shelter – like a womb. Safety. But I couldn't quite do it, I couldn't back off, no matter how sane and sensible that would have been. I had a feeling I was being trapped into such action. Forced into it; frightened, like a child being told stories.

I crossed the empty garage cautiously. Outside lay the drive, covered with loose stones. At least that would give me plenty of warning; I would hear sounds on those stones if anything moved.

I was out under the overhanging porch when I heard the wild scramble over the path. Loose stones went flying. Something had started from low on the ground, belly flat down, in shadow, on the earth, I think. And a second later it was moving fast, still low, still in shadow, hardly seen . . . in fact, *was* it seen? Did I see what launched itself down the path, hitting the ground at speed, coming like the wind, as the moon went and night swallowed the sight leaving only the sound?

And what a sound! Not just a wild howl any longer, but the baying of an animal; baying and snarling. A ferocious noise, racing towards me, bestial, murderous – I turned . . . half-turned. I couldn't find the garage door behind me. I heard my breath come like a sob. I'd just stepped away from the damn door . . . where *was* it? Where was the handle!

I got my hands on it as I heard the thing come up behind me. I knew it was going to spring. I had my knife. I could drive it off . . . two inches of rusty blade to keep at bay . . .

But I didn't turn. Still groping for the handle, I found it! I was in the garage, with the door shut and my back against it, ramming the bolt home, when the creature hit the outer side. The whole framework shook: both doors moved! I could feel it. They bulged in . . . The bolt was never going to hold!

But it did. And the snarling raging outside – only a few inches away, I realized with horror – rose to a crescendo. A second bolt fitted into the floor, and I had nearly got this into place as well, when the door shook with a crash that jerked the bolt from the ground. I hammered it back with my heel. Fear, real fear, gave me speed and strength.

The bolt was in. By the time the third attack came, both were holding firm. I pressed against the door with all my weight, prepared for a fourth impact, but it didn't come. The animal was sniffing under the door, at the gaps where the two leaves overlapped. Sniffing, snarling, scratching. There was no doubt, it was there for the kill. The stench from outside was nauseating . . . sweat, blood, saliva. I don't know how I was so sure, but I could identify them all.

There was a silence. I thought it had gone. But then came the sound of scratching from further along the building, followed by a furious noise of something scrabbling for a hold.

This time I nearly despaired. I was shaking with fear! It was trying to get in at the stable-door that led into the old stalls with the manger. The top half of that door would swing open easily, it wasn't even on a latch! I heard the door go back with a clatter, and there was a howl of another kind. A bay of triumph, as though the creature knew I was trapped, then a wild chase across the cobbled floor in the old stalls. One fragile door stood between us, and I knew it would never hold. A rusty lock hung on it loosely. The door withheld the first onslaught of scratching and snarling, then it splintered.

I had two choices: I could get back up the stairs, for I knew *that* door would hold. It opened outwards, and was solid oak, the locks heavy metal. I could pile rubble, bricks, furniture, against it like a fortress, and I'd be safe there until help came. Bridges would be here in the morning. But I need not be driven in there like a rabbit in a warren. I had my second choice.

I jerked the bolts out, threw open the garage door and raced up the path towards the house. I could get in by the kitchen, it was never locked. I had a gun in the bookcase, and I'd blow this bloody animal . . . I was going at speed, nothing could have caught me. But I stopped dead in my tracks, for the path was barred. Just ahead, taller than ever before – baleful as something from Hell, the man was standing up above me . . . high above. And behind him, the soldier . . . I think the soldier. And a third figure . . . the other man. A grim trio, right across the path. And more behind – the woman, with not a jot of pity in her eyes. And suddenly the noise behind me, the baying . . . And I just had time to look . . . but I didn't see . . . not clearly, not for sure. Darkness engulfed whatever it was, but I had the idea of a huge dog, bigger than an Alsatian, wilder, but the same breed. A more primitive dog, baying, snarling, going for me in the dark . . . with a collar round its neck. *That* I was sure of. *That* I did see. A metal-studded collar. So it was a guard dog, a wild, savage, guard dog. Trained for one purpose – to kill. And as it came for me, I got this stench right up my nostrils, enveloping me, suffocating me, and I went down on the ground. I was going to get torn to bits.

Someone was screaming. It wasn't me, I could hardly breathe. Screaming, shouting – a girl's voice by the sound of it, and in the dark I could hear the whistle of a lash, once, twice, again and again . . . The baying turned to a snarl, and the snarl to a whimper – an angry, treacherous whimper, but the killer quality had gone out of it. I couldn't see the figures. Moonlight came again, and they were gone.

The garage door was open . . . just as I had left it. The stub end of the knife was on the floor. The door from the stable was open, the lock dangling against it.

I looked for scratches but it was too dark to be sure. Too

dark. And I was too dazed – shaking like a leaf. Blood on my hands. From what? Where I'd fallen on the gravel?

I could hardly get up to the house. I kept looking back, expecting to see something. There was a vague outline . . . was it the girl with that dog pulling at its leash? I didn't know where imagination ended and reality began.

I had never been so pleased to see another human being as I was to see Bridges that morning. I stood at an upstairs window and watched him as he started his work. He always knew exactly what he wanted to do, and he got on with it at the same constant speed. Nothing hurried Bridges; nothing slowed him down. He went from the walled garden to collect some tools, and I knew he'd pass close to the stables. Perhaps he'd notice signs of the night's events. Perhaps he'd stop. Little escaped his attention.

But he didn't appear to notice anything out of place, and I saw him trundle a wheelbarrow back to the walled garden.

I went from window to window, scanning the whole area before going downstairs. I don't know what I anticipated as I looked from bush to bush along the drive. Bridges saw me and called, 'Morning. Going to have a bit of rain later on.'

I went to see what he was doing in the walled garden. It was unlike me to be so interested.

'Got to clean it up this time of year,' said Bridges. 'Going to need a bit of manure. And a bit of lime.' I think he was uneasy in case I interfered with what he was doing.

I had to go back into the stables, but I was unwilling to go alone. 'Spare me a few minutes?' I said.

'What's that, then?'

'I need a bit of advice in the stables.'

He shot a look at the buildings. For two pins he'd refuse. 'It won't take long,' I said. 'I might need a hand.'

'What is it, then? That plastering?'

'We might have to lift something.'

He muttered under his breath, but he followed me.

We went into the garage and I took a quick look round. There was very little to suggest what had taken place the night before.

One of the outer doors was still shut, as I had left it. I looked at the bolts and the paintwork. It was hard to say what was just flaking paint and what had been scratched off by the dog's claws.

Bridges saw me examining it. 'Could do with a lick of paint,' he said grudgingly. 'I'll get around to that. Come the weather, I can't get on with things.'

The bolt on the door to the stalls was hanging by one screw.

'Don't really need that, we don't,' said Bridges. 'What we got to shift then?'

'Upstairs,' I told him.

He did some more grumbling under his breath as he followed me.

I was surprised to find nothing had changed in the flat above. So much had happened. To have been so terrorized and have so little to show for it. Only the ashes of my fire indicated that I'd been there last night.

Bridges looked round the room. 'What, then?' He didn't hide his impatience.

'I thought about getting this fireplace out.'

He looked at the chimneypiece, cemented to the wall. 'Take some shifting, that will.' He examined the plaster and cement I'd already scraped away. 'That's going to take a day or two before you can think about moving it,' he said. 'It's going to want levering out.'

I left it at that. Bridges had served his purpose: the spell of the place was broken. I didn't feel any sense of fear as he went clumping down the stairs, still muttering.

I had another look at the garage and the drive under the porch. The gravel had been kicked up a bit, but that often happened. The mail-van used this piece of the drive to turn on, and sometimes the spinning wheels sprayed up the stones. There was so little to confirm what I had suffered. Except the broken knife on the floor.

There was no reason why I should not continue with the work I had started the day before, but I had something on my mind.

I went up to the house, phoned the office, and asked them for the Munich number where I could get in touch with Sarah. While they were looking it up, Freddie came on the phone.

'Sorry about yesterday,' he said. 'Things were getting me down.'

'So they should,' I told him. 'You've been holding the fort for all of us.'

'Forget it,' he said. 'You're getting in touch with Sarah?'

'Trying to,' I said.

He sounded pleased, so I didn't have the heart to disillusion him.

I got through to Sarah a little later, in her office in Munich.

'Hello, Nicky.' She sounded a little wary.

'Hello, love. How's it all going?'

'Making progress. How are you, Nicky?'

'Making out. Just. With you so far away.'

'I'm sorry.'

'Don't be silly. Someone has to work in the firm.'

She hesitated. 'Yes.' That was all she said.

'How long do you think you'll be there?'

Another slight pause. 'We can't be sure.'

'How's Hans?'

'Very well. Did you see my report?'

'It's not exactly business I'm phoning about,' I told her. 'I'm down at the house. One or two things have come up. You know, while I'm involved in this it might be better to finish things off completely. You remember the flat in the stables?'

'You mean where the groom stayed?' She sounded doubtful.

'That's right. The room at the end. There's that big modern chimneypiece in it, that somebody put in during the war.' Even as I explained this I began asking myself what all the fuss was about. Why had I gone to the bother of making this call? I was making a mountain of a molehill.

'I remember.'

'The thing is, I had just started to do the alterations – you know, take it out to make the room more in keeping with the rest of the place . . . and then I seemed to remember that you liked it as it was. Is that right?'

'That's all right, Nicky,' was all she said.

'But am I right? Was that the fireplace you thought was very splendid?'

'It doesn't matter.' I wondered if she was placating me.

'I haven't touched it yet. Just had a look to see if it would shift.'

'Oh yes?'

'I thought we might find a place for it in the house.'

'I see.'

'I thought it could go in one of the main rooms.'

'Is that what you're phoning about, Nick?'

'Well, yes. I had this sudden thought – just as I was about to start on the wall, it flashed into my mind: "This is the fireplace Sarah said she liked."'

'Don't worry about that.' There was a tiny pause, then she said, 'Have you seen anything of Bobby?'

'He turns up.'

'Recently?'

'Not so much recently. He's moved back to town. When did you say you were coming back?'

'It depends. There's a letter in the office.'

'I was there yesterday. They didn't tell me.'

'You were in the office yesterday?' She was suddenly interested. 'How were things?'

'Not so hot. Freddie has too much on his shoulders. My fault. I told him I'd soon be back, full-time.'

'When is this, Nick?'

'When do I go back? Pretty damn soon, I think. A couple of weeks.'

There didn't seem much more to say. I had tried to keep things on a cheerful note, but she sounded distant. It was like speaking to a stranger. Well, I thought, I'd done what I could. And she didn't sound as though she cared. After all, quite a long time had passed, a lot of things had happened, since we'd gone through these rooms together. At least I had cleared the decks, and had put to rest a sense of guilt. Sarah was no longer interested in what happened to the bizarre chimneypiece.

I scratched a line along the wall that marked the inset of the fireplace, unable to decide the best way to tackle the job. I didn't want to harm the chimneypiece itself. I sat on the floor and marvelled at it, wondering who the forgotten soldier had been.

I had three metal wedges and an iron lever, and my plan was to hammer the lever into the wall, get the thin edge into the tiny gap I had made in the plaster. Then I could edge out the heavy framework.

I could have sworn I'd brought up the lever with me. I had a whole trug full of tools, and I tipped the lot of them on to the floor. The wedges were there, and the hammer, but no sign of the lever. I went through them again but it wasn't there.

I went down the stairs, cursing myself for this waste of time.

'Thought you was up there,' called Bridges.

I nodded and went into the tack room. The lever was on the bench, where I'd put it. There was also a sledgehammer, which might be effective. I took it as well.

Bridges saw what I was carrying. 'You busy up there, then?' he said.

I went up the stairs. Something about Bridges suggested I was ineffectual, and that annoyed me.

The plaster still lay on the stairs where I'd cut it away from between the balusters. God knows what I trod on – some hard lump, and my ankle turned over. I fell a dozen steps in one wild movement, landing against the stair door. I wasn't sure if I was badly hurt; I lay a moment.

'What you done?' shouted Bridges, lurching in. 'Something would happen like that,' he said. He tried to help me up. I was all right until I put my weight on my foot.

'You hurt yourself, then?'

'I'm all right.'

'Should take it easy,' he said.

'I've twisted my ankle. I'll be okay.'

He looked at me sharply. 'You gone on too long up there, and down the flight pond. You don't get proper meals, that's what my missus says. That's what's wrong.'

I looked at him in amazement. 'Don't be ridiculous. I tripped on something.'

178

He stalked off grimly. I couldn't think what had made him angry.

I managed to get up the stairs and along the corridor, each step a stab of pain, but I brought the lever and the sledgehammer with me. I lay on the floor and let the ankle throb. It took a long time to become tolerable. Even then I couldn't put any weight on it. I stood on the other foot and tried to bang the lever into the wall. It was useless.

'Going, then,' shouted Bridges under the window. 'Night.'

'Thanks, Bridges,' I shouted back.

I heard his bicycle going over the gravel, and threw aside my hammer. This task wasn't going to be finished this evening; it wasn't even going to get started. I piled the tools back into the trug. I was very angry that I'd made things so difficult for myself, for that was what I'd done. Sarah didn't care what happened to this place, nor what I did to it, whereas my friends, the family, were waiting anxiously for me to begin. So why didn't I? Just a token start . . . drive the lever in, knock in one of the wedges? I chose the easiest, the smallest; then I tossed it back in the heap and limped downstairs and up to the house. I didn't want to be in the stables after dark.

17

Something that Bridges said must have stung me, for I hobbled into the kitchen, concerned to make myself a good meal. I opened a bottle of my favourite wine, a Pommard, and took it through to the living-room. The central heating was pounding away like the engine of a liner, as it seemed to do on cold nights. The warmth of the room and the glow of the wine were accentuated by the chill outside as it grew dark.

My ankle was painful, but a sense of returning well-being gradually took the sting out of it. I pushed aside my plate after I had finished, and wished Mrs Bridges had seen what sort of a meal I had had. I put on some music and sat back to finish the bottle of wine. I had a reel-to-reel tape on which were recorded a couple of symphonies and some incidental music – several hours of playing. But I didn't hear it all. I fell asleep with a glass of wine undrunk and the orchestra fading into unconsciousness.

I woke uneasily, thinking something had gone wrong with the recorder, but it was still playing softly. I recognized the piece and knew I had been asleep for over an hour. I couldn't think what had awakened me, unless it was the tape. The music might have been affected by a change of speed? I sat listening, but it played perfectly. Nevertheless, I knew something about it had seeped into my sleeping mind, another sound, something I had not expected. Perhaps I had noticed an instrument that had previously escaped me: that can happen if a recording is played on a more sensitive machine. I concentrated, but nothing seemed to have changed. The alternative was that the other music I had heard – for that was what I supposed it to be – must have been part of my sleep, a dream.

I saw I had still the wine to finish, but I no longer felt like it. The remnants of sleep were still on me. I decided to go to bed. I was about to get to my feet, testing my ankle cautiously, when I heard the sound again. It wasn't music, but it took me a moment to realize it was someone crying.

I turned to the tape deck in amazement. Was it possible that there had been someone crying when we made that recording? A child, perhaps? We'd done it in studios near the office. The crying had been faint: had I been mistaken? I limped to the machine. The tape was half-way through, the music faultless. I looked round the room. It was here I had first heard the footsteps in the hall; that seemed a long time ago. Anyhow, the sound had not come from within the house, it had come from the tape deck on the coffee table by the window.

I had put on the table-light beside the tape deck, and the rest of the room was in shadow. I never felt the need to light the corners of this house. It wasn't alarm nor fear that I felt as I stood in the semi-darkness. Sadness came over me; tears welled to my eyes and tasted in my mouth. Was that the answer? Was it my own cry I had heard? That was too far-fetched, for my way of thinking. The likely answer was that I had imagined it. Besides, the sound had gone as I grew more wakeful, so the mystery vanished.

I crossed to the tape to switch it off. The sound of crying was soft, muffled, but close, quite distinct. My hand froze above the switch. The music played on; the crying persisted. It was as though the sobs were being choked back, softly, despairing. It wasn't merely my hand that froze, my heart froze too.

I turned off the tape and for a moment both music and sobbing stopped, but then the faint crying started again. So close, so soft; it might well have been in the room. We had curtained the tall windows with heavy velvet material, a warm, rich extravagance, blanketing the room against future winters. I knew what I was about to see, and was appalled by the premonition. I did not want to look, but I twitched the curtain aside.

The garden lay under black shadows. The single light in the room was mirrored in the glass, making it hard to see beyond. The crying stopped. I put my face to the window and peered out. Something moved in the shadows of nearby bushes, like a wisp of smoke in this light. A flutter of lace – something lacy in a puff of air. As it moved away it seemed to evaporate, but not before I caught sight of her young face, tense and white; her looks drawn. One quick look at me, and she vanished. It wasn't exactly an accusation, more a look of bewilderment, of betrayal. But what betrayal? I called out against the glass, 'What betrayal?' I had done nothing to betray her, had never hinted at her existence.

I stood at the window, face pressed to the cold glass, forcing myself to peer into the night, to conjure her out of shadows – because I had to tell her how wrong she was, how much she meant, how I could never betray her or her family. As I stood there, unable to identify the cause of guilt that overwhelmed me, I heard the distant snarl of her animal – for I knew it was her dog: it was she who had come to my rescue, who had pulled the brute from me, whipped it into submission, risked herself, I suppose, as it threw itself towards me in its fury. And with that thought, I understood what the betrayal was. They had taken me to the stables, asking that I should restore the rooms to the state they had been in, in their day. But I hadn't done this; I hadn't even made a start. My gratitude had been so slight that I had delayed, procrastinated, lost tools, nursed an ankle – done anything but show I was a determined and loving friend. Insignificant though that might seem, I guessed it was the cause of her sobbing. That was the betrayal that had left her so wretched.

I started to call to her, to shout through the glass, knocking on the window. But it was useless. She had gone. Wind blew over the lawn and bushes rustled. A cold sky reflected a cold earth. The year seemed to be dying, or was already dead. I was moved with pity – pity even for the soil and the dry leaves circling round the base of trees.

I had a despairing feeling that this time I might have left things too late. Perhaps there was a season in which this pale reflection of a past life could be fanned into a glow. And perhaps that season was past, through my delaying. I went upstairs, blaming myself, yet at the same time still in two minds – in many minds, for I had no passionate urge to do their work in those stables as I had been willing to do all they asked at the flight pond and pagoda.

But I would have done all I could to silence that sobbing.

I put everything else out of my mind except the brief glimpse I had had of the girl's face at the window. Anything to ease that pain. Even when, next morning, I looked with admiration at the chimneypiece, standing in front of it, taken aback for a moment – it was almost a museum piece – I could still see the look she had given me, hear her soft cry.

I set about the work cautiously: it was too good to destroy. This meant chipping away the wall into which it had been fixed, breaking up the fire cement around the stonework. I used a chisel. The wedges and lever were too clumsy. This took longer but there was less danger of cracking the panels. It took time to clear the brickwork, but it was a neat job. I was very pleased.

It was late afternoon before I realized how long it was taking, but that didn't worry me. I had solved a problem. I would restore this room to its old character, and I would save Sarah's fireplace. I don't know why I still thought of it as Sarah's; she had already told me it didn't matter to her. But the thought was lodged in my mind. She had liked it once, and I wanted to keep it for her. Nevertheless, I was surprised to find how little I'd done at the end of the day, and I was too tired to brush up the dust and chippings that littered the room. My ankle had begun to hurt again. I was hungry. It was time to stop. Besides it was growing dark, and I no longer felt at ease here once the sun had gone.

I decided to leave the tools and stacked them against the wall. As I was doing this I thought I heard voices. I stood a moment to listen. Perhaps someone had come to look for me, a tradesman or someone? But there was no sound. I was going to call out when I heard the noise again. It wasn't exactly voices, but it gave that general impression. There were no distinct words, more a sound, an imitation of speech, a man speaking in anger. Repetitive. Rhythmic. Definitely in anger.

I went to the window, and looked over the orchard. There was no one there. The sound faded; I looked towards the walled garden. Still I couldn't see anyone, but the voice was clearer. A man was very angry. And there was also an occasional lighter sound, a woman's voice, also in anger, like a muted chorus chiming in to support him. That was what it was like . . . a passage of threatening music. Formidable.

My heart jumped as a third voice sounded. It was just a suggestion, an instrument underscoring the others. Muffled, despairing. The same sobbing as the night before.

I threw the tools aside and ran down the stairs. Their anger was more than echoed in me. I guessed what they were doing – blaming her, accusing her, because I had not completed what they had wanted. Did they forget that I was still a creature in time and space? I was living, I could be exhausted, I had the capacity only of those who still had vitality that could be used up, could be depleted. Life needed time to recuperate. They had forgotten what was possible for the living since they had been so long dead!

I threw open the garage door. The voices had come from just

outside, from shadows along the drive. I was not surprised to find there was nothing there.

I was still angry when I got back into the house, aware of the pressure that was being brought to bear. Should I get the wretched business over? After all, who would be any the better off for the time and trouble I was taking? What misery was I causing somewhere in the dark out there? I simmered down after a bit, and sat in the living-room with a drink. It wasn't as if I was trying to save a great work: it was splendid, yes – but not art at its best. Perhaps some modern gallery would like to take it. It was wrong at Longwood. They were quite right, these past owners; it should be demolished. If this daughter of the family was taking my part and so bearing the brunt of their anger, there was no point prolonging the matter. But I couldn't make a decision. Vague considerations delayed me. In the back of my mind – what was it? Something prevented me carrying out what they asked.

The room was warm, the whisky comforting. I no longer had an appetite for a meal, eating peanuts with my drink. Perhaps Mrs Bridges was right after all – I wasn't having proper meals. I went into the hall and collected from the big rosewood table a batch of letters that had been lying there for weeks. I have no idea why I collected them at that moment. Then in a distant fashion, with an alien curiosity, I began reading. They were addressed to me but I felt I was reading the correspondence of a stranger.

For the first time I understood how disastrously my business had been affected. From week to week clients had grown bewildered, then angry. I felt as though I were reading events in a novel. There were reports, letters requiring my approval, letters asking for replies, letters of concern. Letters from Sarah. Was I all right? *Was I all right?* Why did she ask that?

Amongst them was a scrap of paper: I read, '*Beautiful chimney in the stables. Have you seen it? Out of place. Idiotic. The best thing in Longwood.*' I had put that scribbled note from Sarah amongst the rest of her letters. Was that what had preyed on my mind?

I read on. Other letters – gossip from Germany – discussions about business – suggestions about new ventures. Then three short letters, growing more urgent, asking about me. Sarah was on the point of coming home three times; each time she had changed her mind. I had the impression that she had been stopped. I wondered – did she really no longer care what I did at Longwood? It appeared she was staying in an apartment in Munich: there was a telephone number under the letter-heading. The simplest thing would be to speak to her. Good God, I told myself, things had surely not gone so far that we couldn't talk to each other!

I rang the number a couple of times, but there was no reply. It would be about ten o'clock in Germany. Sarah might be at the theatre, dining – out anywhere.

I had another number for Hans; perhaps he would know where she was. I could leave a message with him.

He wasn't in. A housekeeper tried to explain, but my knowledge of German was slight. 'Out,' she said in English. She took her time over the next sentence. 'He is out.'

'I'm trying to get in touch with Miss Foster. Sarah Foster.' I wasn't sure if she had understood me. 'Miss Foster. The English girl.'

'She is out.'

'Do you know where she is?'

'She is out,' said the housekeeper firmly. 'She is out. Herr Haupmann is out.'

I couldn't get any more sense out of her. I wondered if she meant they were out together. What other meaning could there be? Otherwise how did she know Sarah was out? Probably the woman hadn't understood what I was talking about. Besides, why shouldn't they be out together? Someone had to look after Sarah while she was in Germany.

I decided to phone again later, but when the time came it no longer seemed important. After all, what could I find out? Sarah would be as guarded as last time we spoke. She was no longer spontaneous; she wouldn't tell me what she really wanted done. She would wait to see what I wanted, what I would say – and then she would make it easy for me. She never used to be like that.

I felt very low that night, depressed, as though I'd been deserted, sick with a feeling of guilt – as if I had committed a crime I had forgotten – or as though I were about to commit a crime.

18

I slept late next morning; I would have slept longer but I heard Bridges at work outside.

I joined him.

'Walking all right, then, I see.' Bridges nodded at my leg.

'It's fine,' I said. 'Lucky for me you were there.'

He took that comment a little grudgingly. 'Got to be careful on them stairs,' he said. 'You can go on too long at some things, specially if you ain't used to that sort of work. Long hours you been doing. Down that wood, up those stairs. Not even in the fresh air, up there.'

He was his own taciturn self, pushing off with his wheelbarrow, heavy with rubbish and weeds, a muttered grumble just below his breath. He was a powerful little man, wiry, with long arms and bowed legs making heavy going in big hob-nailed boots. There were times when I felt he was my lifeline to the outer world, and there were times I would have gladly cut that lifeline.

I hung around the walled garden, pretending to examine the work he had been doing. He was surprised and a little suspicious, eyeing me from a distance as I went from vegetable bed to fruit bushes. For two pins, I felt, he might have asked me what I was doing. I paid him, but he operated under his own steam. He'd worked this ground for many decades and, in a sense, it belonged to him.

My real purpose, I realized, was to delay getting back to the stables. I hadn't made up my mind what to do, in spite of many resolutions. But it couldn't be put off indefinitely. I went back to work, collecting the tools I had stacked in the trug.

I began slowly, determined to preserve all I could for Sarah. The fact that she now avowed no interest made no difference. She might have washed her hands of the house, of everything in it, me too for that matter, but that didn't affect this resolution. I wanted to fight for a flag after the battle was lost.

But as I picked at the plasterwork down the sides of the panels, I was aware of another loyalty, and my senses were alert for any sound . . . any sight. I was on edge, ready to protect an abused ghost. How ludicrous! How could I have any effect on what happened in her world! And yet, I *had*. I had come to her protection, as she had to mine. The thought filled me with a hope. I couldn't put it into words. But we had shared contacts, shared some joy, were aware of each other. What more was possible?

So I made haste slowly, finishing clearing one panel before starting the next – and they were aware of what I was doing. Not that they were with me in the room. I don't think they were able to tolerate that. It was a day of slow, steady progress. A tremulous pressure would come, then go. Perhaps they had learned a lesson, for there was no tension when I downed tools. I heard Bridges wheel out his bike.

'I'm taking your advice, you see, Bridges,' I said. 'I'm knocking off when you do.'

He was grimly pleased. 'You'll get much more done that way,' he said. 'Got to pace yourself, you have. Can't do nothing all at a rush, just do yourself in. Got to take it reasonable.' He went off hurriedly as though he had allowed himself too much approval.

I guessed he was right as I made a cup of tea in the kitchen. Perhaps I ought to go out for a meal – the local pub, or further afield. The phone rang. It might be Sarah. Perhaps the message had got through that I was trying to contact her.

'Hello, that you Nick?' It was Bobby Everett's voice. 'Glad I caught you. I thought you might have moved back to London.'

'I'm still here.' I was careful not to sound welcoming. The man was thick-skinned; he should have realized from our last conversations that I didn't want to keep up this contact.

'There's been a change in my plans,' went on Everett cheerfully. 'I have to go back to Lewes in the next couple of days. You may remember I was sitting in on some of the work Andy Delmar was doing.' I guessed what was coming, but gave him no encouragement. 'I thought I'd see if you were still in the district. It would be nice if you could join us for a meal some time. We owe you hospitality.'

'Think nothing of it.'

'The Delmars would like to invite you back while I'm staying with them.'

'It's not a good time,' I told him.

'Oh. They'll be sorry to hear that.'

'The company is in poor shape. It's my fault, and I have to pull it together.'

'I quite understand. I'll tell them. They'll be very sorry.'

'Yes,' I said, 'I'm sorry, too.'

'Tell you what,' Everett sounded cheerful again. 'I'll give you their number. If you look like having an hour or two free, give them a call.'

'I've got the number,' I told him.

'Sorry about your company,' said Everett.

'How long are you going to be staying with them?' I wanted to know how long I'd have him on my doorstep.

'Not long. A few days. Maybe we'll be able to meet.'

'I'm not sure,' I said. 'Maybe.' I put the phone down. Surely he must realize I didn't want him around!

The call put paid to the idea of going out for a meal. The thought of Everett back in Sussex – how far away? Ten, twelve miles? – created an emergency. I had always felt he was a threat – vaguely at first, but now I saw it clearly. He had been brought to Longwood by Sarah, and every time he came an east wind blew through the place. Everything chilled, went grey; life drained away; certainly the life of creatures existing on the fringe of my consciousness. Everett was their enemy, his presence destroyed them. Was it possible this was his purpose? Was that the reason Sarah had brought him, that he still returned? Was he waging some sort of war? I couldn't see how this could be, for neither he nor Sarah had any knowledge of the beings with whom I shared my life. If they didn't know, what could they attempt to destroy? And yet – in some illogical way – I guessed the truth was hidden here.

Everett was going to be in the vicinity. What had to be done must be done quickly, before his shadow fell over us all.

I had felt uneasy about going to the stables after dark ever since the night of the dog. But I shrugged that off. The job was urgent. Besides, I would be doing what the brute's masters wanted.

I went up to the groom's flat. Perhaps I worked faster – perhaps with a little less care; anyhow the rest of the cement and plaster came away quickly, and the soldier's fireplace was chipped clear. It was made of stone, and proved to be very heavy. I'd brought a flask of whisky with me, and deserved a drink. As I took a swig I had the first awareness I was not alone. I shone the torch round the room. There was nothing there, of course. But what lay against the window? Night, and the grimy glass, blanked everything off. However, the atmosphere was friendly, and there was a growing sense of warmth around me. I got the levers and wedges, and drove them into the wall. Sweat ran off me as I tried to force out the complete structure.

It had been standing for about forty years, taking root. Efforts on my part made little impression. My muscles trembled as I struggled to budge it, and the room swam. But it finally moved! The crack along the wall opened a quarter of an inch wide. My heart hammered, not just with exhaustion; I was elated!

The torch was on a chair, shining on the wall as I worked. Now I took it and peered into the crack. It took a long time to get used to the light, but gradually I began to see the outlines in the recess. God knows what I expected – some gruesome secret. Some skeleton of the past. Everything was covered with grime, and it was impossible to know exactly what was there, but there was something – a small fireplace, modest, with a mantelshelf. Was that all? It was similar to the fireplace in the tack room downstairs, and it seemed no adequate reason for this wave of relief from my unseen audience. Or had they been so offended by the soldier's work that they could not rest until it was destroyed?

189

For my part, I felt it had been a great effort for little. But it was a moment I was happy to share with them – this rush of feeling like a little puff of wind . . . this breath of life. After all, these stables had been standing in the grounds of Longwood before they built the present house. They must have loved them and resented all changes. I understood and appreciated that. And yet, caught up in this silent excitement, something nagged at me. Sarah had asked me to keep one thing, this object of their dislike, mundane, domestic – just a fireplace, for all its 1920s art.

The thought sobered me. I backed off from their triumph, and they noticed. The wave of pleasure died down, jubilation trembled, dissipated. I wasn't sure, but in the distance I thought I heard the snarl of the dog. Faintly – far away.

I went back to the chimneypiece and looked through the crack. There was hardly space enough to see anything. I put all my strength into the next effort, and the stone panels shifted perceptibly. I could now put my fingers into the space beside the wall. The noise of clapping was almost real; delighted, spontaneous clapping. I steadied myself to get my breath back. There was no sound of the dog.

The next attempt to shift it was less successful, but the space was a full inch by the time I sank into the chair. A moment later I *did* hear the dog. Far away, true – but it snarled angrily: I could hear it because the applause had died. Only one pair of hands was still clapping – girlish, proud, lacking circumspection. And then even that sound trailed off. The dog howled. I began to make a calculation, coldly determined to put a suspicion to the test.

I went back to the wall. It was easier now to shift the object, since I could get a proper grip with my hands; I could get my shoulder against the wall and use my full strength. It would be much easier. Encouragement welled up around me. Then I went and sat down. The dog bayed.

The hair rose on my neck. I had to make one more test. Once more I moved the chimneypiece, engulfed by a sense of love and approval; and once more I moved away in cool hostility, to the sound of vicious snarling. Closer now, much closer. The case was proved.

I heard the animal scrabbling outside of the stables. Oh yes, it was *that* close, the pressure that intense. It was all or nothing: either arms stretched out, across impossible divides, towards me, or the terrifying wolf-snarl circled the building. One way hate – the other love. I was not prepared to tolerate it.

The animal must be directly under the window. How long before it came racing up the stairs? I strode to the chimneypiece and pushed it back against the wall.

A ghostly world was struck dumb; the silence that followed was more eerie than the noise before. And then some sort of hell broke loose. I was stunned by the noise in my head: the dog throwing itself against a door, shaking bolts, the rattle of chains, an uproar of angry sounds. A scream; a single voice sobbing; then blows, vicious, angry, blows. A turbulent uproar. I had taken them off guard, and their reaction was fearful. But I was equally determined. Did they think I was to be intimidated? What did they think I was? Besides, what could they do to me?

I was heading for the door when that thought stopped me in my tracks. What *could* they do to me?

I remembered the feelings of force I had run into before. I remembered the dog. I didn't *know* what they could do. Perhaps I had reason to fear.

I picked up the lever, a short iron spike, weighing it in my hand, and then went along the corridor and down the stairs. The hound was going mad; someone was screaming; someone else was shouting. I pushed open the garage door and swung the lever up to shoulder height.

The night was still, cold, windless; white wisps hung in a great bowl, and a sweep of stars reached dark horizons. There was no sound – not a whisper, not the rustle of a leaf. Nothing moved. Was it true? Had I only to face my fears to destroy them?

I walked back to the house with the iron spike at the ready. I hadn't worked out the logic, but it seemed to me that if something were able to attack, then I would be able to defend. I hung on to that thought, keeping calm and on my guard.

Nevertheless, I was shaking by the time I got into the house.

My shotgun lay on top of the bookcase; I loaded it, and went back out. I walked up and down the drive from the house to the stables; I did it a dozen times before the feeling went out of me, and then I fired one shot into the dark. One shot whistling through the trees might bring them to their senses.

I was still in the garden when I heard footsteps on the drive.

'That you?' shouted Bridges. He was pulling on his jacket, and he viewed my gun anxiously.

'What's up, then?'

I was surprised to see him.

'Where exactly do you live, Bridges?'

'Along them cottages. What's the matter, then?'

'How far away?'

'The cottages? Hundred yards.'

'Sorry I woke you,' I said. 'I thought there was something out here.'

'What something?'

'A fox, perhaps. It was dark.'

Bridges looked suspicious.

'Or a badger. Sorry about that. Thanks for coming.'

'I wouldn't bother with badgers,' said Bridges grimly. 'Lots of them about . . . Not sensible to go shooting in the dark.'

He stumped back down the drive, still pulling on his jacket. I went into the house, and put the gun away. I was sure I wouldn't want it again.

19

I must have dropped off to sleep for a couple of hours just before dawn, but I was not at all tired. I seemed to have had a sudden surge of energy and I was very pleased with what I had done. I was completely in control of the situation. I caught sight of myself smiling in a mirror – everything was easy this morning. Just having faced that fantasy in the dark had lifted a weight from my mind; I was walking through the house with a springy step, singing scraps of a dance tune as I made breakfast.

When the phone went and I heard Everett's voice, I knew I could handle him without getting angry. 'Sorry, Bobby. This is the worst of all days to call me. Why don't you give me a ring when you're staying in Lewes?'

'I'm on my way there now,' said Everett. 'I'm in Tunbridge Wells. I shall be passing close to your place in half an hour.'

'Much though I'd love to see you . . .'

'Sorry to insist,' he went on, 'but I have to have a word. It's about Sarah.'

It was so unexpected that it took me off-balance.

'Sarah? What's the matter?'

'I'm very worried about her.'

'What's wrong?' Anger was mixed with my alarm. What the hell was Everett bringing to disrupt my life now?

'You don't know where she is, do you?'

'I've got a number.'

'I've been ringing it. She isn't there.'

'She could be out.'

'She's been unavailable for several days.'

'Are you sure?'

'You haven't been in touch?'

'No.'

'I think we ought to meet, don't you?'

'I'll be here.'

Everett drove up to the front door in a very short time.

'Come in. I'm having coffee. Like some?'

'Thanks.'

He still had the bland look about him, but he was watchful and seemed nervous . . . that is, for a man so passive.

I asked, 'What about Sarah?'

'We've been in touch from time to time,' he said. He seemed to be working out a puzzle. 'She started phoning me more or less every day a few weeks ago.'

'Whatever for?'

'She wanted to come home.'

'She wanted to come back to England? Why did she have to tell you this? She never told me.'

'She seemed to think you didn't read her letters. Besides . . .'

'What?'

'She wanted my advice.'

'I don't see why.'

'She did. Then afterwards she tried to get me to agree with her.'

'I don't get it.' I reminded myself not to let him make me angry. 'What was the problem? Something I don't know about?'

'I said it would be best to stay on and finish the job she had gone to do. She took a little persuading, but she stayed.'

'Thank you very much. I don't see what business it was of yours . . .'

'She asked me. I couldn't refuse to talk to her.'

'Sorry. Right. Go on.'

'She stayed. Then, as I say, she started phoning every day, wanting to come back. She wanted me to say she ought to.'

'Why didn't you? What's the bloody mystery?'

'I thought she was imagining things.'

'Like what?'

'She was worried about you.'

I put down my coffee. 'Whatever for?'

'She was concerned about the way things were going in the company. That was understandable – you and Freddie were concerned yourselves. But I said that in my opinion you were just taking what we call in the States a sabbatical. It's very common over there, though it isn't here. You had been working very hard for years, and obviously had decided to take time off. Sarah said it was so completely unlike you: I think that was what troubled her. She couldn't understand how you could change so much. She kept expecting you to get back to work. "It's not like Nick," she kept saying. Everything you did – you know, staying down here, being so isolated, so solitary, letting the work drift, and "letting everyone down" – that's how she saw it. And she couldn't understand why.'

I had recovered as he spoke, but for some reason I kept stirring my coffee, head down, so that he couldn't see my eyes. God knows why I did that. What could he see in my eyes?

'How is she now?'

'That's what I don't know. She got more and more insistent that she must come back and see you were all right. I pointed out that even when she had been in England she had stayed in London, and you had lived down here. I thought it best to make it plain that none of her friends now seemed to think the marriage was going ahead. I think it was Freddie who said, "Can't understand these two. The great loves of their lives, and now the whole bloody affair is dead as a doornail."'

'You told Sarah that?'

'I think it was she that told me. These things happen; I don't think anyone passed judgements.'

He made it all so dry and factual, like a story out of yesterday's newspaper. *He* certainly seemed to pass no judgement. The odd thing was that for the first time I had a sudden yearning – a terrible feeling of loss. What had happened to Sarah? What had happened to me? She could have passed the window now – a stranger. Was life, were relations, *that* unreal, *that* meaningless, *that* transitory? I couldn't accept it, but it was I who had made them so.

Everett was still talking, sipping his coffee thoughtfully, debating this problem. He seemed aloof, abstracted, and at the same time involved. He was all of a piece, that man: it was as I might have expected him to react. 'I have to admit I tried to put your point of view – what I thought might be your point of view. I said, after all business wasn't everything, you had proved your capacity, you'd made a fair fortune, and been a success. You had had a very satisfactory youth.'

'What's that supposed to mean?' Almost objectively he had made the praise sound like a criticism.

'Just what I say: you had played the young man's game with skill, talent and energy. You had both ridden on the crest of this wave for several years. You'd fallen in love – so I had reason to suppose. It had been an ideal time in your life. I don't imagine that there was any view of life to come that could promise

195

anything better. Now all there was to look forward to was marriage, consolidation of the business you had put on its feet, settling down, becoming a more mature and stable member of society. Nothing really to compare with seven . . . ten . . . fifteen years of such excitement.'

I don't think I took my eyes off him. It was all so impersonal – he might have been dissecting a frog, pointing out its innards. Or he might have been discussing a stranger, someone else, certainly not me. And yet . . . he *was* talking about me. Taking the mask aside; saying the things I didn't want to hear.

'You think she assumed the marriage was off?'

'Oh, come on, Nick, that was pretty obvious. You found a dozen reasons to delay things. What else could she think?'

'Then she was wrong. Why should I change my mind?'

'Your mind probably stayed the same. But maybe when it came to the point you didn't really *want* to give up being a young man.'

'Rubbish.'

'Possibly. It's just one explanation. There could be others.'

'Did you talk this sort of crap to Sarah?'

'It was Sarah who talked this sort of crap to me.'

'I find that hard to believe.'

'It's not all that uncommon. Nobody wants to give up the more exciting for the lesser.'

'God, man, I'm not a child!'

'No one supposed you were. It's just that reality – you know, day-to-day existence – isn't so attractive as the dream.'

'The dream! What dream?' I was scathing.

'The promise. You know – the struggle to get there. The real excitement is the race; some men find the prize a disappointment. *Any* prize. Nothing lives up to the promise. After all, the gamble of putting the company together was fun, and since it's been successful it hasn't been anything like so exciting, just a pleasant way to make a living. The same thing with Sarah: the living together was wonderful, the coming together. But is that all life is about? Does one have to settle down to marriage like the rest of mankind? Or is there another way?'

'Like what?'

'Each to his own fantasy. Some people manage to live in their own particular unreality for ever, and never come to terms with life. You might say, they never live it at all.'

He was treading so close that I wondered if he had guessed . . . but what could he guess? No, it was just a general statement. Everett knew nothing. Nothing about the real reasons I was staying in this so-called isolation, nothing about the choice I had to make. The unique, fantastic choice!

'Anyhow,' he was saying, 'whatever the reason – and it's not crucial – the relationship had changed, and Sarah had to accept that, as I tried to tell her. She thought she ought to help you . . . but she didn't know what to do. I suggested she'd have to accept that people change, that they can fall out of love as well as in.'

'Did she believe you?'

'I don't think so. Women are like that. I suppose that they think themselves – as women – infallible. The magic had worked between you, and it would always stay.'

'What did you say?'

'I said perhaps you'd found a stronger magic.'

At times the man took my breath away. But it could only be a manner of speech.

'I haven't found another woman, if that's what you mean.'

'I never supposed that.' He looked up at me from his coffee cup – clearly, steadily, almost gently. It was a destructive moment. For a split second, I could have blurted out what had happened to me. But the moment passed.

I changed the conversation.

'You don't know where she is? What do you want me to do?'

'I thought you ought to know. She told me last week she was coming here . . . to Longwood. She kept asking about your health.'

'That's nonsense, I've never been so fit. You should see the work I've been doing.' I almost spoke of the chimneypiece.

'Yes, I said you were in splendid condition. But she seemed to think it might be psychological.'

'Gone off my nut?' I couldn't help laughing. Everett allowed himself a slow grin.

'An emotional upset. You see, she's trying to make sense of

197

something that doesn't make sense to her: why you should have lost any feeling for her . . .'

'That's not true.'

'Perhaps it's as she sees it. And seeing it that way, she looks for an explanation that can make things understandable. So – what *has* caused you to drop her, to delay, postpone, the marriage until it is no longer likely? What keeps you alone in this great house and garden? What drags you back here, so persistently, so irresistibly? Not another woman, as you say . . . she doesn't think that. No, there is no rational answer. Therefore, thinks Sarah, the answer must be irrational.' He glanced at his watch. 'I have to go. I know you're very busy.'

That was typical of Everett. There were a dozen things I wanted to ask him now, but he was suddenly in a hurry to leave. I went with him to his car. 'Is there anything *wrong* with Sarah?'

'I don't know. Of course it's natural for her to be concerned about you, but this goes too far. You're a grown man. What danger can you be in?'

'She thinks I'm actually in danger?'

'Something like that.'

'What sort of danger?' I was quite bewildered.

'I don't know. It's a vague, general feeling, I believe. She plays it down; it's a bit hysterical.'

'I'm not in danger here.'

'Of course not. That's why we have to be concerned about her. Sarah is very controlled, but this attitude to you . . .' He shrugged.

He was about to drive off. Perhaps he saw how shaken I was, for he hesitated, and tried to sound reassuring. 'There might be a perfectly reasonable answer why she doesn't answer the phone. I'll try again this evening, or I'll contact your friend Hans. Don't worry too much. At worst she may have suffered an emotional crisis: too much work, perhaps. She should have tried your antidote – time off. Or perhaps she can't accept that the affair is over. But one recovers from such things.'

He went, leaving little comfort. Everett trailed disaster in his wake. He might just as well have said that I was responsible for anything that happened to Sarah. I had a disturbing fantasy that she might have lost her memory, and be wandering all over Germany. I tried to forget it; but finally I had to call her number in Munich. I tried it a dozen times during the next hour. There was no answer.

I was loath to call Hans, but I had no option. The housekeeper answered and recognized my voice.

'Herr Morell?' Then she said, 'Fraulein Foster?'

I had a great sense of relief. I said slowly and clearly, 'May I speak to Fraulein Foster?'

'Out,' said the housekeeper.

'Still out?' Did she understand what I meant? Could she speak English? 'Let me speak to Herr Haupmann.'

'Still out.' She was very emphatic.

'Still out? Do you mean, both are out? You mean – out together?'

'Herr Haupmann out. Fraulein Foster out. Out. Still out!' She was very angry or very anxious. There was nothing more I could learn from her.

So once again a visit from Everett had left me in a state of indecision. He had gone on to Lewes, and would be with Delmar. I had the telephone number, and was on the point of calling him to unload my anger. But what could I say? On the face of it, he'd come to me because he expected I would be concerned about Sarah. And so I was. For the first time in months I forgot my passion to get back to work in the garden or stables. Sarah preyed on my mind. Everett had made it sound as though she had had a breakdown, and if she had, it was owing to her efforts to hold my little empire together – to keep faith in the face of rejection. In his dry manner Everett had already written off any future life Sarah and I might have together. What he didn't know, what no one knew, was that I had had no choice in what I had done. I was the instrument of people who would pass into eternity without me, creatures drowning in time – how could I turn my back on them? Sarah's love had been my life; but to them I was life itself.

It was no use belittling this battle. I cared! I wanted to reconcile two worlds – two goals had to be achieved, or those five spirits would sink back into the frosty earth – this time for ever? I couldn't leave them to such a destiny. I couldn't throw off their claim on me.

It was late before I was able to leave the house and walk down to the stables. Maybe I was being manipulated, maybe I was just a catspaw, but I had to go.

It seemed a long time since I had last been there, when I had tested the pressures and inducements put upon me. Fear and love had been a stick and a carrot the previous night, but since then I had stalked the garden with a gun and perhaps they had learned a lesson. Surely they must know by now that they were in my heart and what I did was out of an eternal, human sympathy? Surely they would never set the dog loose on me again, nor use the girl's tears to win my efforts? Still, I was cautious. We had made mistakes before, both parties. It was surprising only that we had been able to communicate as well as we had done, and no surprise that we had sometimes misunderstood each other.

The fireplace was back in its alcove where I had pushed it. I was surprised to see how neatly I had jammed it into its original position. I had used all my strength, and the line of chipped plaster was all that indicated what I had done. I ran my hand over it. It was flush against the wall; only the crack running up both sides and along the top picked out the chimneypiece as not belonging to the whole. Perhaps I was growing more used to it, but it didn't seem so out of keeping as I had once thought. I wondered what Sarah would think about it. Would she prefer it in a room in the house? I sat on the floor and pondered about that, but in my heart I knew she would like me to leave it where it was.

I was still sitting there when I became aware of how cold it had grown. The light had gone, but that didn't bother me now. I collected paper and wood from the garage below and lit a fire in the grate. The room was soon warm and I felt safe, content; but I still did nothing about the fireplace. My car was parked in the garage, and when I went down later to collect more wood, I brought up cushions and a rug from the car. Lying on them by the fire, I knew I would be told what to do.

I was surprised to find I was falling asleep. The room had

grown very warm and close. I enjoyed the snug feeling of the place, with its uneven floor and grimy walls, like somewhere I'd been as a boy; it was an illusion of camping-out.

I didn't sleep. Lying with my hands under my head, gazing at the firelight on the ceiling, I seemed to be recovering from something, convalescing. But from what? Peace and warmth seeped into me, and I wondered if the same process functioned with the family. Did they take time to recuperate? Or were they inpervious to time? Beyond time? Perhaps they didn't use energy? Though I felt they did – how else could they get in touch with me?

I went down to the garage again. I knew now what I was looking for, but I wasn't quite sure why. I wasn't getting a clear message.

Bridges stored tools on shelves along the wall. I collected a tin of cement filler and a trowel.

I looked at my watch. It was just after two. Through dirty windows I could see bright moonlight. I felt a need to be as quiet as possible, but the stairs creaked noisily – I wasn't sure why I had to be so secret.

I squatted down beside the fire and opened the tin. The mixture was fresh; I stirred it with the trowel, still keeping at bay the implications of what I was about to do. If I kept the idea from *my* mind then it wouldn't be so obvious to the onlookers. And I knew they were there.

It almost worked. I scraped out some mixture on the trowel, and began smearing it along the edges of the chimneypiece. The crack I had made was hardly more than a quarter of an inch – not entirely regular, and in some places the plaster had fallen away – but the filler covered everything. It began to dry in the heat of the fire.

Then I felt something welling up around me. The atmosphere pressed in my ears; it was something elemental – uncontrollable – anger! A great hubbub started to mount . . . then stopped dead. The anger vanished, the wave of sound was gone. For a few seconds the world was as mundane as ever, with no power or force that was not totally normal and explicable. Was it as simple as this – that all I had to do was make a stand, decide

I would not sacrifice this poor object because once Sarah had delighted in it? Could I make this decision and yet keep their confidence? I continued to work, cementing the cracks, stroking the trowel over the wall, till it was possible to see what it would look like – exactly as Sarah had first seen it.

I had won a battle! They would have burst upon me if they had dared: the first flush of fury had sounded, but it had gone. A pricked bubble, that fury. I continued working, and as I did so I became conscious of a growing loneliness. The air thinned . . . I could almost count them as they left. The soldier, quick, angry, but disciplined – under orders to go without protest, marching almost. The scholarly man shuffled after him. The man and the woman were hesitating, then going slowly – sadly in fact – hardly believing I should so desert them . . . betray them.

I waited for the last of that little group to go. Was there still a special bond between us, in spite of what I had chosen to do? Did she know why I had made this choice? Perhaps not. Perhaps she might then have gone first.

But she hadn't gone, I was sure of that. The air still carried a special gentleness; wistful, romantic. She could hardly credit that I no longer played the shared game.

I worked on, noticing how quickly I was becoming tired, scarcely able to raise my arm, having difficulty in spreading the mixture across the wall. It was as much as I could do to keep my eyes open. This was one way of stopping me, I knew it! But I was an automaton . . . nothing would stop me. I was doing this for Sarah, for our future life. I was not to be sidetracked . . . not to be beguiled. I would not turn my head, nor give a glance at the white shadow that was somewhere behind me . . . close, with a whiff of perfume, the vague flutter of material – muslin? Chiffon? I sensed it floating – I didn't see it, I didn't look, I would not turn my head. And I knew she had risked some frontier that neither I nor any of the others had dared to test. She had pressed against a divide. Had she crossed it? Was she nearer? Were we? If I turned . . . if I just glanced to show her my understanding, which was the only way in which I could return her gesture, *her love* . . .

I would *not* look. That was what she was asking of me, so I was determined not to do it . . . But why? It was a small gesture in return for so much. Surely such innocence deserved something.

God knows why I was so resolved; it wasn't like me to be so puritanical, unbending, and so ungenerous, though the perfume was by my shoulder and the room swam with her presence. She was telling me something. Something I had never expected, that stopped my hand in mid-air. A whisper, the words indistinct, but the meaning . . . the implication . . . the bewildering knowledge that she too understood that we were alone for the first time. Nothing made sense at that moment, but the innocence was surely gone! The last trick was being played. No one – no *man* – could win it.

Something brushed against my cheek. Nothing in the room could have done that. There was a gentle pressure close to my mouth, something falling across my face, a wisp of hair. A wisp of hair – a touch like a kiss.

I knew it wasn't possible. That was the one barrier nothing could break through. But I felt the touch . . . after she had gone. Oh yes, I knew she had gone.

I got up with my hand to my face, and made my way out of the room, and down the stairs in the dark. Then to the house, dazed . . .

I stood in front of the mirror in my room, and took my hand from my face. I don't know what I expected to see. On my cheek, close to my mouth, was just the faintest impression; like a brush of lipstick in our own times, a smudge. A mark. But this wouldn't rub away. It was not *on* my skin, but in it. It wasn't clear, but I could see it – a bruise . . . in the shape of two lips.

20

'May I speak to Dr Everett?'

'Is it important?'

'Or perhaps you might tell him Nick Morell phoned. He could call me back.'

'Hold on a moment.'

I was through to a switchboard; there was a muffled conversation at the other end, then Bobby Everett came on the line.

'That you, Nick?'

'Sorry to bother you. Is this a bad time?'

'That's all right. Anything wrong?'

'I wondered if you'd heard from Sarah.'

'Not a thing.'

'You said you were going to phone her last night.'

'I did. And I called Hans. He's not there either.'

'I'm getting a bit worried. One or two things have cropped up, things I'd like to discuss with you. You know – about what might have happened. I wondered if there was any chance of you dropping round?'

'I'm sorry, Nick. I'm up to my ears.'

At other times it had been difficult to keep him from calling. Now when I was concerned to see him . . .

'I'm thinking of going across to Munich.' It was best to make sure he realized how important the matter was to me. Sarah was our one point of contact. I couldn't tell him why I really wanted to talk to him.

'I'm not sure that's a good idea.' He sounded cautious.

'She might be in trouble. I must do something, and I thought you might have some ideas.'

'I'll talk to Andy and see what the programme is. If I can get away, I'll let you know.'

'It could be urgent,' I told him.

'I understand. Of course if you think you ought to go . . .'

'Okay. I'll wait for your call.'

The last thing I wanted to do was go to Germany: I had other things I wanted to talk about. Perhaps Everett wasn't the right man, perhaps Delmar would be more knowledgeable. But I could contact Delmar through Everett. Besides Everett must know something; he was a doctor, specializing in nervous diseases, I assumed. That was what a neurologist did, wasn't it?

I walked backwards and forwards in my study, talking to myself. I hadn't done that before, and as I caught sight of myself in the mirror I grinned. I was a classic case!

I'd spent a long time in front of that mirror that morning. Not something I usually do, but today was different. The mark on my cheek was still there. I touched it gently. I could have put my finger on it with my eyes shut, for it tingled. Sometimes I thought the spot was warm, sometimes cold – as though I had placed ice against my skin. I couldn't identify the feeling; it was like no sensation I had had before. I scoffed at myself for being light-headed, like a boy going to his first party and getting his first kiss! But the sensation stood up to my mockery. The mark showed no signs of fading.

I hung about the house waiting for Everett to return my call. But no call came.

I had no idea how long he and his associates stayed at their work, but I guessed that staff at the clinic, or the University, or wherever it was he and Delmar spent their time, would probably keep office hours. There had been no call by half-past five, so I phoned again.

'Mr Morell? There's a message for you. Just a moment . . . Yes, here it is. It's from Dr Everett. Shall I read it to you? "Will be at seven Georgina Road between eight and nine. Care to join us for a drink." '

'Is Dr Everett there?'

'Oh, no, he went a long time ago.'

The message might have lain there forever if I hadn't phoned.

I checked and found the address in Brighton, a few miles beyond Lewes. It was now after six. This was not as I had planned things, but it might be best to go.

The street was close to the seafront, just off a spacious Georgian square. The once splendid houses were now divided into apartments and offices. Number seven had solicitors on the ground floor, and accountants above, but one name by the entrance smacked of Everett's world – a medical partnership. The door was open so I went up. The apartment door was open as well, and the rooms beyond were crowded. The atmosphere was one of *bonhomie* and tobacco smoke. They were mostly a collection of young to middle-aged men, with a smattering of women. They had been dining and drinking well, and had reached a cheerful stage in the evening.

I was pleased to recognize Ruth Delmar. 'Nick! I didn't know you were here.'

'I've just arrived.'

'You've nothing to drink. This way.'

'Actually I'm looking for Bobby . . .' She didn't stop to listen, and we headed for a bar in the next room.

'Try the champagne. It's real, I don't know why. There's a new president or something. Cheers. Andy's here, and Bobby. I think Andy's now on the committee. Big deal.' She thought it was a great joke. I realized I was many glasses behind everyone else, but I had no intention of catching up.

'Let's find them,' she said. 'Whoops! There they are.'

Everett saw us and waved us across. I didn't bother to register the introductions.

'Great you could come,' said Everett.

'Any chance of a quiet word?'

'Of course. Of course.' He edged his way to the other side of the room. 'I suppose you're getting a bit worried,' he called over his shoulder. 'About Sarah. It's ridiculous that they haven't left a message.'

Away from the bar it was a little less crowded.

'Space to breathe,' said Everett. He leaned against the wall with a large glass of whisky. I wasn't sure if he was concentrating.

'I remembered something,' I told him. I had the story planned. 'And it worried me a bit.'

'Oh yes?' Everett was peering over my head at the rest of the crowd.

'You remember the painters?'

'The ones who heard footsteps?'

'Yes. Sarah drove them to London one evening, and they told her about it.'

'I remember.'

'She phoned several times after that, and laughed at the story. But she wanted to be sure I was all right. She didn't care to leave me alone in Longwood after that.'

'So?' He didn't appear to see the connection.

'It's obvious: she must have believed the story about the footsteps, or she wouldn't have worried.'

'I don't see what this proves.'

I nearly told him to put down the glass of whisky, but I stuck to the script. 'If she took that sort of rubbish seriously – seriously enough to worry whether I was okay – it's possible she was not quite herself even then.' I was keeping it very tentative.

'Not quite herself?'

'Look, if something's happened to her in Germany – if she's had a breakdown or something – it could have been building up for some time. She could have been on the verge of emotional trouble, or mental trouble, I don't know much about that sort of thing – that's your area, isn't it? I mean, if she's going to accept the painters' story – some fantasy – doesn't that mean there's something wrong?' I guessed the idea had got through, in spite of the fact that he kept sipping his drink and peering round the room.

He saw who he was looking for, and called, 'Over here.' There was no way of stopping Delmar from joining us. 'Nick has this theory, that Sarah has been building up to a breakdown ever since they went to the house. Maybe she heard what the painters heard. Maybe she had a similar experience.'

I didn't expect Delmar to know what he was babbling about, but he nodded thoughtfully.

I was half-way there. We were talking about Sarah, not about me, so it was safe to go further. 'Perhaps I'm wrong. But suppose she did see or hear something like they did, what does that mean? Is it just like having a dream? Is it completely illusory? Could they *all* be sharing an illusion? It seemed very consistent, didn't it? They heard the same thing several times, and they all said it was footsteps.'

'Sarah too?'

'No, she didn't say anything. I'm just supposing she might have had the same type of experience, and wondered if it would be a sign of anything serious.'

'Mentally?'

'Yes.'

'Have you any reason to suppose your painters are suffering a breakdown?'

'What?' I didn't follow.

'They had several weeks exposed to this situation, which they appeared to believe in. Are they suffering? Or have you some special reason to think Sarah might suffer in a way they don't?'

I hadn't worked out my story to that degree. 'For heaven's sake, I don't know about these damned painters! I don't care about them. I care about Sarah. All I'm asking is, would someone who may have had an experience like that . . . would they be likely then to have a breakdown? Is Sarah vulnerable because of that possibility?'

For two men who had been drinking for some time, they were both well able to pick out the weak points in my drama. And I was, indeed, dramatizing it now.

'Sarah hasn't had such an experience,' said Everett, 'not that we know of. Just the painters. And we have no evidence they are a whit the worse for it.'

'Maybe you're right to be concerned,' said Delmar, 'but not on account of that supposition. Besides . . .' He hesitated, they glanced at one another. I had a suspicion they might not be as drunk as I'd thought, but the idea passed. The feeling that they were putting on an act for me passed as well: after all, I was the one putting on the act. They could have no idea why I should be asking such questions, except out of concern for Sarah.

'Perhaps we could do with a refill,' said Everett. He indicated his glass; it was still half-full.

'You think so?' Delmar was doubtful.

'Perhaps not.' Everett leaned back against the wall.

Delmar looked at me thoughtfully. 'The question of fantasizing, visualizing . . . this experience of an unreality that is firmly believed to be reality . . . very interesting.'

I thought he was about to tell me something, but he stood a little unsteadily – perhaps mulling it over, more likely having forgotten what we were talking about.

'Funny you should bring this up,' said Everett. 'We spoke about it once before.'

'I don't remember,' I said.

'About Andy and his patient, Mrs Palmer in the wheelchair. Another aspect of the power of illusion.'

'Nothing definite,' Delmar reminded him.

Everett nodded wisely. 'I'd put a dollar on it.'

I didn't know what he meant, and wondered how to bring the subject back; but I didn't need to bother.

'Some types of illusion are as powerful as reality. To the person experiencing these states they *are* reality. Measurable reality.'

'What does that mean?'

'Mrs Palmer certainly feels pain. No one can tell her she isn't suffering. Her pain isn't an illusion. The girl who was pursued by her stepbrother . . . she wasn't screaming for fun nor to attract attention. She was fighting off an attacker, defending herself against rape.'

'What girl? What rape?'

'A published case. Nearly thirty when she was referred. Married, and unable to have a child.' He waved aside the facts. 'Not all relevant details. She suffered horrendous fantasies, imagining a stepbrother, much older, attacking her sexually . . . as indeed he had done when she was a child.'

This was a different world to the one I had intruded on, but it was very close.

'The husband brought her in. He had been away from home for a few days, and came back to find her threatening suicide.

He had to wring from her the story that her stepbrother had attacked her persistently during his absence. He had abused her, terrified her, knocked her about . . . she was definitely bruised. Then he raped her.'

'Did they call in the police?'

'He was dead, this stepbrother. Six years previously. Drunk driving at speed. Depends what you call suicide.'

It was moments before I realized the implications of what he was telling me and I couldn't understand my growing excitement. Not at first.

'But you say she had bruises?'

'The body reacts to blows.'

'If he wasn't there . . . if he was dead?'

'*She* saw him. It wasn't the only occasion – he'd appear most unpredictably. Embarrassing on occasions. Socially.'

'With other people there?'

'Yes.'

'Could *they* see him?'

'Of course not. I told you, he was dead.'

I could have told him something about that. But that was exactly the information I was so careful not to give.

'Is that what you meant by "measurable reality"? The bruises on the body were some sort of proof?'

'I suppose so, in a way,' Delmar shrugged. 'One can make much more accurate measurements than that, in clinical conditions. As Mrs Palmer feels pain, so this woman could hear this stepbrother coming. He had a rasping cough, smelled of drink . . .'

'She could smell him?' I remembered the perfume in the garden, in the stables – when she was close.

'The nerves can be wired to record. She certainly smelt what she said she smelt, although none of those testing her could see, hear, nor smell a thing.'

Everett looked at us thoughtfully. 'The thing that interested me was the measurement of the eyelids, flickering at each anticipated blow . . . and the blotch on her arm as though the blow was struck.'

Neither of them noticed . . . I couldn't help it, it was an

involuntary action . . . that I put my hand against my cheek. Had no one seen the outline of that kiss?

It wasn't easy getting any sense out of them: they were disinclined to concentrate, and I didn't want to make things too obvious. I pretended to join the party, carrying a drink around with me. I tried to reintroduce the question several times, but Everett and Delmar had lost interest. I began to think about leaving.

'Here's your man,' called Everett suddenly. He waved me over. A middle-aged man looked at me blankly. 'Dr Edwards will tell you about ghosts.'

Edwards was then more indignant than blank. 'Whatever do you mean?'

'This is Nick, an old friend of mine,' said Everett. 'He's interested in the power of the illusory. His house is haunted . . .'

'That's nonsense,' I said.

'People hear footsteps,' said Everett. 'I don't think Nick believes in such things.'

'He's quite right.' Edwards tried to move away.

'I've read your exemplary publication on the subject,' said Everett.

'It's not about ghosts.'

'But the general public . . . Nick, for example . . . would think it's about ghosts. People walking about at night . . .' Everett turned to me. 'Edwards wrote the paper we were telling you about. The girl with the stepbrother.'

'The dead stepbrother?' I was clearly impressed, and the stranger was flattered.

'She saw him, after he was dead?' I asked.

'She suffered a great deal from her fantasy.'

'But how could she? If there was in fact nobody there?'

'If it was important enough for her to go through the experience, then it was not impossible. Certainly it's not unique. You might say, she recreated an old situation.'

'It must have been appalling for her.'

'In one way, it certainly was.'

'In one way?'

'She had more than one desire, conscious or unconscious, that she had to satisfy.' He too had been enjoying the party but he managed to remain rather pompous and on his dignity.

'So in one other way, she wanted this to happen?'

'Wanted? Yes, for want of a better word.' I was relieved to see that Everett had moved away. 'What's happened in my case,' I said, 'in my house, is that workmen – several of them – heard the same thing. They may even have seen something. That makes any explanation more difficult, doesn't it – there being more than one witness?'

He wanted to go, but didn't wish to be too impolite. 'If for some reason the need is strong enough, and the recipient's in a certain state of mind – emotional, physical, disturbed perhaps – then it's not impossible to create a state in which seemingly inexplicable experiences occur. The powerful experience of the patient in question was that she was dominated by the attacks of her stepbrother when she was young. The consequences were quiescent for years. After she was married, they returned in dramatic form: she visualized the dead man as though he were still there. I'm sure Everett will be able to get you a copy of my paper.'

I was more or less blocking his way as he tried to leave. 'One last point. This is very convincing, understandable, because you say it meant so much to the girl. But what about a situation where there's no cause. Suppose these painters . . .'

'Painters?'

'The workmen in my house, or anyone else for that matter – suppose they saw or heard someone . . . people who weren't really there . . . ghosts as Everett called them. Just creatures from the past, who appear . . . consistently?'

'I really have to go. My companions . . .'

'Why should such figures materialize rather than any others? If I saw strangers from the last century, several times . . . people I had no connection with . . . why should they take *their* particular shapes?'

He stopped with sudden interest. 'You've had this experience?'

'Not me, the painters . . .' If only I had had the courage to admit it!

'I can't comment at second hand,' he said. 'There's probably some incident, a forgotten episode, a shared mythology, a story, or nursery rhymes . . . we draw on childhood. These painters of yours may find a germinal idea has contributed to the character of their illusion. Now I really have to . . .'

I didn't try to stop him as he pushed past.

'Boring old bastard,' said Everett. 'Sorry to lumber you with him.'

Delmar appeared at my side. 'Learn anything?'

'We create our own ghosts because we need them.'

'What about Sarah?' asked Everett. I couldn't think what he was talking about. 'Did you tell him you thought she'd perhaps been seeing things as well?'

'Of course not.'

'I thought that was the theory?'

'There was no point telling him. Besides, I could be wrong. Sarah is probably swanning around Germany with Hans.'

'The treatment worked,' Everett threw up his hands. 'A little party and the patient is restored to cheerful optimism.'

They were both still there when I slipped away a few minutes later.

On the way home I tried to work out the implications of what I'd learned. Neither Everett nor Delmar had been their usual sober, circumspect selves, but Edwards was another matter, and he was a specialist on the subject. He'd written a paper about a girl who had been pursued by a dead man. That corresponded closely enough, for I'd been pursued by dead people – the difference was that she had conjured her ghost out of her own past and I hadn't. Mine had presented themselves independently; they weren't part of a 'shared mythology'; I could remember no nursery rhyme about such a Victorian family. Edwards's theory didn't cover my experience, though I could see how it had worked with the dead stepbrother: something as traumatic as that would leave a deep scar on the abused victim. But I was no victim and I had nothing to recreate; the family that now shared my life seemed to have a separate existence. Could I have used them to bring to life something within my own personality? I doubted it.

I had a very odd feeling as I turned into the drive at Longwood. I didn't fancy running the car down to the stables, so I parked it outside the house and went in.

Immediately, I knew I was not alone.

I stood in the hall, in the dark, softly closing the door behind me, uncertain why I preferred not to turn on the light, but feeling that I might be exposed. Darkness in Longwood had always been a safe and comforting thing, and I expected it to be so now. But it wasn't. Something was different. For the first time in this house, I felt uneasy.

The windows allowed moonlight to fall across the hall. I grew used to the gloom and saw the place was empty. From where I stood I could see the bottom of the staircase. It was as I had left it, silent, empty. Maybe it was just strange to come back to the deserted house after being packed into those rooms of noisy humanity.

This was the hall in which I had first heard the sound of footsteps myself – the dancing footsteps with which I suppose I had fallen in love. I would have welcomed such a sweet and frivolous sound now, but *they* had never come into the house since those first few days. Besides, the sensation I had was not like any I had had in the house before. Never had I moved so cautiously, been so wary, as though an enemy waited behind a door. Could something have happened while I had been away? Were they angry with me because I had left them so long? Was that peacock of a soldier waiting to inflate somewhere in the corridor? I didn't think so, but the warning was there. A whisper . . . as I had once heard a drone of insects. God, yes, now I understood! It was the family who were warning me . . . telling me to be on my guard. The girl was whispering, not from close at hand – there was no perfume this time and nothing moved in the dark. Just an air of anxiety; I caught their fear, and my skin prickled with human alarm.

I glanced at my watch; it was after one o'clock. Perhaps I was tired. Perhaps I had allowed the conversation at the party to influence me. What was it they had said? Was it possible I had some reason to create a fear like this? I could think of nothing. I was not going to remain rooted to this spot for the rest of the night. My instincts could be wrong, these guardian spirits could be wrong. I took a couple of steps softly across the hall. I froze . . . I didn't know why, but I froze. Something was there.

But nothing moved at the foot of the stairs; nothing moved outside. No owl, fox, dog. Nothing.

All right. If I had reason to stand so stock still a second time, what was the cause? And if there was danger, where was the evidence? I looked round the hall. Even in the inadequate light of the moon I could see everything was in place and the windows were closed. I went up the steps watchfully. Evidence might lie elsewhere.

I had counted the rooms in the house. Eight bedrooms, one of which was turned into a billiard room. I guessed there was no reason to go through the rooms over the kitchen: it was a part that could be locked off, and I turned the key that closed it. A wide landing lay under the arched roof, part glass cupola. I was still unwilling to switch on lights, and I could see well enough. All the rooms led from this landing. I headed towards my own bedroom.

The door was shut! That halted me. I usually left my door open. Had I closed it as I had hurried out?

I pushed it gently open. The moon was on the other side of the house, and not enough light filtered through to see clearly. I turned on the light. It was empty, but one curtain had been pulled a little across the window, and there was a slight pressure on the bed where someone had sat. I examined the window, which was shut. The painter had once said to me, 'You should have those windows fixed. Anyone could get in.'

I looked in my bathroom, then I went back on to the landing. Now I was sure I could hear something – faintly, as though something had moved, and then . . . even more faintly, someone was breathing, from a room across the landing. I pushed open the door and turned on the light there too. Sarah turned in her sleep. She was in one of the twin beds. She opened her eyes and blinked at me, uncomprehending. Then she smiled wanly. 'Hello darling,' she said.

21

I switched on the lamp beside the bed. Her fair hair was untidy over the pillow. She tried to lift her head. She looked very tired. I couldn't say anything.

She held out a hand. 'What's the matter, darling?'

'You gave me a shock. I didn't expect you.'

'Didn't you see my car in the garage?'

'I didn't go there.'

'I left you a note in the hall.'

'I didn't turn on the light.'

There were shadows under her eyes, and her hand was hot, moist with sweat. She looked surprised. 'Why ever not?'

'I guessed there was someone in the house.'

'You are clever.' She smiled, but she seemed some distance away.

'Are you all right? Why are you here?' I didn't mean it to sound like that.

'Hans brought me back to London. He wanted to drive me here, but I told him I could drive myself. I didn't mean to upset you. I don't think I'm very well.' It was an effort for her to talk.

'Do you know what's wrong?'

'Just a bit run down. Nothing to fuss about. You know these German doctors.'

'What doctors?'

'I went for a few days to a nursing home, just outside Munich.'

'Oh my God!' She looked so exhausted. I'd never seen her so frail.

'I'm all right, darling.'

She seemed determined not to upset me. I got the feeling that she wouldn't have come back unless she'd really had to.

'Sarah. Sarah, I'm sorry.'

'It's not your fault.'

'You've been doing everything. Holding the whole bloody shambles together.'

'It's not a shambles.'

'Oh, God.' I couldn't think how she'd got here in this condition. Hans must have been mad to let her travel alone.

'Please, Nick, don't worry. I'm a little depleted, that's what he said. He spoke very good English.'

I hadn't kissed her. I could hardly touch her. I was sick with self-contempt. This was my work: I could hardly believe what I had been doing. What meaningless fantasy had so taken over my life that it had obliterated her? What had I thrown away? And for what? The academic puzzle I had been exploring with Everett and his friends was meaningless compared to this reality, this loyalty, this love that I had treated callously. I didn't give a damn how that might sound; at that moment I knew she was the only thing life had to offer. I didn't know how I could repay the debt I owed. And because it was Sarah there was no debt.

But even as I stood beside the bed, still holding her hand, more fragile than I remembered it, even then – like a separate mechanism working under its own steam, pushing forward from the back of my mind to demand attention, pushing into the forefront until I had to take account of it – something was saying, in a whisper growing gradually insistent: what was this going to do to my relationship with my beloved ghosts? What would happen with Sarah in the house? Or was she so ill that she could be safely confined to bed? How would this intrusion . . . I was angry, pushing the thoughts into the back of my mind. Sarah was my life, not an intrusion!

There was no silencing the voice, however. With Sarah in Longwood, could I still continue in my idyllic world? Still work with them? Could I finish the job I had started? Was I to be won by kisses where I had not succumbed to threats? I couldn't blot out these thoughts, I couldn't once and for all finish with that dream. If it went now, I knew it could never be recalled.

I sat on the edge of the bed. Sarah had closed her eyes, which were circled by shadows I had never seen before. This was how she would look when she was old, I knew, and the taste of tears came to my mouth for I loved her with the shadows and the lines that fever had drawn across her face. Loved her, but could not dispel the whisper from my mind. Two conflicting prizes; two conflicting worlds. I couldn't have both.

She didn't move, but just lay breathing a little unnaturally. I put my hand gently on her forehead. She was sweating. I stayed there until I was sure she had gone back to sleep.

I lay awake listening to hear if she was all right. About dawn I slept, but I woke after a couple of hours and went through to see her. She still slept. I went back to look at her every half hour. I was getting nervous, and wondering if I should call a doctor, when she woke. 'I feel much better,' she managed to say but her listless eyes belied her.

'I'll phone the doctor,' I said.

'There's no need. They say I've been working too hard. It's rubbish.'

'I hear he's very good. Just to put my mind at rest.'

'Darling, phone Bobby.'

'Bobby?'

'He's a doctor.' She had struggled to sit upright, but now she fell back. She was weaker than I'd thought.

I got in touch with the switchboard at the clinic. 'Is Dr Everett there?'

'I'm afraid he's in conference.'

'I have a message for him. Tell him his cousin is back from Germany, and that she's very ill. She's at Longwood, and she wants to see him. The message is from Nicholas Morell. Please see he gets it immediately. The last time a message passed between us, it lay around for hours.'

'I'm quite sure, Mr Morell . . .'

I put the phone down and went back to Sarah, who had gone to sleep again. Sweat had made her hair quite damp. If Everett didn't phone soon, I would most certainly call the local doctor.

As I walked up and down outside her room, even the most callous of the voices that spoke to me had the intelligence to keep silent. If the thought of hanging concentrates a man's mind wonderfully, the thought of death had brought mine back to reality abruptly.

There was no reaction from Everett at the end of half an hour. I had begun to look up numbers of the local doctors when I heard a car pull up outside. Everett jumped out and pushed open the front door.

'Where is she?' He was already going up the stairs at a run.

'The guest room. Opposite mine.'

He was by her bed examining her as I joined him.

'What's her temperature?' He had a hand on her brow.

'I don't know.'

'How'd she get here?'

'She drove from London.'

'Christ.' He looked at me angrily.

Sarah looked up, saw him, and smiled. 'Hello Bobby.'

I had a pang of utmost jealousy: I had thrown away everything. But all I wanted was for her to be all right; if she was well again then I'd accept that she was entitled to love anyone. She could even love Everett.

'Make us a cup of tea,' said Everett. I was glad to have a reason to leave the room.

Everett followed me into the kitchen a few minutes later. 'It's more or less what she says. Some doctor in Munich saw her, and told her she wasn't ready to travel.'

'Hans should have stopped her.'

'She would have made the trip on her own if he hadn't flown over with her.'

'I thought you said you'd been in touch by phone? How was it you didn't know she was ill?'

'It's not possible to diagnose by telephone,' he said drily. 'Besides, she didn't suggest then that there was anything wrong. She was perfectly all right until about ten days ago.'

'What's the matter?'

'Exhaustion. Diminished resistance. She's picked up some virus, but she's throwing it off. It's going to leave her weak for a bit.'

We took the tea up to Sarah's room. Her eyes lit up as I put the tray on a table beside her. 'This is lovely. Isn't it lovely?' She was like a child, so ready to be happy, eager to be pleased.

'I have to go,' said Everett. 'I'll drop in tomorrow.'

'Does she need anything?'

'Just rest.'

She took only a little of the tea, watching me as I wandered about the room.

'Are you tired? Do you want to sleep? I'll leave you.'

'Stay.'

I was uneasy, and stood looking out of the window.

'I'm sorry, Nick. I never meant to land on you like this.'

I asked, 'Have you been living with Bobby?' She looked quite shocked. 'I'm sorry. I know you haven't. I just had to ask.'

'Of course not, I hardly know him. We haven't met since we were children.'

'I know. I know.'

'I haven't been living with anyone, Nick.'

After what I had done it was no business of mine: she was entitled to live with whoever she chose. I wondered about Hans.

'No one?'

'How could I? I love you.' My mind was split down the middle. One part was overjoyed that, no matter what I had destroyed, some essence was still safe. I was being offered a gift I didn't deserve: a perverse neglect had failed to kill love. And at the same time, the other part of my mind was cunningly aloof, making judgements, quickly suspicious, telling me this fevered visit was a trick – an attempt to win me back from whatever magic it was that had kept me here, that had divided us. Sarah was in bed in Longwood with all the marks of illness because this was the only way she could win my sympathy and make me feel guilty. Would I give up my mystery, turn back to a humdrum world to look after her? Was this clumsy plan going to succeed? Everett had probably put her up to it; I must guard against it or my secret world would evaporate . . .

I didn't argue with that, I knew it was true. I would have to be careful, rouse no suspicions, appear to go along with this change in events, be pleased to be able to help restore her, do anything to give myself a little time, to keep alive my liaison with the beloved shadows. I guessed that all I needed was a very short time. So many barriers had vanished . . . what else was possible between us?

And the first part of my mind looked on in horror at my corruption and deceit. It was a humiliating insight.

But Sarah had no such awareness, no cruel judgement. She had put down her cup and watched me with loving eyes. 'Is your work finished?'

'Most of it.'

She hesitated. 'You phoned about the stables?'

She didn't ask a proper question, but I understood.

'Yes. That's all there's left to do.'

A few minutes later she fell asleep. Her day was punctuated in this way; she might be talking to me, her eyes would be following me around the room, when her arm would drop on the quilt and she would be sleeping. I tiptoed from the room, something whispering in my head that it was an escape. The house was as good as empty – Sarah was not really there, though I had an alibi in her, confined to bed, hardly able to move, weak, frail, half-awake most of the time. I slipped from the house, conspirators chuckling softly in my ears.

I wasn't sure why I was so secretive. Sarah didn't care what I did to Longwood as long as I was happy. But that wasn't sufficient, for part of what I wanted to achieve was deception. Approval by her, or by anyone, would have destroyed the mystery and the magic. My pleasure in this relationship with the people at Longwood lay in its secrecy, in the fact that it was a conspiracy. Perhaps guilt was part of the pleasure. I didn't stop to think about it, for at times the critical, disapproving part of my mind would take over and deluge me with scorn and contempt.

I knew *they* were trying to stampede me back to the stables, for there were urges for me to complete what I'd started. No more back-tracking, no stabs of conscience, no considerations for anyone, least of all Sarah; the job could be finished with a few marvellous blows with the sledgehammer I had carried around for so long. Get it. *Get it now!* Splinter the wretched monstrosity where it stands. That would be the bold decision – to take sides, show where I stood, for then we should be as one.

That destruction, that shattering impact, was surely a consummation devoutly to be wished?

But I always managed to shy off. Actually, shy off, like a startled horse. I would be hurrying to the stables with that half-formed resolution to be done with it, then something would seem to start up from the ground and I'd literally swerve off – down the path to the flight pond, or into the walled garden where no one followed. Bridges might be there, silent over his earth, grim and muddy, not giving me a second glance – although a couple of times he brought himself to ask, with a gallantry that grated, 'How's the lady, then?' and 'What news of the lady?'

Everett called the following day, as he'd said he would. I left them alone and they were together for quite a time. As he left he said to me, 'Temperature's dropping. She's a little better. It's going to take some time.'

When I went up to see Sarah she was smiling. 'Do you know what Bobby said? He has such odd ideas.'

'What?'

'He asked me if I thought I was ill in place of you.'

'What the devil is that supposed to mean?'

'He thinks you might not be able to be ill, so I'm ill on your behalf.'

'That's *very* stupid.'

'He thinks we can carry an illness for another person. If someone is locked up in an illness . . .'

'Which I'm not.'

'Then someone close can take on the illness, or part of it . . . help to unload the other person.'

'So I'm really the one who's ill, not you?' I scoffed.

'It's a theory. You can carry other things for people, not just an illness. He says children do it for their parents: they take over unrecognized states of mind, unconsciously, and continue to fight old battles for them. You know, carry on their prejudices. Things get transmitted that way. Legends, morality, culture.'

'Has he been here for the last hour talking that sort of rubbish?'

222

'It's very interesting.'

'I thought he was supposed to be a doctor, and trying to get you better?'

'I am getting better. Don't you think so, Nicky? Look, I can sit up.'

She made a brave effort, but soon tired and slipped down again.

'He's exhausted you.' I was angry. I had the old feeling of being threatened that I had so often felt with Everett. 'I won't let him come again.'

'But I want him to. He's a great help. You have to admit, he does make you laugh.' I wasn't laughing, but I was glad to see how she viewed him.

'It's a mad theory,' I said. 'You were in Germany when you became ill. I was here.'

'I don't think that matters if the concern is strong enough. The love.'

God knows her love was strong enough, but I could see no sense in Everett's ideas. Though as usual – as with his damn story about the woman in the wheelchair – his wretched comments continued to harass me. I got the feeling there might be a germ of meaning in what he said. It was true; people did carry ideas for other people. Students carried teachers' ideas; children indeed carried the patterns passed to them by parents; lovers carried hopes and fears for their beloveds. But could Sarah carry an illness for me? If so, what illness? Was she sweating out my fever? Getting rid of poisons that I couldn't get rid of for myself? It was too ridiculous, far-fetched. The sort of hi-falutin' nonsense that would appeal to Everett. For a doctor, it was suspiciously like mysticism, and I wondered how that would be looked on by the medical council. Niggling in the back of my mind was the thought that I should report him, but that I tossed aside contemptuously.

I had meant to make use of my time to finish all outstanding duties that day . . . and that meant only one thing really. But I found myself drawn back time and again to Sarah's room, impatient when I found her asleep. I tiptoed away again, and waited until I heard her move. Somehow I had to destroy this inhibition that Everett had cast over me, like a spell, and the best way to do it was through her.

'When did he say he was coming back?'

'Bobby? He'll be here tomorrow.'

'He's coming every day?'

'Till I'm better. Do you mind?'

'You brought him here deliberately, didn't you?'

'What do you mean?'

'You know very well. You brought Bobby to Longwood that first time. You'd made up your mind to do it – you had a special plan.'

She was eating grapes, watching me. Then she nodded.

'What was behind it? What was the idea?'

'I wanted him to meet you.'

'Be honest, it wasn't just that.'

'No.' She shook her head slowly.

'What else?'

'I thought he might help.'

'Help who? With what?'

'I hoped he'd be able to help you, because I thought there was something wrong with you.'

She was so gentle – it was admitted so softly, so innocently, this great deception, this betrayal. Although I don't suppose she saw it that way, it was. She had brought in this outsider.

'*What* did you think was wrong with me?'

'You changed, quite suddenly. One day you were like you had always been, then you were different. You lost interest in all our old things, you stayed here, you didn't go back to the office: I seemed to vanish from your life. You were a stranger pretending to be Nicholas. I would have been happier if you had fallen in love with someone else.'

'Your friend Bobby told me that he had explained it to you: I was taking time off. And it's possible to fall out of love, without falling for someone else.'

'This was different. Deeper. You suddenly went blank. You were telling lies, putting on an act; there was something you didn't want anyone to find out.'

'Like what?'

'Something about yourself.'

'You're talking like Everett. I suppose you got these ideas from him?'

She shook her head. 'Is this upsetting you?'

'Of course not. Why should it?'

'Because I'm saying you aren't the person you thought you were, not invincible, not immortal. We aren't young forever, which is sad. Bobby says you won't come to terms with life . . . or did he say death?'

'He really is an unexpectedly second-rate philosopher. It's those years in the States and all those spoon-fed, *Potted*, *Digest*-type of books they study over there.'

'You really think that, Nick?'

'I think he should mind his own business. What help did you expect from him?'

'He wasn't much help.' She looked towards the window, to the setting sun where red clouds were fringing the skyline, suddenly very sad; wistful. My heart went out to her. Why did I persist in this angry interrogation when she needed rest?

'Bobby said that something simple – like the fact we were going to get married, or a change of house or job, something like that – can trigger off unexpected things in people. Like a depression.'

'He thinks I was depressed?'

'He thought it was possible you were fighting off depression. That you had turned to something else to save yourself from it.'

'To drink, perhaps?'

'No, to some sort of unreality. He said, to "fantasy".'

I looked at her blankly, trying to read what she thought in her eyes. But she was heavy-lidded, tired.

'That's very astute,' I mocked.

'He doesn't think it now,' she said.

'Oh? Why not?'

'I don't know.'

'He's a specialist isn't he? In this sort of thing?'

'Not really, he's a neurologist. His friend Andy is the specialist.'

'What does Bobby think now?'

225

She shrugged. She made an effort, but she was very tired. 'Maybe you had a breakdown. Maybe you just wanted to drop out, got tired of making money, and backed off from all the pushing and shoving. It might be a crisis in your life, and you want to change direction. He thinks it's no big deal. That's what he said.'

So the expert had been fooled: the idea of living a fantasy as an alternative had been considered and discarded. I must have played the part better than I supposed.

'What do *you* think?' I asked.

'I guess he knows what he's talking about.'

It was a moment of triumph . . . a triumph for the elated, cunning creature hugging itself in the back of my brain.

'So we can still get married?' I said.

She was lying back, sleepily, but now she opened her eyes, wide, caring, but a little wary. 'I don't think so,' she said.

'Why not?'

'Not yet.'

'Why?'

'*I* don't know . . . But you know, don't you?'

She wasn't being clever – this was not a trick. Lovingly she had put a finger on the heart of the pain. There was nothing I could say. No matter who else I fooled, I couldn't fool her.

22

My moment of triumph was shared of course; I should have expected that. The elation was evident as soon as I left the house. I had decided to walk under the window behind which I knew Sarah was sleeping, to stay within earshot . . . if she needed me, if she called out. But as I stood there I was aware of the amusement in the air. I had cleared all decks, and now shared a secret that was eternally safe. No one suspected what really bound me to this place. Wise men of science had been proved fools. The balding and bespectacled man was bowing and bobbing his admiration by a line of shrubs, just beyond my line of vision, suggesting I was as cunning as they were, outwitting those who had been set to watch me. Everett, and no doubt Delmar, had suspected a version of the truth, and had discarded it. There was an invisible rubbing of hands: I was a match for my own generation; now to the business of theirs.

I didn't want to run foul of the family now. In fact, one half of my mind was all for racing down to the stables faster than they themselves. One mighty swipe, the chimneypiece would be demolished, and the story would be over. I smiled my readiness. There was a sense of excitement, a rush and tumble of activity. Perhaps they were all there, perhaps even she was. It was an excitement that smacked of hysteria. They were rushing and I was responding: *don't stop or delay!*

I went a few steps with the invisible tide, down the path towards the stables. Then I stopped. I wasn't sure what I'd heard. A sound from Sarah's room? They assured me not. So a step or two more, then I found I'd stopped again. I was a man being manipulated by strings. Bridges was at the gate of the walled garden – what must he be thinking of this erratic stop-go along the drive?

'Any better today, then?' called Bridges. He hardly knew Sarah, yet he was genuinely concerned about her. I doubted if he'd ask the time of day if I were ill.

'Coming along,' I called back. 'It's going to take time.'

A curt nod from Bridges, and he disappeared into the garden.

I was aware I was alone, motionless with indecision. Lacking the courage to go and do my worst? I doubted that: I didn't think it was lack of courage. Lack of commitment, perhaps? Waiting for the impetus . . . still uncertain. If their shared love and dedication was not enough to sustain my resolution, what was? How could I be persuaded to finish the job? And at that moment for the first time at Longwood I felt deserted. An air of malice blew up from the woods. The tops of the trees shivered in a north-east wind, and the cold got through to me. I felt really on my own. It was foolish of them to use such tactics – if that was what they were doing. They should remember that they had tried coercion before, and it had failed.

But this time a wave of terror swept over me, sudden physical panic. I spun round, desperate to confront them, to restrain them – pleading. Yes, I was ready to do exactly what they asked – I mouthed the words – I would smash anything for them. Only in God's name, they must not . . . they must not . . .

I didn't finish the thought, racing into the house and up the stairs. Sarah was in her room, at the window, struggling to raise it; she had opened it about a foot. The cold air whipped in.

I grabbed her. 'Sarah! Love. What is it?'

She didn't see me properly. Her eyes were clouded; perspiration shone on her; her hair was matted. But under her nightdress she was as cold as ice. I led her back to bed, unsteadily, feebly protesting, trying to draw her arm away. 'So hot. I must open the window, Nick! I'll be better if I open the window.'

'I'll do it. Stay in bed. Keep warm.'

I opened the top of the window a fraction. 'I'll phone Bobby. See what he thinks.'

She was vehement, spitting out with sudden malice, 'No. I don't want him.'

I was shocked.

'Sarah, he's looking after you.'

'I don't want him.'

She wasn't even looking at me properly; she was focusing over my head.

I went cold and spun round. There was nothing there. I might have known they never came into the building.

'What is it?' I asked. 'What are you looking at?'

'Nothing.' She turned away, and I knew what she'd meant when she spoke earlier about my lying. When I thought she was asleep, I closed the window again, and fastened it.

I walked to the stables, taking time, *willing* that I should be observed. I went to the front and stood there, whispering. I said, 'Don't you dare,' very softly. But the orchard and the long wood and the winter-chilled world were frostily aware and listening. It was loud enough for them to hear.

'Night, then,' shouted Bridges.

I was sorry to see him go. I had a hostage in my house, and for once I could have done with another human creature to give protection to its own kind.

I couldn't get Sarah to take anything to eat or drink that evening. She pushed aside the rest of the grapes and said they were bitter. I didn't take much myself. I sat down in the sitting-room with the door open, so that I could see the foot of the staircase.

I heard Sarah twice, and both times I found her moving like a sleep-walker across the room. She was angry, like a drowsy child, when I led her back to bed. It was late before I went upstairs myself. I could hear her breathing deeply across the landing. She seemed to be at peace. I tried to keep awake, but I fell asleep listening to her.

Somewhere in the house something was sliding over the wooden floor. It was shuffling, stopping, darting forward. I heard it in sleep, bringing an image of people moving over sand. I sat up, startled. There was silence – I must have been mistaken. Then the wild sweep over the floor again. What in God's name was it? Leaves being blown in autumn? From the foot of the stairs? Something fluttering over the flooring? In the hallway, where she had danced? Nothing moved now.

There was no sound of breathing from across the landing.

I ran into Sarah's room. The light was on and the room empty. I shouted, 'Sarah! Sarah!' There was no reply; the strange shuffling started again.

I went down two stairs at a time. The front door was open, the north-east wind blowing in bursts, letters from the hall table scudding across the floor. I shouted for her down the corridor, but I knew she must be outside. I raced into the garden. For a moment I wondered which way she had gone, then I had no doubts. The wind went through my pyjamas like a knife, as I turned down towards the stables.

There was no sign of her. The top half of the stable-door was blowing in the wind, hitting the rusty latch like a hammer with each blast. I ran over the loose gravel, with crowing laughter in my ears. We had been successful! I was expected to join in the crescendo of delight, for our conspiracy was safe, and Everett and his agents would never be a threat.

I went up the stairs, my heart pounding with effort, and saw her at the door of the room. God knows what she intended, but she had the rusty broken knife in her hand. She didn't seem to recognize me and lifted it to defend herself. I grabbed her wrist and took the blade from her. She started to push past me, but I held her. She was dressed only in her thin nightgown, and her body was as cold as a corpse!

I don't know what I screamed into the dark. I don't think it made sense. But the gauntlet was thrown down to them all now, challenging those hidden faces.

She fought with me all the way to the house, and she was so frail, her blows so feeble, that I had hardly the heart to grip her tightly. But I had to. The front door was still open, wind blowing letters over the floor. As I pulled her up the steps into the hall she yelled at me, looking her hatred: 'The dog! The dog!' A meaningless and hysterical scream.

I slammed the front door behind us and she passed out. But *what* dog did Sarah know? I carried her upstairs. I couldn't risk leaving her alone, so I took her to my bed and tried to bring her round. I rubbed some warmth into her arms and shoulders; I wrapped blankets round her. She hardly breathed for hours. I thought she had frozen to death.

At dawn, as the sun flickered on pale clouds, she opened her eyes. It took her a moment to realize where she was, then she smiled.

'You've brought me to our bed, Nick. How nice.' She went back to sleep almost immediately. I wrapped myself up and sat beside her. It was hours before she came round.

I spent the morning sitting watching her. I put a chair by the window and looked through some of the letters that I collected from the hall floor. My mind wasn't on them – I was far too shaken – but for the first time in a long while I felt a return of interest in my work, in what the company was trying to do. It was a secondary concern: every movement in the bed concentrated my attention. She was restless, jerking, turning, in an uneasy sleep. Every now and again she tried to say something. I leaned down to listen, but it was meaningless. About mid-day she started sweating again. I got a handkerchief and went to run it under the tap, thinking it might help to bring down her temperature. When I went back into the bedroom, Sarah was outside, in the hall, shutting the door behind her. She must have taken the key for I heard her turning it on the outside.

I ran to grab her but the door was already locked.

'Open the door, Sarah! Open it! Sarah . . .' No answer. I could hear her on the stairs.

I was angry and alarmed. Something about her frightened me. It was like dealing with an animal, cunning, unpredictable. I wondered if she had really been asleep – had it all been a long-drawn-out charade to catch me off my guard? And why? She knew I was doing my utmost to help. I heard the kitchen door close. What the devil was she doing? I had the feeling she was no longer sane.

I remembered our bathroom had a second door to the landing, cursed myself for loss of time, and ran back. I went out of the second door, down the stairs, and along the corridor to the kitchen. She was searching in a cupboard where I kept household tools: I didn't think she'd even known it was there. She looked startled, like a trapped animal, bewildered that I had been able to follow her. She had a pair of pincers in her hand, and threw them at me, but they went wide. She was scrabbling for something else when I got my arms around her. She gave such a howl of pain that I nearly let go. She started to fight again, but, thank God, was too weak. The strength went out of her and she lay limp as I carried her back to bed. The key was in the lock; I put it in my pocket.

She was unconscious in the bed for hours, which alarmed me. But it was better that way as I could watch her. I didn't know what the hell to do.

'I was never like this,' I was saying to myself. 'God knows, I wasn't like this.' But I wondered; I wasn't sure. Had I in fact been as obsessed? As cunning? As ill? It was as though I had infected her; she had caught my disease. What was happening to her? Was she seeing them? In contact? What in God's name were they plotting?

I was completely cut off from contact with them . . . excommunicated, if that was the word. But I could feel the malice in the air. Now they had a weapon I could not match. They would go on using her, abusing her, until she dropped dead or they got what they wanted. Was I prepared to stay in that fight, while Sarah was destroyed? Let them win this bizarre squabble: Sarah and I could take up our lives again, fantasies over, back to normality, as though nothing had changed. Why was I so stubborn, why must this struggle go on? Why did I feel the heart of our very beings was at stake? That was surely an exaggeration – let it go, let them assert their mastery. They held all the cards.

I locked the bathroom door, and the bedroom door, so that there was no way out, and went downstairs to phone Everett.

'Hello. How is the patient?' he wanted to know.

'Her temperature goes pretty high, off and on.'

'She'll do that for a couple of days.'

'Are you coming to see her?'

'I'll be along later.'

'She's restless. Gets out of bed. I don't think she knows what she's doing part of the time.'

'Can you keep an eye on her?'

'There are problems.'

'Anything particular?'

I didn't know what to tell him. 'I think she's troubled about something.'

'We know that, don't we? She's disturbed about you.'

'Well, I'm okay and she isn't,' I said sharply. 'We need to do something for her.'

'Like what?'

'I don't know, I'm not a doctor.' He seemed to be throwing things back on my shoulders.

'I think you can help,' he said blandly.

'How?'

'For a start, what you're doing now must be a great comfort to Sarah. To realize how much you are concerned about her will suggest she is still loved. I think that has something to do with what's wrong.'

'Look, Dr Everett,' I said, 'she's trying to slip out of the house. She's managed it once – in her nightclothes.'

'Any idea what for?'

I was back on the spot again. What could I tell him? That she was on the side of those I had once thought angels and now knew to be devils? He'd think I was out of my mind.

'Did you say to her she might be carrying my illness?' I asked him.

A slight pause. 'We discussed the theory.'

'Would it have to be physical illness?'

'What's that?' His surprise was obvious even over the phone.

'What sort of a disease? Just physical? Or can people take over something mental? A breakdown?'

There was a change in his voice. 'Look,' he said, 'stay with her. Keep her warm and quiet. I'll be over.'

I went back to the bedroom. Sarah had her eyes shut and seemed to be asleep. Apparently she hadn't moved. I went to the window and closed the curtains slightly. As I turned, I saw she was watching me. 'Why did you lock the doors?' she asked.

'If you go outside you'll make yourself really ill.'

She lay quiet for a long time.

'What were you doing?'

'I phoned Bobby.'

She tried to control it, but that made her very agitated. 'He's no use as a doctor,' she said. 'He did nothing for you.'

'I didn't want him to.'

'Neither do I.'

'Have you seen the girl?' I asked.

That took her off guard. For a moment she was shocked, and stared at me, her eyes unclouded momentarily, showing she understood. Then she said, 'What girl?'

There was no point saying any more. They were here somewhere, so I had to be careful. I was tempted to try to communicate with them through Sarah's mind, but I had no idea what that might do to her.

'You haven't told me all the changes you've made,' she said.

Sometimes it was like talking to Sarah; sometimes she seemed a stranger. I was cautious. 'I'll show you when you're better.'

She seemed to be making up her mind about something, then

she said, 'You know what you phoned about? The fireplace in the stables? You can take it out. Destroy it. The old one is still there. I don't really like that ugly modern one.' She was smiling gently, as if to make things easy for me.

'I do,' I told her. 'I like it. It's a symbol.'

'What of?'

'I don't know. Integrity. Human obstinacy – love – indestructibility. Something.'

Her eyes went cold, and she turned away.

'The place was so beautiful in the old days.' Even her voice was different. Momentarily she was the beautiful ventriloquist's dummy.

'How do you know about the old days?' I asked.

She turned to me, and for a moment it was Sarah, tender, pleading. 'Nicky, it would be easier for me . . . for both of us.'

'To be intimidated?' I asked. 'To be destroyed? There'd be nothing of us left.'

She whispered, 'I'm frightened of the dog.'

That made my blood go cold. What were they doing to her? I jumped up. 'Look,' I said, indicating the room with a sweep of the hands. 'There's no dog! They can't get into the house.'

She looked at me blankly. 'Who?' she asked.

I couldn't say anything, the ground was shifting too fast. I knew I wasn't going to resolve anything by reason. It was beyond reason. There had to be another way. Perhaps Everett could help.

There was no sign of him by evening. I phoned the clinic again, but got no reply. I'd had nothing to eat all day, and Sarah had refused everything. I was getting very tired, and a little panicky. I had never had a moment of fear for myself all the months I'd been alone in this house, but now I was terrified for Sarah, and I knew I was frightened of her as well.

When Everett did come, it was after nine o'clock. 'Sorry, there was an emergency,' he said.

'This is an emergency,' I told him grimly.

I went upstairs with him but he said he thought it best if he saw Sarah by himself. About twenty minutes later he came down again. 'Has she been talking to you?' he asked.

'What about?'

'Have there been any people here today?'

'No one. Not even Bridges.'

He was very quiet for a moment.

'She's in a bad way, isn't she?' I said.

'It's a crisis,' he admitted. 'A healing crisis.'

'What the hell is that?'

'She's using everything she's got, all her power, all her energy, to throw off her illness. The whole of her body is concentrating on eliminating something unwholesome. One's best chance is to let the body do what it can for itself.'

'And what if that is not good enough?'

'I don't think we have any reason to suppose that.'

Something snapped. 'Well I have! The odds may be stacked against her. It might be more than she can cope with. She's only got her own strength . . .'

'That's all anyone has.'

'But there's more than one against her. There can be other forces, other spirits.'

'The painters' noises?'

'For God's sake, they weren't the only people to know about them! I knew. I know! And they're devils . . . trying to do things to her . . . and to me – through her. What can your healing crisis do against that?'

'I should think it will do enough. Whatever devils there are are of our own making, don't you think, Nick?'

I stopped shaking. 'I don't know,' I said. 'I just want her to get well.'

'Given a chance, we can cure ourselves,' said Everett. 'We just have to know the truth about ourselves. Unfortunately that's probably the hardest thing in the world to know. The fever sweats out the physical poisons; the mind has to sweat it out its own way.'

He was going . . .

'You're *going*? Leaving us in some sort of . . . limbo?' I was quite shaken.

'What else do you want me to do? I can't fight your devils for you. Sarah is trying that, isn't she? Your help should be sufficient.' He hesitated, then he said, 'Look, if you can't cope, give her one of these. It will help her to sleep.' He dropped a couple of pills into my hand.

He drove off, and I was face to face with monsters.

I remembered Sarah and ran upstairs; but she was safely in bed.

We didn't speak about Bobby. I found myself talking about the house. And then she said, 'Why didn't you fiinish what you were doing? It would have been better.'

I knew what she was talking about. 'It would have meant the fantasy was more important than you were.'

'You've made a confrontation out of it.'

'It *is* a confrontation. Right against wrong. Good against evil.'

She mocked, 'You're right and good?'

'They are corrupting.'

'If you really cared about me, you'd do as they say.'

So! There was an admission. '*They?*'

She spun on me viciously. 'Yes. They! You know who I mean. You were infatuated, in love! You would've done anything for her!'

'Not anything.'

'That fireplace!' she scoffed.

'I told you it was a symbol. Of us. Of you and me. Of change. Of life. And they knew it.'

'It was vanity! Just your pride. You did everything else they wanted.'

'I couldn't shut my eyes any longer to what they were doing, to what they were. Ruthless, cold, inhuman. Nor could I shut my eyes to my own collusion and corruption. My obsession.'

She was in despair. 'Nicky, you know what will happen to them if you cut yourself off? They'll die . . . really die. You brought them back to life; don't let them disappear forever!'

I was swept by a sense of loss which I tried to brush aside. It wasn't sane. I wanted quit of them. All of them!

'Let them go.'

'Nick, they're dragging me with them!'

My skin prickled. 'That's not possible.'

236

'Feel my hand, Nick. That's why I'm so cold. They're going to earth.'

'Listen, Sarah, Bobby says . . .'

Her fists were clenched, her arms tense, resisting unseen assailants, hands that held on to her as though she were a raft in a sea and they were survivors struggling to stay afloat. She fairly howled, 'What does Bobby know? Don't take his word, don't trust him, don't risk me!'

I put my arm around her – the image persisted – to keep her afloat; she jabbed out a hand, I jerked back, but I got part of the blow. I couldn't see with one eye. She raced for the door. God, did I never learn! Sarah wasn't inside that skin . . . certainly not inside that head.

But the frail body was too weak to do all she – or they – wanted. I caught her on the stairs and dragged her back. 'Nicky, Nicky, do as they ask. They're suffocating me.' She looked dreadful. My heart broke: I couldn't go on letting her suffer. I held her down on the bed and pushed one of Everett's pills between her teeth. She kept them clenched. She tried to spit it out, hitting blindly at me, jerking her head from side to side. She tried to bite me, but I got the pill into her mouth. She nearly choked. I was taking no risks: I got the second pill. The fight was over, and she swallowed it. I held her so that she couldn't sit up. A few minutes later she was unconscious. I pulled the bedclothes over her, and left.

What they were doing was blackmail, but I had no choice. It wasn't *me* they were threatening, it was Sarah, so there was no way to challenge them now. They would tighten the screws on her, and real or not, she felt that pain. Woman in a wheelchair, I whispered to myself.

It was dark along the drive. They could have come at me, dog and all, out of the pitch-black and I would have scattered them in their hideous unreality. They must have guessed my mind as they saw me turn towards the stables. I was sure they were there – perhaps pacing me step by step as they had done before along this same fifty yards. I didn't care to look; I wanted no part of their schemes. I was there for Sarah's sake. One heavy blow with the sledgehammer, and the air would be rid of the echoes that had dogged me for months. And Sarah would sleep easy.

But although I didn't look left or right – scorning to use the trick we had devised together – I knew they were hurrying alongside, crowding in as I neared the stables, exalted, excited; it was as though I could hear the noise of their triumph. It went against the grain. Perhaps Sarah had been right when she spoke of my vanity, perhaps my stand against them was nothing but a matter of pride. I was not to be exploited, abused, by them – not even when infatuated. They had made use of that infatuation; I had been a catspaw; and now, for one more time, I would still be the catspaw, lending them the muscle and power which they didn't have. Then they could vaporize out of my life.

It seemed such an easy decision, now, that I asked myself why I had held out so long? Did it really matter what a few ghosts achieved against my will? Was it so destructive of my being? Why should it degrade either Sarah or me? My protest had been vanity all right.

Had it? Had it? Another voice whispering: surely I was finished with voices! But it wasn't willing to be silenced – it was unhappy about blackmail, telling me I had held out against them because I sensed their corruption. When the price asked became clear, I wasn't ready to pay. They were not to brush Sarah's whim aside as of no account; I was not prepared to pretend it was worthless – it counted in my world. That was the rock that had broken the waves of fantasy.

I wished there had been some way of successfully holding out. But now there wasn't.

This time I wasn't sure that I entered the stables alone. This time the narrow staircase was so crowded I could hardly breathe. Had their triumph overcome some obstacle? Could they now come within four walls?

It didn't matter. I walked the dark corridor to the forlorn little room.

The sledgehammer stood against the wall – moonlight picked it out, and I couldn't pretend not to see it. There were too few permutations now. No chance to fall over my ankle; no delaying, consciously or unconsciously. The hammer weighted nicely in my hands, beautifully balanced – heavy-headed, thick-shafted. One well-timed swing would shatter the stone panels. That would be all they wanted – gesture enough. They had had the grace to leave, I could feel it. I was alone in the room.

I hadn't started to swing; I can't pretend such a last second had arrived before something, God knows what, came into my mind. No other way? Was there *no other way*? Did we – it was 'we' now, Sarah was in every calculation – did we have to capitulate in this slavish way? Did these shadows of humanity, fixed in time and prejudice, rigid in themselves, did they dominate the life, the ripples and echoes of later generations that had swept on after them, did they still have the power to control us with ice-cold hands? I couldn't believe it. Not even now, when I heard the cry from the house, the sound of a nightmare, the growl of the dog? There had to be another way.

I don't think I had clearly conceived what it was as I swung the hammer, but suddenly it was light as a feather; I could have cleared a path through an army with it at that moment. There *was* another way! I was still swinging it as I went down the stairs, through the garage, into the garden . . . a big warning swing that would keep even shadows at bay. The world was sharply silent, undoubtedly startled! They didn't have time to tighten the screw of their blackmail for I was heading off down the long wood – scene of our first meetings, ground of our shared triumphs, swinging the hammer like a broomstick over my head, intoxicated, for the idea was becoming clearer, shaping itself every step of the way. And silence was turning to alarm – an incredulous hiss of questions, of warnings, anger, outrage. And then a wild uproar of which not a vibration broke into real sound, but which was there, surging round me, in my ears, like a mob enraged. They must have guessed, peeped into my brain, caught a glimpse of the awful crime I was going to attempt. And they were going to break barriers to stop me – time and space would be no protection! Their fury rose; they were determined to reach out, cross the uncrossable, physically hold me.

And I felt that hold! Now, when I no longer dreamed or desired it, or marvelled at it, they managed to rouse something against me . . . What to call it I don't know. A pressure? A wall of air. A gale of wind, confined to inches, just a strip of the atmosphere that blocked my way through the woods and had me at a standstill, trying to make headway, being forced back . . . It was like a door closing on me.

Had I thought about it, I would have been shocked and helpless, for it was unbelievable – and it was happening! But if I could be so forced, so physically manhandled, pushed back step by step, then I could retaliate. That was simple logic. I took a step away, and swung the sledgehammer. What it hit I don't know; I could see nothing. But the impact was enormous. The air vibrated; my hands jarred. Something shattered like glass. I could believe the sound of a scream . . . a scream of rage, and a hubbub about me. But the way forward was clear, and I hurried on.

Moonlight tinged the black water of the flight pond. That was something to skirt round; no doubt I might finish up there, in that deep fathom of mud. One slip, and I'd never be up again! But there was no movement, no attack. If they were going to make a last stand it had to be now, for I was almost at my goal. The rush came when I thought the danger over, and I was sent spinning into the water. I held on to the hammer like grim death. That was all there was between me and the foul pond if this bizarre enemy could get at me.

I came ashore, from knee-deep, and was ready for them again.

But they changed tactics . . . this time the cry from the house was so real that I nearly raced back. But how could I hear such a distant cry? It wasn't possible, it could not have been Sarah. The trick served to heighten my anger. I swept up the hammer and swung it, a broadsword in battle. The woodwork of that delicate little balcony was scattered . . . The long days of work, the autumn hours, the love and tenderness that had gone into it. Now matchstick splinters! The pagoda itself stood, unprotected, the last outpost of this family folly.

I didn't dare to wait in case I lost resolve. The sledgehammer was hampered in mid-air – it was being wrested from my hands – parade-ground orders deafened my brain. But I hit back; the first blow grazed the pagoda, while the second took the balustrade apart. The air was one despairing wail. I could have cried myself, but their wickedness had been too deep, and now was unforgivable. What was charming had to go with what was evil. My third blow was unopposed: the heart had gone out of my enemies. I finished off the business with shattering blow after shattering blow. There was no sign of the pagoda as I turned for home.

I'm not sure what I expected; I hadn't thought that far ahead, but I suppose I'd put the clock back several months. There was no Victorian folly in the garden; no evidence of our work together. Surely that returned everything to an age of normality, as though they had never been? They would surely vanish as their monument vanished?

For a moment or two they were indeed stunned. The enormity of what I had done must have bewildered them. Perhaps in those few moments there was a chance that they would evaporate like smoke, there being no reason left for them to survive. But I was wrong.

It took those few moments for them to recuperate. After all, they would have no more faculties, no greater talent, now, than they had had in life. They had not been fast-thinking, quick-witted, inventive; what they had been was powerful. And it was that power they remembered now.

I was hit by a tornado, a crescendo of energy, a great charge of electricity. It was actually none of those things, but there is no other way to convey the impact of what swept out of the wood and threw me against a tree. The trunk behind me seemed to sag, though all round the bushes hardly trembled: no wind was blowing through the long wood that night. What hit me was more elemental then the elements.

The sledgehammer was snatched away and sent spinning into the pond . . . bubbles of marsh gas broke on the surface. I knew I would be next to go. A blast sent me across the muddy patch towards the water. I grabbed bushes, branches, bracken; I hung on. They tried to tear me away. I prayed it couldn't be done without offending physical laws. The vegetation, this tree, was beyond their power. I held on for life, for grim death . . . they couldn't prise me from it.

But I had to get back to the house. They knew where I was, but I couldn't see them. But a sudden inspiration – a wild hope: why couldn't I see where they were? I would have a chance if I knew where the weak links lay, the plump man, for example. Where was he? How was I being attacked? In a body? Encircled? It was essential to know, and I had a way of finding out. I had managed it in this very spot on a late summer day, when I had first seen the images as visions flickering into being. I had seen them only on the margin of my vision. I could do that again.

They didn't seem to realize what I was doing as I looked into the darkness. Night made the process more difficult . . . but it worked. It worked! Images on the margin of vision . . . on the edge of the water the bald man was standing, the scholar, anxious, uncertain, looking at his fellows for instructions. At the woman hurrying, a figure of vengeance if ever there was one, hurrying to take cover amongst trees, great skirts billowing, making her appear huge, a demon. Shouting soundless orders, pointing, instructing, her face blotched and ugly as it looked towards me – black hair beginning to uncoil, heavy eyebrows glowering. I wondered that I noted such detail, but it impinged itself on me. She was the force to reckon with, she was the drive for revenge. For that was all it was now – revenge! What else was left for them in my world? I was no longer their ally. The masks were thrown aside, the daggers drawn. Punishment had to be handed out, a backlash for defiance. As a last convulsion before oblivion, she was determined I should not survive.

I kept up the scanning exercise. Along the path, blocking escape to the house, stood the soldier. Who was he, I wondered? Their son? A friend? The girl's intended? Formidable in his peacock uniform, with sabre and jangling steel, more than ready to put in the knife . . . I was still looking for enemies, and the older man appeared, detaching himself from shadows as I scanned the black under the trees. Heavy, dictatorial, he would swat me as he might a fly, if only he were able to do it that way. I thanked what little fortune I had that they couldn't break through axiomatic material laws; they couldn't just use brute strength to murder me.

And the girl? There was something, another figure beyond . . . I shrank back from searching further.

I had two choices. Either I just denied that they existed, just walked to the shelter of my own house, denying the whole experience, which wasn't real while I was part of reality . . . Or, second, I could make a dash for it. I knew where they all were now. If I kept away from the path, made a run for the trees alongside the field . . . And I went off like a man doing a hundred yards! I had gone twenty before they reacted. Then none of the four moved, but another figure, screaming, screeching, leapt across my path, white, with streaming hair, fingers scratching at my eyes! What could it be? I went back against the iron railing that divided the garden from the field, and I held tight. The power that tried to dislodge me was a second too late. I held on . . . held on . . . Was I going to be able to make my way like this, crossing a checkerboard like a chess piece, in despairing leaps? I'd never make it. A wild howl in the distance, the sound of a chain. But I'd faced the dog before, and somehow I knew he couldn't come again. It was his masters I had to fear now.

A moment's quiescence. It seemed that they too might need to draw breath. And then off I went – on another stumbling charge through the bushes, with the undergrowth tangling round me, thorns tearing my clothes, thorns like nails going deep into my skin, with blood on my hands and legs, creepers pulling me to a standstill, gorse gripping me like a prisoner. They billowed out of the wood on all sides; the puffed-up soldier, brutal, above me; the woman huge in her fury; the two other men filling all space in the dark round me . . . Sarah had cried out that they were suffocating her, and now I understood as the air drained away, evaporated. It was impossible to breathe . . . I was going down – drowning without water . . . in the distance the dog still baying.

Perhaps I was wrong, perhaps he still threatened . . . And not a soul, human or otherwise, dead or alive, to help me this time – knowing my strength was failing, my heart going like a hammer. I was going to be found dead in this wood, dead of a heart attack. Bridges had warned me. What was it Mrs Bridges had said? I wasn't getting proper meals? I was doing too much . . . unused to the work? It would all be so explicable.

But at least I'd drawn their fire. This was their last gasp. Without me, without my help, my living energy, they could do nothing. Even if I didn't make it, Sarah would be safe. 'Sarah is safe' I shouted. It took the last drop of air I had in my lungs, but I shouted, 'You can't touch her.' It was all I could do, a final defiance. But it struck deep, for there was a crack in the weight that bore down on me, a crack and an inrush of air. I gulped, I heard my throat rasp, and I rushed up to some incomprehensible surface, breathing, lashing out, kicking clear of roots and rubble. I ran. Bushes whipped in my face, wind rocked me like a blow, but I ran. It was for life this time. Devils of my own making, Everett had said . . . how did I unmake them? How to expel them from my garden, my being, my mind?

But nothing caught me. Nothing touched me. Pressures eased, like a balloon fizzing into space. I was running on a dark night along my own path to my own house. Even the dog was silent. Was it true, or were they round the corner? Swooping ahead to reappear? Devils could do anything.

I was so weak I couldn't have resisted them any longer, all the strength had gone out of me. But they weren't there. The moon came out, and I could see that nothing lay between me and the front door. Longwood was mine, my home. I walked up the stone steps and into the house.

23

I went upstairs to our room. The light was on; Sarah was just wakening. She lifted her head as I came in. 'Hello, Nicky,' she said. She was wan and pale, but her eyes were clear, and she looked at me with love. I put an arm around her gently and kissed her. Her cheeks were cool, her forehead no longer ran with sweat. Her kiss had a sudden passion, but her body was frail beside me. She was weak with fever, but the fever had gone.

We lay together like survivors after a storm, a shipwreck, an earthquake. Very shaken, thankful to find ourselves together and alive. The intimacy, the happiness of the past few years came flooding back. We felt that whatever catastrophe had swept through our lives was over. We were wrong – this was a respite, a false dawn, but we didn't guess it.

'Where were you,' she wanted to know, 'when I was asleep?'

'Burning a few bridges,' I said. 'Breaking them up, anyhow.'

She seemed to understand. It had often been like that with us – no need to explain things, each understanding the other.

'Have they gone?' she asked.

I wondered how much she knew about them, and how? But this wasn't the time to ask. 'According to you, they must have gone,' I said.

'According to me?'

'You said I'd brought them back to life, and that if I cut myself off from them, they would die forever.'

'I said that?'

'Here, in this bed.'

'I don't remember.' She was staring, eyes wide with wonder.

'What's the matter?'

'It's hard to think what I really remember and what was a dream.'

'But you did see them?' It was a comfort to know this was something else we shared. 'After all, Mac and his painters only *heard* things. It's reassuring to know it isn't just me . . . I'm glad in a way you saw them too.'

She said, 'Only the girl.'

'Where?'

'At that window. That's all I saw.' She turned to look out at the night. It was beginning to show a grey, cold cloud.

'You saw her?' I don't know why I was so shocked at the thought.

'She's beautiful, isn't she?' said Sarah.

'I've scarcely seen her,' I said.

She looked at me in disbelief.

'Not properly,' I went on. 'Yes, once, at a distance. Across the pond in the wood. Fair hair, fair skin, green eyes.' I had to think exactly what I had seen. 'Somehow I know, though, what she's like. What she's wearing when she's running beside me. And once, a brief look over her shoulder, in the dark, in pain.' I remembered, the night they touched my heart with her crying. 'She kissed me,' I said.

Again the look of disbelief.

'Didn't you notice the mark?' I touched the side of my cheek beside my lips. Sarah lay close to me. 'There's nothing there.'

I got up and crossed to the mirror. The mark had gone. I felt a sense of relief, for a last link had vanished. Their world was withering away. But as I stood by the glass I was aware of another feeling – a pang. Not exactly of regret . . . not quite a longing.

'You're right.' I lay holding her. She seemed so slight; she had burnt up a lot of energy . . . I would have to look after her. 'Bobby went off and left us,' I told her. That still preyed on my mind. 'He must have known the ship was sinking – or listing badly – yet he went.'

'Yes, he would,' she nodded thoughtfully. 'He told me not to come back from Munich, said you had to work things out on your own. Now he would judge we would have to work it out for ourselves. He says that's the only way to overcome weakness.'

'Where does he pick up these snippets of philosophy? Christmas crackers? Old calendars?'

'You don't like him, do you?'

'I think I'm jealous of him.'

'That's nice.' She began softly kissing me, eyes, ears, neck. I lifted her aside very gently. 'You're not fit for that.'

'I soon will be.'

I was beginning to suspect we might be home and dry too soon. The victory had been too easy; the hatred that had struggled to destroy me in the wood would hardly have deflated so quickly. Perhaps they were outside, still at the windows, willing a way in which to come in. She caught some of my thought.

246

'I wonder why they were here? What roused them?'

'The empty house? New owners?'

'You think they were always here, waiting their opportunity?'

'I'm not sure. You know some young people, children, seem able to rouse spirits, poltergeists . . . maybe it was something like that. When the past is disturbed, it appeals to immaturity, instability.'

'Us?'

'Most likely me. Perhaps you need the combination . . . uneasy, dead spirits and the compatible living.'

'They didn't materialize for the painters. Not properly.'

'They didn't get the right response. I didn't realize it, but I welcomed them. I escaped into them.'

'Escaped from me?'

'From myself. From that part of myself you were forcing me to become.'

'I'm sorry, darling.'

'Don't be silly. It's as things ought to be.'

'You're beginning to talk like Bobby,' she said.

'He's not *always* wrong,' I joked.

She was quiet for a moment. 'Who were they?' she asked.

'The people who built this house.'

'What brought them?'

I heard myself answer, 'We did.' I couldn't think how I was so certain, spoke with such authority. 'When we restored this place, it was like breathing life back into them.' How could I know such things?

'But how did they get here?'

I had to tell her the truth. 'Through the crack in my soul.'

She understood, but she added, 'Ghosts don't just appear and batten on you because you don't feel well.'

'I'm sure that's true,' I said. 'They couldn't have just come from nowhere.'

Outside, there were streaks of dawn. I was still uneasy. 'Something else Bobby said . . . about a case he had. Fantasies are created, they don't come from nowhere. In his case, this woman's fantasy came from her past. The creatures, the people at Longwood, must be my creation, but they don't come from *my* past. Yet I brought them to life. It's as though I have known them some time . . . I must have had a model, or a memory, something I've forgotten.'

'Can you think of it?'

I shook my head. 'I've no recollection . . .' I had a sudden vision: a pile of old papers. In the tack room at the stables? Hadn't I put them some place? It came back in an explosion of memory. 'I know where they've come from,' I said. 'An old photograph, of a family on the lawn outside the house. Very old – very faded. You could hardly recognize anybody in it.'

'What did you do with it?'

'It was with papers. Plans of the gardens, deeds, maps, that sort of thing. They were mildewed, sticking together. I put them in a place to dry.'

'Where?'

'In the cellar. Beside the boiler. Behind the oil tank. I'd forgotten.'

'You're sure?'

I nodded, and began to get up.

'What are you doing?'

'I'd really like to destroy those things.'

'What for?'

'The photo, certainly.'

'What difference will that make?' She was getting anxious.

'I just want quit of everything to do with them. If their origin is destroyed, that will be the end of the matter.'

'It's already the end of it,' she said, holding on to my arm with both hands, pleading in a way.

'It's all right. Look, the sun's coming up.'

'I'd rather you didn't, Nick.'

'It's nothing. It's our house, not theirs. We're the new people at Longwood. The past must learn to accept the present.'

'Tomorrow would do . . .'

'Sarah, please! It's on my mind. I knew there was something disturbing, and it must have been this. They've done all they can, to both of us.'

'Darling, you don't have to prove anything.'

248

'I'm not proving anything, I just want the loose ends tidied up. We're going to be very busy over the next few weeks. I've let our little company go to pot and we're in for a tough spell getting our customers back. We aren't going to have any time for this sort of thing.'

I was smiling reassuringly, but she was still anxious. She let go my hand.

'It shouldn't take long.' But she was silent as I left the room.

There was no use my trying to fool Sarah. She knew what I felt I had to prove. This was nothing if not a test: this was the final thread that had to be broken. There was no single part of me that yearned after the miraculous; I no longer had doubts or vacillations. But no regrets, and no mercy either. I knew where my fantasy had been born, and I knew I was going to rip it to shreds.

I went downstairs, through the hall, along the corridor, an executioner. Revenge for their attempt at revenge. There was no space for more than one master in this house.

I stood at the top of the cellar steps and remembered the first night I had slept in the house alone. I had gone down these stairs to switch off the central heating; there had been something on the steps – a brush – I remembered – and I had tripped over it and fallen. Something had caught me in mid-air. Would the genius of the place still cushion my fall? Was I amongst enemies or friends? Whichever they were, I had to set the pattern now. I don't know why the hair stood up on the back of my neck as I set off down those steps. I had fear in my bones. Not of anything fantastic, anything unreal . . . fear such as a grown man has when he knows he is in a dangerous trap and may not survive. But I had no choice, I had to go down, hand feeling for the light switch. I couldn't find it; then when I did, it didn't go on. What the hell! Enough light filtered through the window of the old wine-cellar and fell across the stone corridor to show the door opposite that led into the boiler room.

I went down step by step, testing them in turn as though they might give way. The fear was a tingle that ran along nerves and seemed to daze me a little. I tried to shake it off. I had a charm which I found I was whispering to myself softly at each step –

'The eye of childhood fears a painted devil.' That was the magic, the scripture, that would ward off evil. And I had to believe in evil now!

But there was nothing, no one, in the corridor, only the cold dawn coming through the windows . . . and the strange silence that is reminiscent of someone holding his breath. It was that sort of silence, and I knew what it meant.

I threw back the wine-cellar door, so it hit the wall behind. The window was high on the wall opposite for the room was below ground level. Below ground level! Of course it was, all cellars were. But below the ground, under the earth? Again the sense of my body suddenly chilling. The room was bare, empty. I told myself not to be so childish. 'The eye of childhood . . .'

I crossed over the corridor into the boiler room to collect the papers and the photograph. And they were there! All five of them, in shadow against the wall, waiting, watching for me, expecting this. And to be honest, so was I. It was only a second or two of silence – of motionless silence – but it seemed a long time, a great age while the world heaved under me, a wave of duration that almost moved the stone below me – the swell of an ocean of time.

Each pair of eyes looked enmity and hate, looked devils at me. I was such danger to them, the ultimate threat. I sensed it, and if one could be sorry in such strange circumstances, then I was sorry for them. The guillotine was falling, but I could stop it; it only needed my blessing. A change of heart would win me back to their seductive Eden, to be in bliss again.

I had a clear passage to the big oil tank and the boiler. *They* were ranged along the other wall, all eyes turning as I moved, in unison, some communal spirit directing them. Like birds in a flock, rising together . . . I was uneasy to have to head past them, to have them for a split second behind my back. I moved fast, as fast as I could in the dull light, across the rubble on the floor, among stacked garden-chairs, boxes, other equipment. Then I was round the back of the tank and saw the pile of papers against the wall. They seemed stunned, too static to move. Was the rigidity of death already setting in?

I thumbed feverishly through the papers . . . I missed it the first time . . . I was so scared, head turning every second to look over my shoulder, jerking round for fear of shadows between me and the door. So scared . . . but it was there! The photograph! Even fainter in its dried condition, sepia-tinted, yellowed, with cracking edges, but clear enough to see the proud family. Father in his portentous authority – tall, straight as a soldier, straight as his faded soldier son who wore a fearsome look as part of his uniform; the plump and scholastic cousin or uncle who bowed a bald head slightly in recognition of a fractional inferiority – all knew their places, indeed. There stood the dark-haired *grande dame*, powerful in her own right, the centre of all life – or all death, as I suspected. And a dog merging into fainter edges of the print . . . There they were, four and a dog. My eyes held off from the fifth figure – even at this stage I could hardly bring myself to look, for to look was to sign a warrant. She was wearing her Alice-in-Wonderland dress down to her ankles, white and long-sleeved, the dancing-shoes just visible, a picture of innocence with sly eyes that I knew were green and long fair hair down her back. Smiling with an archness that I'd seen in the long wood, secretive, with a promise that could never be kept, sidelong in its deception. The devil's bitch.

They were all behind me, shadows one on top of the other, ranged behind each other, blown-up in rage, passionate in a fury of destruction; the storm about to be let loose on me. I had no time for pity, nor for fear. I lifted the photo. 'It's you . . . *you* . . . A hundred years ago when you were alive. When you lived here . . .'

They came at me in a wild sweep of movement, each with aspects of individual hate, an instinct to kill in each of their different ways. All deadly. The soldier was – as was his right – first to the fray: I couldn't see what the weapon was that whirled down in a terrifying sweep above me. I had to take my eyes off him momentarily as I ripped the picture across his face . . . ripped it, and saw him go screaming back into the mêlée of his family's shades. I ripped it again . . . just in time, as I had heard the howl of the dog coming at me, unseen, out of the dark. I tore it again, and again, in a frenzy myself, as frantic as the sea of shadows that came at me . . . And as I looked up, an assassin sighting his victims, I saw them go down, fall back, the photograph cutting across their fantasy existence with every fresh tear . . . bald man and powerful dame. Then, still coming at me in these unending, massive seconds, the father, a stick raised like a club but never falling, as he became a scattering of paper scraps over the cellar floor . . . And worst of all, startling in her transformation, riveting me in a moment of helplessness, the girl rose from the disintegration of these vanishing shapes, long hair streaming, ribbons and bows undone, eyes flashing a special loathing, dress awry as she reached out, long fingers seeming longer, her nails at my eyes, her face distorted . . . a witch. Truly a witch! This pretty little girl had melted my heart, and made me long to live in other times. The pity of it! That the picture was so shattered, had ended like this. A tiny fragment of the photo was still in my hands – just her smiling face. One of the family who had tried to invest Sarah. No sound . . . no last wild cry . . . the room was empty . . . white bits of paper were at my feet . . .

I groped my way to the door, shaking. I looked back, expecting to feel something for a lost dream. But I didn't. Nothing. Except relief. I was standing on firm ground; the stone floor just a stone floor, in a workaday world. And I thanked God for it.

I tried to go up the stairs, but I was suddenly giddy. Nothing abnormal, nothing mysterious. Anyone can feel giddy.

I was a heap on the stairs when Sarah found me. She hurried down in her nightdress, and helped me to my feet. I hardly remember her taking me to the floor above, and on up to our room.

I woke hours later. She was dressed and standing by my bed with a tray of something hot to drink.

'Whatever were you doing down there?' she asked.

But I think she knew. In a sense she had been with me.

Bridges was in charge of the cars, parked like an army parade up and down the drive from the house to the stables. He was very pleased with himself. 'Always done it like this,' he informed everyone. It was the first time I had heard him chuckle.

I left the others in the house. The reception had grown into a party that spilled into every room. Sarah was managing things to perfection, Hans was growing theatrically jealous, and the others were expressing their happiness in different ways. Some of them, I suspected – Freddie, for example – were also expressing their relief.

It was a wonderful wedding as weddings probably all are, but during it I found a convenient moment to slip away.

I took one of the guests with me; for, after all, we had some business to discuss. We walked around the house, gauging the expanse of outside wall.

'Take a bit of covering,' said the painter thoughtfully. 'Take a bit of time.'

'Got any help now?' I asked.

'Could get Joe. Lost Alf, but could get another couple, you know. We've grown a bit since this job.'

'Oh, I know. With your quality of work you'll get big.'

'Nice of you, guv. But it's still going to cost you a packet.'

'Don't worry, Mac,' I said. 'We're picking up the pieces. Two or three months and we'll be making money.'

'Two or three months? That'll fit nicely. Pressure-paint the outside? I'll give you a price.'

We moved on round to the front. The painter viewed the house thoughtfully. 'Something's changed, hasn't it? Seems different.'

I knew that myself. 'Been exorcised,' I said.

'Oh yes?' He looked up at the outside, expressionless.

'With love,' I told him.

He gave me a dry look, then returned his gaze to the building. We stopped on the lawn in front, and he stood for a few moments, looking it over, taking it all in, the tall pink-white walls, from floor to floor and side to splendid side. I thought he was doing some sort of a professional estimate, but then he shook his head with slow appreciation.

'Bloody house,' said the painter admiringly.